Blood Brothers III

Jim Crow and the Gilded Age

Ronald E Pressley and Nancy P. Holder

1122 Creations

Copyright © 2021 by 1122 Creations Knoxville, TN.

All rights reserved.

No portion of this book may be reproduced in any form without written permission from the publisher or author, except as permitted by U.S. copyright law.

Contents

Foreword	VI
Introduction	VII
1. A NEW ERA BEGINS	1
2. JIM CROW	5
3. THE GILDED AGE	11
4. JIM CROW IN MEMPHIS	15
5. THE DEPRESSION OF 1873	21
6. PARKER'S JOBBING	25
7. HARRY COMES HOME	31
8. DECISONS, DECISIONS	35
9. THE PLAN	39
10. WORKING THE PLAN	49
11. THE ROBBER BARONS	55
12. LABOR UNIONS	59
13. THE PRODUCE SHED	63
14. NEW CUSTOMERS	67
15. GEORGE ARMSTRONG CUSTER	73
16. THE COMPROMISE	77
17. THE WRONG HEROES	81
18. PARKER JOBBING BEGINS	87
19. OPENING DAY	93

20.	THE SOUTH LEGISLATES SEGREGATION	97
21.	LENORA TAKES CHARGE	103
22.	THE GREAT RAILROAD STRIKE	107
23.	THE INTRUDER	113
24.	CANNERY BEGINS	119
25.	FIRST BATCH	125
26.	WHO IS ALMA MAE ROGERS	131
27.	BESSIE AND JOHNNY	137
28.	JOHNNY COMES HOME	141
29.	THE BARONS VISIT	145
30.	SILVER RETURNS	155
31.	INNOVATIONS	159
32.	WHITE HOUSE EASTER EGG ROLL	163
33.	SWING LOW SWEET CHARIOT	167
34.	ANOTHER ASSASSINATION Tuesday, July 5, 1881	173
35.	THE EVOLUTION OF GEORGE WILHELM PRESLEY	177
36.	ELECTIONS 1880	183
37.	ARTHUR IS PRESIDENT Monday, January 2, 1882	189
38.	MOURNING FOR A MENTOR	193
39.	TARIFF ACT OF 1883	199
40.	AMERICAN FEDERATION OF LABOR	203
41.	SUFFER THE LITTLE CHILDREN	207
42.	THE SALVATION ARMY	211
43.	THIRD GENRATION	217
44.	ELECTION 1884	223
45.	CLEVELAND IS PRESIDENT	229

46. HARRISON IS PRESIDENT	235
47. FAREWELL ADDRESS	243
48. EPILOGUE	249
Acknowledgments	254
About The Authors	255

Foreword

There is no requirement to read the first two books in the Blood Brothers series to enjoy this final book, Blood Brother III; however, the authors would encourage you to do that.

We have included some pertinent facts about the earlier days of the Presley family and Will's journey through his memories and dreams. The narrator occasionally refers to past events and their significance.

The authors' disclaimers made in the introduction to BB II remain applicable to BB III.

While we intend to be historically correct concerning all actual happenings, settings, and societal norms, we are not infallible. If the reader detects any anachronisms, please do not allow them to ruin the story. Better yet, let us know, and we may be able to make revisions.

Our story requires the use of particular dialects, which we have also attempted to write in a fashion that is true to our characters' period and socio-economic level. We apologize if any of the dialogue seems offensive. There is no intention of disrespect as we both hold all human life to be of value.

Introduction

*Blood Brothers, A Family Divided i*s the story of the Presley patriarch, J.W. Presley, an impoverished Irish teen who dared to make the treacherous journey to the new world with nothing but a contract of indenture.

Blood Brothers II, Reconstruction, Racism, Riots, Ratification followed the personal development of the prodigal son, Will, as he sought ways to atone for the burden of his activities in the American Civil War.

Blood Brothers III, Jim Crow, and the Gilded Age chronicles how the dramatic advancements, inventions, and socio/economic changes affected the second and third generations of the Presley family.

The last quarter of the nineteenth century would present the Presley family with new challenges and opportunities.

For Senator G.W. Presley, the personal challenges would involve balancing his legislative duties with his inherited responsibility to protect and promote his father-in-law's business while simultaneously being a positive role model for his children and a supportive husband to Lenora.

The opportunities would include continuous efforts to influence his fellow Senators, seeking expanded opportunities for the Parker enterprises, and rescuing several family members from dead-end situations.

At times, the load seemed more than he was capable of carrying. He always remembered his roots as the son of a sharecropper. How he had been elevated to the upper house of the Congress of the United States of American was still a partial mystery to Will Presley.

Chapter One

A NEW ERA BEGINS

When he sat down at his Senate desk in the Capitol Building, Will Presley glanced at the calendar. It was Tuesday, January 2, 1877. Uncertain, anxious, and, yes, fearful of the future, he contemplated the beginning of a new year.

First, the Presidential election of November 1876 was still undecided. Electoral votes in Florida, South Carolina, and Louisiana were in dispute. A Congressional committee would decide the outcome.

Second, the Depression of 1873 was still raging and even growing wider. The influx of people into cities, generated by the Industrial Revolution, had created a terrible situation for unemployed workers. They had left their farms and moved to the cities to fill the factory jobs which had been plentiful. Besides, many more immigrants entering the country had added to the problem.

Third, Parker's Farm, owned by Harry and Alice Parker, Will's in-laws, struggled for survival. Geared to provide food products to the War Department, demand had waned because of the Armed Forces reduction. Most of the farmworkers employed by Parker were laid-off, at least temporarily.

Then, on December 27, one week ago, Harry Parker had a heart attack and was now in a D.C. hospital in intensive care.

Lastly, Will was concerned for his family members down in Graham, North Carolina. Roaring Fork Farm harvested timber and raised tobacco, both of which were now in low demand.

Homebuilding and commercial construction had ceased; therefore, lumber was plentiful, and there were few orders. Even the tobacco that had been a booming export product had withered. Will's family struggled to survive. Although able to raise vegetables and pigs for their food, money sources had dried up.

Alice Parker had been making daily trips to the hospital to visit with her husband. Will's wife, Lenora, had three children to care for and depended on Will to make the necessary business decisions.

"Alright, now Will," he thought to himself. *"Just take one thing at a time. The Presidential election is beyond your control. Congress will decide on the Electoral College dispute.*

"Parker's Farm can produce enough pork meat to supply some local General Stores and restaurants. Neighborhood grocery stores in D.C. could use our produce. When the vegetables are ready to harvest in the Spring, we can sell those, too.

"I'll discuss all this with Lenora when I get home. Harry and Alice will be involved in any decisions we make, but not until he comes home from the hospital.

"If we can develop these additional outlets, our laid-off employees can be brought back to work. We will need to find somebody to manage the farm because Harry cannot physically do that anymore.

"I wonder how Pete and his new wife are doing on Roaring Fork Farm. Lillian is Martha's youngest sister, so I reckon they get along alright. Still, Billy Bob and Willadeen are in charge now.

"Would Pete and Lillian consider moving to Falls Church to manage Parker's Farm? He has been a farmer his entire life and knows how to farm. Could Billy Bob handle Roaring Fork without Pete?

"Adam, Thomas, Jedediah, and Johnny Junior are men now and can help Billy Bob with the tobacco and timber crops. Pete might relish the idea of moving to Falls Church and establishing himself as his own man.

"Not having another family to be dependent on Roaring Fork to supply a living might make things easier for the rest of the family. I don't know how Lenora and the Parkers will react to this idea, but it's worth considering and would solve many problems for everybody concerned.

"Getting Parker's Farm back up and running full speed would enable us to assist some of the people in Falls Church who don't have a dependable source of food. Lenora has mentioned that we might be able to provide food for the poor folks in our community.

"Thank the Good Lord that my salary from the Senate has allowed us to have everything we need in this time of depression when many folks don't have what they need. Pastor John talked about when Jesus said, 'Inasmuch as ye have done it unto one of the least of these, ye have done it unto me.'

"Well, I reckon it's gonna be a busy year or two for the Presley/Parker bunch."

Will walked out under the dome of the Capitol building at lunchtime. He encountered two of his friends, Congress members from Virginia, Jim Hall, Falls Church, and Jeremiah Jones, from Hampton. Will had served with them before he became a Senator.

"Hello and Happy New Year to both of you," he smiled and extended his hand. "Are you men heading out to lunch? If you are, I'm buying it today. I'd like to talk to you about the Electoral College dispute."

"Yes, we are on the way to lunch, and that is the subject we were just talking about," Hall answered. "There's a little café just down the street where I like to eat. It's quiet, and they have great sandwiches."

"Yeah, Presley, I haven't seen you in a long while. We've got some catching up to do." Jones was smiling broadly.

When the three men entered the café, the owner immediately recognized Hall. "Greetings, and Happy New Year to you, Representative Hall. I don't believe I know your associates."

"Well, allow me to introduce Senator Presley and Representative Jones. These men are my colleagues from Virginia."

As the owner looked disdainfully at Jeremiah Jones, he said, "I don't serve blacks." Richard Blair, the owner, was a Confederate-sympathizer from Maryland.

Hall snapped back, "And I don't do business with bigots or biased people. Let's go, gentlemen, and we'll find another place for lunch." Staring at Blair with anger in his eyes, he retorted, "I won't be back, and my friends in Congress won't either."

When they left the café, Hall apologized to Jeremiah. "I had no idea he was so prejudiced. The war has been over for twelve years."

Jones smiled wryly and said, "It's not your fault Jim. I've been dealing with this my entire life. This Jim Crow business is what I have problems with."

"Tell me about that, Jeremiah," Will looked puzzled.

"Well, it's a long story, and we have more pressing problems to discuss right now. There's a little sandwich shop close to the Capitol building. We can get a sandwich and take it with us back to the office," Jones answered. "I usually have lunch there."

After eating lunch in Jeremiah's office, Will asked, "What is the discussion about the disputed electoral votes. What are your colleagues in Congress saying?"

Jim Hall spoke. "As I understand it, by midnight on Election Day, Samuel Tilden, the Democrat, had 184 electoral votes, one vote short of the necessary 185 to win. Besides, he led by 250,000 popular votes. The disputed votes were in South Carolina, Florida, and Louisiana."

"One of my cousins, who is a Representative from South Carolina, claimed that Democrats had intimidated black voters and scared them away from the polls," Jones informed them. "There was a shooting in which five white men died."

"Didn't the Fifteenth Amendment guarantee black men the right to vote?" Will was incredulous.

"Absolutely, but Southern Democrats still tried," Jones shook his head.

Hall replied, "There is talk of removing all Federal troops from those three states and effectively ending the Reconstruction effort. If the Republicans agree to that, the Democrats will not contest those electoral votes, giving Rutherford B. Hayes the necessary total. That will give us another Republican President of the United States."

"Do you gentlemen believe this compromise will be accepted?" Will wondered.

"I will not vote for that," Jones emphatically stated. "That agreement will allow Democrats to get away with voter intimidation."

"Yeah, but we can resolve this issue and move on to something else, Jones. My Father says that politics is the art of compromise, and this is the perfect example of a compromise," Jim asserted.

"Man, that's a tough decision. I'm glad that you guys in the House have the responsibility for solving it," Will commiserated. "When do you think it will come to a vote?"

"That all depends on Speaker Randall. He's from Pennsylvania and was elected Speaker last year," Hall answered.

"Now, Hall, you and I are good friends, and we agree on most things, but on some things, I will not compromise. Allowing those Rebs to go back to Jim Crow is my main one. I'm sorry, my friend," Jones respectfully disagreed. "I will represent the desires of my constituents."

"And I will serve mine, too," Hall answered him. "I believe that we need to move forward from Reconstruction. We've been involved in that for twelve years now. This recession is crippling our nation, and somehow, we must try to mitigate that issue."

"Nobody ever said it was easy to govern, just that it was necessary," Will ended the conversation.

Chapter Two

JIM CROW

As Jim Hall and Will rose to leave the office, Jeremiah spoke to Will. "Presley, if you're interested, I'll tell you about Jim Crow."

"Yeah, I'm interested. I have always been an advocate for equal rights and treatment for black people under the law."

Jones began slowly and softly. "It all started sometime in the early thirties with a minstrel show. A white man named Thomas D. Rice painted his face with some black stuff and around his mouth with some white stuff. It was foolish-looking, but that was the point he was making. They called it Black-Face.

"Black people were objects of ridicule. In the comedic portion of his show, he made us all look like shuffling, lazy, good-for-nothing sluggards.

"Rice was a song-and-dance man, and by all reports, put on a good show. It was so well-received that some black men who wanted to do song-and-dance adopted his style.

Jim Crow

Thomas D. Rice

"It wasn't long before all black men were called Jim Crow as a nickname. I've been called Jim Crow on the State Assembly floor and even here in the Capitol building.

"I never make a big issue of it, but I give a stern, disapproving look every time I hear it. I fear that when all troops are withdrawn from the Southern states, black codes will be re-enacted in state legislatures."

"So, what do you think we in Congress can do about state laws?" Will asked.

"Maybe the only thing we can do is be supportive of our colleagues in the Virginia Assembly and assist them if they contest these actions in the courts."

Making a mental note, Will thought, "*That's another problem I hadn't thought of. Maybe Harry can give me some insight into handling things. It might be a while before he's well enough for me to burden him, but I trust his judgment.*"

Turning to Jeremiah, he said, "My Paw used to say. Just do the best you can with what you got. I reckon we'll handle each situation one at a time when we encounter them.

"How widespread is this Jim Crow business?" Will asked.

"It's all over the South. I know Rice has done shows at Ford's theatre right here in D.C. He's played in Richmond and Hampton, I know for sure. But others are repeating this character in New York and Boston, and Philadelphia. It's an unflattering portrayal that people begin to believe.

"Do you remember Rufus Brown from Glenmore Plantation?"

"Yes, I do remember Rufus. How is he doing?"

"He's doing fine, but he's distraught with these Jim Crow insults. As a Representative from his district, he deserves the respect of the other State Representatives. Because he was a slave before the Thirteenth Amendment, the white boys think he is somehow inferior and treat him differently. They openly refer to him as Jim Crow.

"If a State Assemblyman can't get any respect, he's afraid these bigots will feel free to re-enact those old black codes but call them Jim Crow.

"Well, the Fourteenth and Fifteenth Amendments should settle that matter. Those amendments outlawed black codes. If they try to bring them back, the courts can rule on their constitutionality."

"Yeah, they can do that, but dammit, why do we have to keep fixing things?" Jones asked rhetorically. "It just gets so frustrating that these people persist in taking advantage of us. It seems they think whites are superior to blacks and that God ordained it that way."

"Preacher Henderson, my stepfather, used to say, we are all God's children," Will added.

"Yeah, but we're, also, full-fledged citizens of the United States of America," Jeremiah reminded him.

As Jones talked, Will was thinking, *"There's not much I can do about this situation, but I can listen as Jeremiah talks and be supportive of my friend."*

"Say hello to Rufus Brown for me the next time you see him. If he ever wants to visit me at the Capitol, I will be available to him."

"Will do, Presley. Rufus voted for you to become our Senator, and I'm confident he will support you again in 1880 when you're up for re-appointment.

"I enjoyed having lunch with you today, Senator. Please stay in touch with me throughout this Congressional session."

"It was good to see you and Hall today. I miss the camaraderie we had in the State Assembly." Will smiled and shook his hand.

Arriving home after finishing his first day back at the office after the holidays, Will drove the buggy to the barn to unhitch the horse. Ronnie and Randy raced out to greet him (the boys raced everywhere they went.)

"Daddy, Daddy, I won. I got here first," Randy exclaimed.

"He pushed me before we started, Daddy. That's not fair," Ronnie complained.

"Well, maybe you'll win next time, son," Will consoled him. "Both of you give Daddy a hug, then let's go see Mommy and little Mimi."

"Mimi hit me today, Daddy," Randy tattled.

"Why did she do that, son?" Will asked suspiciously.

"He was playing with her doll and wouldn't give it to her," Ronnie tattled.

"What did Mommy say," he quizzed them.

"She said it was Mimi's doll, and I had to give it to her. But I had it first," Randy explained.

"She was playing with my rubber ball, so I played with her doll."

"Mommy said that boys don't play with dolls, but girls can play with balls. That doesn't seem fair to me," Ronnie defended his brother.

"Come on, boys, we're going inside and see if Mommy has supper ready."

"She doesn't, Daddy. Mommy took us to the hospital to see Papaw, but they wouldn't let us kids in," Ronnie explained. "Mamaw had to come to sit with us in the lobby so Mommy could go see Papaw."

"Alright, let's go into the house, boys."

Racing ahead, Ronnie burst into the house. "Mommy, Mommy, Daddy's home."

Mimi ran to Will and hugged his legs. "Daddy, we went to the hospital to see Papaw today, but they wouldn't let us see him. Mommy and Mamaw saw him and told us what he said."

Lenora smiled and said, "Welcome home, Senator. Did you have a good day?" She kissed him lightly on the lips.

"Yes, but it was a disturbing day, too. I had lunch with Jim Hall and Jeremiah Jones. Hall suggested a small café close to the Capitol, and when we got there, the owner refused to serve Jeremiah. Said he wasn't in the habit of serving blacks.

"Hall showed his righteous indignation, and we left, but the bias is still there. You remember what we encountered in Memphis twelve years ago, don't you?"

She nodded her head, and he continued. "Well, it's just as bad as ever, and it's rampant right here in our nation's Capital."

"You must remember, Will, there are many, many people living here who were Confederates or, at least, sympathized with them. Folks are still talking about the *lost cause*," she reminded him.

Have you heard about Jim Crow?" he asked her.

"Of course, I have. Minstrel shows have played at Ford's Theatre for years. Timothy D. Rice, who developed the character of Jim Crow, played there too. I never saw him, but many other people played him here, including some black song-and-dance men. Why did you ask me that question?"

"Jeremiah Jones told me what you just said. I had never heard about Jim Crow. We didn't have minstrel shows in Graham, and the only time I went to Ford's when I lived here, I saw John Wilkes Booth.

"Jeremiah said that Jim Crow had become a name used by haters to deride all black people. Supposedly, he's a lazy ne'er-do-well who moves slowly and is a sluggard.

"He thinks that if all Federal troops are withdrawn from the South, black codes will be re-instated. Jim Crow laws will replace those black codes.

"Do you remember Rufus Brown from Glenmore Plantation?"

"Yes, he was a freedman, a former slave, wasn't he?" she recalled.

"That he was, and now he is being treated as an inferior by his colleagues in the State Assembly. They are passing laws that provide for separate facilities for black people in public buildings, on public transportation, and in public schools."

"Will, don't you remember that the educators in Memphis wanted separate schools for the black children. They thought the children would be intimidated by white children."

"I *do* remember that, and I questioned it, but we have a different generation of school children now. Those ideas of separation applied to the brand-new schools we built.

"Now we have schools funded by taxes which are levied against everybody regardless of their race. White schools get more funding than black schools and are much better maintained.

"I can't do anything about state laws, but I can be supportive of Rufus and my other friends down in Richmond. The thinking is that this kind of discrimination will become more widespread as time goes on.

"We have more immediate problems at Parker's Farm and with our furloughed employees, too. This Depression has been ongoing since '73, and, somehow, we must try to alleviate that," Will continued.

"It's been a problem since the railroads got over-extended as they built rail lines to the west. J, P. Morgan, the Wall Street banker, kept providing railroads with cash for expansion. He was getting money from European investors and feeding it to these railroads.

"By September of that year, railroads started defaulting on Morgan's loans, then the stock market panicked and crashed.

"To be fair, the same thing was happening in Europe. It was a worldwide depression. That's another reason the money dried up.

"That's how and why it happened, but now, it is our responsibility to take some kind of action to change it.

Chapter Three

THE GILDED AGE

C hristmas morning, 1876, dawned with a new covering of fresh snow. The crisp, cold air felt exhilarating to Will Presley as he stepped out onto the front porch with his first cup of coffee of the day.

He and Lenora had placed presents for their children under the Christmas tree. Anticipating a delicious dinner with his in-laws, Will felt a sense of happiness and contentment.

Life was good.

Hearing squeals of delight from his children as they discovered their presents, he smiled and went inside.

"Oh, Daddy, look what Santa left for me," Mimi exclaimed as she showed him the small crib for her doll.

. "Now Maggie has a place of her own to sleep."

"Yes, Princess, you and Maggie have been good girls this year. I know she'll love it."

Ronnie and Randy rolled their eyes at each other and snickered. They had secretly watched their mother wrapping gifts for all of them but kept it from Mimi.

The boys received cowboy clothes, including chaps, made by Ralph Pendleton, a tailor who had a shop downtown. Pendleton also created costumes for the actors at Ford's Theatre.

Bouncing into her grandmother's house ahead of the rest of the family, Mimi cried out, "Mamaw, Mamaw, look at Maggie's new crib. Now she has her little bed and doesn't have to sleep with me. Santa brought it to me."

The boys strolled in, and Alice exclaimed, "Lookee here at Mamaw's two cowboys. I like your new clothes."

"Yep, I'm Jesse James, and this here's my brother, Frank," Ronnie said smugly.

Alice smiled but said nothing.

When Lenora and Will followed their children into the house, Alice welcomed them. "Merry Christmas, children. I'm happy to see you today.

"Harry's in the gathering room, Will. You can join him there. Len, you come into the kitchen and help me finish dinner."

"Oh, I love the aroma of apple cobbler cooking, Mama. Thanks for making it for us," Lenora was gracious.

"I knew you liked it, and the children love fried chicken. Christmas is a memorable day, and I want everyone to have what they like on this day," Alice explained.

After dinner, the whole clan moved into the parlor, and Alice carried wrapped gifts for the Presley family.

"Alright, Mimi, you are first. I hope you like it," Alice smiled. "Now, here are gifts for you boys. I hope you will read it.

"I didn't forget you and Will, Len. I know that both of you enjoy reading."

Harry just quietly watched, then reached for a cigar and lit it. Alice noticed the cigar, frowned, but said nothing.

Mimi tore the wrapping off the box. Alice had given her a tea set."What is it, Mamaw? It looks like cups and plates."

"Yes, Sweetheart, it's a tea set. You and Maggie can have a tea party."

"Look, Mama, Mamaw got us a book with a leather cover and gold on the pages. What is it, Mamaw?" Randy was curious.

"It's a Bible with gilded edges on the pages. Down toward the bottom, it has your name in gold, too. Ronnie's is the same. That way, you won't get them confused," she assured them.

Lenora gingerly opened her package. It contained a book by Louisa May Alcott titled *Little Women.* "Oh, thank you, Mama. I've wanted to read this book for a long time."

"Well, I went into the Book Nook, and Becky, the owner, suggested this book. It has been available since '68 but is still a popular seller.

"Alcott lived in Concord, Massachusetts and is closely associated with Emerson and Thoreau, the Transindentualists."

Will opened his package and asked, "Alice, what is *The Gilded Age?* I've heard of Mark Twain, but not this book."

"According to Becky, it's a satirical look at what's happening in our country today. Everybody has been trying to get rich since completing the Transcontinental Railroad in '69, the Second Industrial Revolution, and the westward expansion. Pundits have called it the Golden Age, but because only a few have gotten rich, Twain dubbed it the Gilded Age."

"And I believe Twain is correct," Harry retorted. "Only a few Industrialists who have conspired to monopolize the key industries have succeeded, while the rest of us struggle to survive. I've heard it called Social Darwinism."

"Yes, I've heard that, too." Will nodded his head.

"Daddy, what is *Social Darwinism*?" Lenora asked.

"Princess, Darwin was a naturalist who espoused a theory that in nature only the strong survive; he called it *Survival of the Fittest.* Many people have seized on this theory to explain why only a few have become rich. They deserve it because they are intellectually and physically more assertive, and the weaker ones should and must be subservient to them.

"Workers and labor unions and minority groups have pushed back against this sentiment and opposed it. But, many in government have opposed any involvement in aiding poor or disadvantaged folks."

"But Daddy, didn't Jesus say that when you help those in need, you have, in effect, aided Him?" Lenora asked. "And today, we celebrate the birth of Jesus."

"Yes, Princess, that's correct, but Congress doesn't always follow Jesus' teaching."

"Presley, when you finish reading Twain's book, I'd be interested to know your reaction. Is this the Gilded Age and not the Golden Age?" Harry spoke rhetorically.

Two Days Later

When he finished breakfast, Will started to walk down to the barn; he saw Harry coming out of his house. When Harry reached the bottom of the steps on the   fromt porch, he grabbed his chest and moaned in pain.

Will started to speak to Harry, then saw his knees buckle. He fell to the ground. When Will got close, he could see Harry gasping for breath and holding his chest.

Yelling for Lenora to tend to Harry, he ran to the barn, hitched the horse to the buggy, and quickly loaded Harry into it.

Shouting to Lenora as he started toward the front gate, "I'm taking Harry to the hospital in D. C. I'll get word to you about his condition as soon as possible."

Chapter Four

JIM CROW IN MEMPHIS

Very shortly after the 13th Amendment ended slavery, the southern states decided to lease convicts for labor. Peonage (convict labor) became a profitable business. Hundreds of white men were hired as police officers and given the job of arresting blacks, who were found guilty of violating *Black Codes.* Following their arrest, these men, women, and even children, could be leased to plantations where they would harvest cotton, tobacco, or sugar cane.

Some of those arrested were leased to the owners of coal mines or railroad companies. The states received payment for every prisoner who worked for the businesses.

More than 800,000 blacks were part of peonage or re-enslavement through the prison system. This practice continued until the 1940s.

The states who profited from the peonage system justified the practice by using one phrase from the 13th Amendment. Neither slavery nor involuntary servitude could occur except as a punishment for a crime.

The federal government took no action as *Black Codes* were established to appease the angry white southern farmers.

A few examples of Black Codes include:

It was illegal for a Black Preacher to address a congregation without special written permission from the police.

Being without a job was considered vagrancy or loitering.

In South Carolina, a male child whose parent was considered vagrant could be apprenticed to an employer and held until 21.

Willie Johnson's Construction Company had prospered in Memphis. Norville Hill had aided him in establishing the business before he and Charlotte left Memphis to return to Knoxville in 1868.

Li'l Georgie, his brother, was a twenty-five percent partner in the business, and his mother, Bertha, and his sister, Anna Lou, worked for him. When construction on a house was completed, the women gave it a thorough cleaning and prepared it for occupancy.

Will Presley and Norville Hill had employed Willie and Li'l Georgie to build the Freedmen's Schools in Memphis. The two brothers, Willie and Georgie, were freed slaves who had lived on a plantation picking cotton.

After their freedom was granted, they moved to Memphis and survived by doing odd jobs around the cotton warehouses on Front Street. They quickly learned the building trade, chosen by Lenora, Will's wife, as laborers on the school projects.

Norville had been their foreman and trainer in the school construction. He continued to work with them after the schools were finished.

Transitioning to building houses in the South Memphis district where the freed blacks were segregated, there was a great need for affordable housing for black folks.

Norville convinced a few white landowners to build houses and rent them to South Memphis residents for investment income and fair land use.

Norville, and his wife, Charlotte, moved to Knoxville, where they continued their work with the Freedmen's Bureau.

When they moved, Willie and Georgie pursued additional home construction using funds they managed to save from their paychecks from working for white landowners.

Life was good, but then, things changed.

In Tennessee, the Freedmen's Bureau was still operating in Nashville, Memphis, Chattanooga, Knoxville, and Pulaski. Still, many Jim Crow laws became *De Jure* (established by law), and many others were *De Facto* (existing in fact, if not legally in the law).

When the State of Tennessee was re-admitted to the Union, Home-Rule was re-instituted. So legislatures and town councils returned to the pre-war era's rules and laws. Discrimination and ill-treatment of blacks, once again, was the rule rather than the exception.

Vagrancy laws were again enforced against blacks. Any black person, male or female, who was unemployed was jailed and sentenced to work on cotton plantations for poverty wages. Many females were charged with prostitution and detained for months without a hearing or trial.

Georgie spoke to Anna Lou when she walked into a house he was building, "Where you been, girl? I ain't seed you in three days."

"Them Irish cops done put me in de jail. Said I'se a vagrant 'n a 'ho. I'se jist walkin' down Beale street goin' home afta work.

"He tried ta git me ta go in de alley 'n pull my underpants down, but I wuddn't do it. That's when he say I'ma 'ho 'n goin' ta jail."

"Momma been worried 'bout you, 'n me 'n Willie has too. I didn't know where you wuz.

"How'd ya git outta jail, girl? Ya ain't got no money ta pay yo' way out," Georgie questioned her.

"Dat Sargent at de po'lice station say I'se jist stayin' dere ta git free food. He gittin' tarred a feedin' me, so I say let me go home 'n my Momma wud feed me.

"He say git yo' black ass outta here 'n go home ta yo' Momma."

"Ya needs ta be a stayin' close ta me 'n Willie. Maybe they be leavin' you alone, then. Hand me them nails ova here; then you head on home 'n tell Momma you all rite."

Willie entered the building just as Anna Lou started to leave. "Where ya been, girl? Ain't seed ya in days. We been worried 'bout ya."

"It'sa long sto'ry big brutha. Git Georgie ta tell 'bout it. I'ma-goin' home 'n see Momma."

"Where ya been, big brutha?" Georgie asked Willie.

"Been down on East Beale street at a lynchin'" Willie had tears in his eyes.

"Who dey hang dis time?" Georgie frowned.

"Ya 'member Ralphie Phillips'" Willie asked.

"Didn't dat boy work some fer us?" Georgie remembered.

"Uh-huh, he sho' did. Wuz a good worker, too." Willie nodded.

"Whut'd he do ta git hisself hung?" Georgie got nervous.

"Him 'n dat li'l white girl, Susie Dunn, wuz a courtin'. Her Daddy caught 'em settin' on a tree stump. Daddy claimed Ralphie wuz tryin' ta kiss her 'n she didn't want 'im to."

"Dem two's been a courtin' eva since dey wuz in same school class, nigh on ta two yeahs now. I seed 'em holdin' hands walkin' down de street," Georgie related.

"Yeah, I know dat, but why'd he hafta git a white girl?" Wuddn't ther' no black girl he cudda had?' Willie asked.

"Sho wuz. He's a big strappin' ol' boy, real strong, 'n a hard worker. But ya know, when dem girls start ta makin' goo-goo eyes at ya, it's hard ta say no, 'specially fer a seventeen-year-old boy," Georgie replied.

"Dey strung 'im up on a big oak tree rite in his own front yahrd. His Momma watched tha 'hole thang. She wuz screamin' 'n cryin' terrible loud. Li'l Susie wuz too." Willie was crying openly. "Damned white folks won't give us a chance, a'tall."

"Dat boy cudda amounted ta sump'in one day if he cudda kept his britches on," Georgie was teary-eyed. "It'sa damned shame, I'ma tellin' ya."

"Willie ya gotta tell Momma 'n Anna Lou ta take ta ridin' de streetcar, dey don' need be walkin' no mo'," Georgie told him. "Dem po'lice'll let 'em alone if dey ain't walkin'."

"Dat streetcar ride costs a nickel each way, gittin' ther', then gettin' home. That's a dime every day," Willie shook his head.

"Stop bein' such a tightwad, Willie. That's my Momma 'n my sista we talkin' 'bout. Jist give 'em each a extra dime when ya pay 'em. It ain't gonna break us," Georgie insisted.

"Yeah, I guess ya gotta good point, li'l brutha," Willie conceded. "But dey hafta ride in de back of de streetcar."

"Yeah, I know dat, but it sho' beats walkin'," Georgie was emphatic.

November 3, 1868, Election Day

"Er ya goin' down ta dey court house ta vote taday, Georgie?" Willie inquired.

"Whut ya mean, vote?" Georgie was puzzled.

"Taday's when dey vote fer President a de United States, Georgie. Ulysses Grant is a runnin' as a Republican agin' Johnson. I'sa gonna vote fer 'im. Ain't you?"

"I ain't neva voted afore, 'n don' know how," Georgie grinned.

"Ain't none o' us knows how, but I'm a-gonna learn. Come on, li'l brutha we goin' to de cawtthouse ta vote."

"We ain't got no five dollas fer no poll tax. How we gonna pay dat?"

"Billy Jackson's got sum a dem poll tax receipts. Said de mayor give 'em ta 'im, 'n Ulysses Grant hisself paid fer 'em."

"Hey, wuddn't Ulysses Grant here in Memphis fer a while back durin' de war?" Georgie remembered.

"Sho' wuz. He de boss man ova Fort Pickering 'til Lincoln sent 'im back ta Washington," Willie replied. "I'm a-gonna vote fer 'im 'n de mayor too. De mayor's de one whut give dem receipts ta Billy."

"Kin we take sum a de men who work fer us ta go vote, too?" Georgie looked conspiratorially.

"I don' see why not," Willie grinned. "Why'd ya ask that?"

"If Billy Jackson know we got a lotta votes fer de mayor, he might ease up a li'l bit on us 'n Momma 'n Anna Lou. Tell his po'lice ta let us be."

"You right, boy. Git all 'er men ova here. We gonna take 'em all to de polls wit us. I'ma make sho' Billy tells de mayor how many votes we brung wit us."

"Now yer talkin', big brutha."

Billy Jackson was a tall, heavy-set black man with a small mustache but no beard. He was bald but always wore a derby hat and held a black cigar in his mouth but seldom lit it.

Working as an errand runner for the mayor, Billy was accorded respect in the black neighborhood. An exaggerated air of superiority gave him a touch of arrogance, too. But, still, it was good to have friends in high places.

Willie and Georgie led their group of six workers to the courthouse's front and encountered Billy standing on the steps.

'Well, well, lookee who's here," he smiled. "I'm delighted ta see de Johnson bruthas comin' out ta vote. Did'ja brang all dese otha men wit ya?"

"Yas, Suh, we sho did, Billy, 'n we all gonna vote fer de mayor and Ulysses Grant. Ya be sho' 'n tell de mayor we brung 'im some voters taday," Willie confided.

Leaning closer, he whispered, "We don' know nuthin' 'bout votin'. This de first-time fer all us, so ye'll hafta he'p us."

"Don' ya worry 'bout nuthin'. Nobody gonna question long as ya got dem poll tax receipts. Dem people know wher dey come from."

"Hey, Billy, dem I'rish cops been messin' wit my sista. Kin ya speak ta de mayor 'n git dat stopped?" Georgie inquired.

Grinning broadly, Billy bragged, "It's as good as done already. I'll tell de mayor taday.

"I got a bottle a red-eye ova in de carriage. I'll git one fer ya, but ya gotta share it wit yer boys. Only my special friends gits one a dem.

"Now don' open it 'til ye git back home. Don' want dem I'rish boys puttin' ya in jail."

When Willie's crew of men walked into the polling room to vote, one of the poll workers roared, "Looks like we got a bunch a Jim Crows comin' in ta vote."

"Yas Suh, ya do, 'n we got poll receipts ta prove it," Willie bluffed him.

"Yep, I see you do, boys. Come on in here," he said with an embarrassed look on his face.

After Willie's men had voted and left, a poll worker looked at his friend and said, "If all these black boys start votin', things 'er gonna change around here."

"Yeah, but long as we can keep 'em votin' our way, it'll be alright. Them poll tax receipts work real good."

Chapter Five

THE DEPRESSION OF 1873

"Will, what caused the Great Depression to start here in America?" Lenora asked as they talked about the country's problems.

"Here's what I understand from listening to my fellow Senators when they speak on the floor of the chamber and what I hear from briefings from my staff.

"It's complicated but, it all started with the rampant expansion of the western railroad. You know, the first transcontinental railroad caused a boom in the economy. Workers were hired, the lumber business boomed, the steel business boomed, and everybody was making money, including the workers.

"Laborers could make a lot more money working for the railroad companies or the steel mills than they made working on farms. Consequently, they left their farms, moved to the cities, and bet their lives on the business boom's continued success.

"Government land grants, and subsidies to the railroads, fed the boom. A feeling of euphoria overtook common sense, and folks were expecting everything to be successful and make the principals involved instantly rich.

"Over expansion and wild speculation caused banks to lend money without judicious forethought, so they overextended themselves. **Jay Cooke and Company** had agreed to finance the Northern Pacific's new line to the West. In September 1873, the bank failed.

"With Cooke's failure, other banks failed and caused a domino effect. Railroads dependent on bank loans failed. When railroads fell, other businesses that depended on the railroad employees to buy their goods and services fell alongside them.

"Wasn't that when you first went to Congress?" Lenora furrowed her brow.

"Yes, I was there, and I voted for the subsidies to the railroads. They needed lots of railroad ties, fuel stops, and facilities along the way. Our country needed the transportation link to the west. I must admit that my family in Roaring Fork being in the lumber business influenced my decision, too.

"Of course, the Great Chicago Fire back in '71 and the Great Boston Fire in '72 ruined the economy there, but it did create a huge need for lumber in those cities. My family back home benefitted from their disaster."

"Isn't it always the case that some benefit while others suffer?" Lenora commiserated.

"Yes, it is, my Sweet Lady, but that is beyond my control." Will shook his head.

"Because the federal government discontinued silver as money and moved to a gold standard, it negatively affected the economy. A lot of silver mines in Nevada went out of business.

"The Germans were hurt badly too because they supplied silver to most of Europe. It caused a major slowdown all over the continent, so the depression spread worldwide. It's complicated, but folks are struggling everywhere."

"What are you going to do about it, Will? What can you do?" Lenora was deeply concerned.

"I am going to start right here at Parker's Farm. If we can expand our business by starting Parker's Jobbing, we can help folks in our town and community. We'll hire some people, and hopefully, we can supply some extra vegetables and meat to those who are going to bed hungry right here before our eyes."

Lenora's face contorted as she said, "The Federal Government gave subsidies to the railroads, didn't they? Why can't they supply some money to feed these starving common people?"

"Many of our elected representatives believe that helping businesses grow will create jobs for working people. It's called Capitalism-a free-market system."

"I think that people should have jobs, too. It creates a sense of worth for ordinary folk. But what about those who can't find a job?" Lenora was frustrated. "People can't buy things they need if they don't have money, can they?

"It seems to me that the government should help the little people, too."

"Now, Lenora, I wish I could wave a magic wand and solve all of these problems, but I don't have one. What I can do is talk with John and Jim Hall to get their opinion. I do not believe they will support government intervention for ordinary people."

"But Will, it just does not seem right that poor folks are suffering while rich folks are getting richer. I read a newspaper article the other day about Andrew Carnegie. He is a multi-millionaire because railroads are buying his steel-much of it with Federal Government subsidies.

"Cornelius Vanderbilt is wealthy because he owns steamships and many of those railroads. John D. Rockefeller controls most of the oil industry, which fuels those railroads. J P Morgan's bank is supplying money to all of these men, so he is rich now, too," Lenora retorted.

"That's the way the system works, I reckon, Sweet Lady. As I said before, I will discuss it with the Halls and my colleagues in the Senate. We'll see what happens."

Lenora smiled and said, "I know my ideas are new and maybe a little bit radical, but I speak from my heart. Jesus said, I*nasmuch as ye have done it unto the one of the least of these, my brethren, ye have done it unto me.*"

"You know more about the Bible than I do, Lenora, but I must work with what is doable in the Senate. I promised you that I would introduce a bill in the Virginia Legislature about Women's Suffrage, but it didn't go anywhere. I'll try, but I'm not optimistic.

"You know that President Grant reduced the money supply, which caused interest rates to go up. This reduction caused many farmers who depended on seasonal loans to go out of business, too. With a restrictive monetary policy, I don't think more government spending will take place."

"You mean unless it benefits the rich plutocracy," she replied scornfully.

"Plutocracy? What do you mean by that?" Will had never heard the word.

"Plutocracy means 'rule by the rich,' when a small group consisting of the wealthiest people in a society rule by their wealth. Plutocracy is a self-reinforcing system. Once a group of wealthy people is in charge, they can use their money and political power to change the rules to serve their wants and needs best.

"A small group of rich folks now controls our country. That's why Grant reduced the money supply to drive up interest rates. The big banks in New York are profiting by that," she explained. "I heard people in the War Department talking about it when I worked there."

Wryly smiling, Will suggested, "I reckon that motivates a lot of Senators. Many of them meet regularly with prominent people in business from New York and Chicago. Lots of people are impressed by wealthy folk who can invest in their districts back home. I don't like the system, but I'm gradually learning how it works.

"I'll speak to John Hall at church this Sunday and ask if I can visit him and Jim in the afternoon. Next week, I'll talk to Jeremiah Jones to see if any Congressional sentiment exists to help people in need. We'll see what happens."

Approaching John after church, Will smiled and extended his hand. "Good morning John, how are things at the Hall farm?"

"We are surviving but struggling like everybody else in these parts, Presley. How about you and the Parker farm?"

"Well, Harry is not well, as you may have heard, but we are trying to hold things together. If you are available after dinner today, I'd like to ride out to your place for a chat. Will Jim be there?"

"Yes, he usually comes by on Sunday afternoon to catch up on the latest family happenings. I'm certain Jim would like to see you, too."

"Alright, I'll come to your place after dinner. Lenora will have the kids, and Alice will be busy with Harry, but I'll be there about mid-afternoon."

Chapter Six

PARKER'S JOBBING

Lenora joined him at the kitchen table, and he said, "I had some thoughts today about how to alleviate our problems here on the farm.

"How do you like the sound of Parker's Jobbing?"

"What are you talking about? Parker's Jobbing?"

"Yeah, jobbers act as wholesale companies for General Stores and Grocery Stores. We can provide seasonal fruits, chicken, and pork almost year-round using salt curing or smoke curing the meat as we have done for the War Department.

"Of course, we would need to increase our capacity, but by expanding distribution, we can bring our furloughed people back to work. Somehow, we must do our part to overcome this economic depression.

"This will be our fourth year of watching people suffer through these challenging times. I believe, too, that the Presley clan in Graham is having difficulty. Timber and tobacco have slowed in demand, and their markets are suffering.

"Sure, it's a big departure from our usual activities, but these are unusual times."

"Will, I'm not certain Daddy can assume the additional responsibilities of another business," Lenora shook her head.

"I thought about that, but do you remember my brother, Pete?" When she nodded, he continued, "Pete has been a farmer his entire life and knows how to do it. He has a new wife, Lillian, who is Martha's sister.

'They might consider moving to Falls Church to run the farm and oversee the increased production. We already have experienced workers who know how to do it. This plan could be an important move to help us, and at the same time, help my family."

"How could this help your family?"

"If Pete and Lillian will come to help us, the Presley family will have one less family to feed and provide a living. Buck and Johnny's boys are men now and work in the timber and tobacco crops with Billy Bob. Andy got married and moved to the farm operated by his wife's family.

"Maw and Preacher John are living in town, and Maw's still teaching, and John's still preaching. It would just be Billy Bob and Willadeen and their young'uns and Martha and her young'uns depending on Roaring Fork Farm for a living."

"Now, you know we can't make that kind of decision without talking to Momma and Daddy," she was skeptical.

"Yes, and I would not even begin until we can get their approval. Harry has a long recovery period, and Alice will be busy with his care, so we will wait until his health improves. We have some time to think about it, but the sooner we can begin, the better. The growing season will start in March, a couple of months from now."

"Did the medical folks give you any indication about Harry's recovery time or when he can come home?"

"Yes, the doctor said two or three more days in the hospital, then bed rest at home for a month or so. He won't be able to return to normal activities until late Summer or early Fall," Lenora looked worried.

"Momma was concerned about running the farm because you have Senate responsibilities and don't have time. She doesn't think she can do it alone."

"Although the Senate does not convene in the Summer and Fall, I do have things that demand my attention. My thoughts today were almost identical to Alice's. That's why I thought of Pete."

"Well, it might solve our problems, but I don't think we should mention it until Daddy improves. He must be involved in any decisions," Lenora concluded.

"I am in total agreement with you on that, my Sweet Lady."

"How would we go about acquiring more customers for our products?" she asked him.

"The first thing I will do is talk to John Hall. He has been providing beef to the grocery market for years. I know that Jim works with him when Congress is not in session. He could provide some good contacts, too."

"It's all about having contacts, isn't it," she mused.

"It is. Harry told me that when I first considered entering politics. When Harry introduced me to John for the first time, I was impressed at their estate's grandeur. The Hall family is very influential and is what I would consider rich," he remarked.

"This Industrial Revolution we're experiencing has created several rich families," Lenora observed. "Morgan, Vanderbilt, Carnegie, Rockefeller, and others have become extremely rich. Are you suggesting we might join their ranks?" she was incredulous.

"Who knows? It might happen, but probably not," he smiled. "It is a nice thought, though.

"My primary goal at this point is to put the farm back on solid footing and get our people back to work. Then, too, I want to assist the people in our community who are struggling to survive.

"If at the same time I can help my brother and other family members, that would be an additional benefit," he sighed.

"When Momma comes home from the hospital, I'll invite her over to have supper with us. We'll get the latest news about Daddy and share our ideas about the farm with her. She will know how Daddy will react and tell us when to approach him with it," Lenora told him.

"If we decide to proceed, I would like to make a trip to Roaring Fork to meet with Pete and Lillian. A decision of that importance should be made face-to-face. You know they will have a thousand questions.

"Maw and Pastor John will be impacted, too. Billy Bob and the others at Roaring Fork should have their opinion listened to, also," he shared with her.

"Daddy, Daddy, are we goin' to Roarin' Fork and see Mamaw and Papaw John. It was fun when they came to visit us." Ronnie was excited.

"Wait a minute. I'm not sure you children can go. You can't miss school. Mamaw Parker will be here to take care of all of you while we are gone. Your Father and I will be busy taking care of business down there."

Lenora continued, "Now you two boys watch for Mamaw Parker to come home. When she gets here, run out to the barn and tell her we want her to come and eat supper with us."

"Can I tell her, Momma?" Randy begged. "Ronnie always talks before I have a chance."

"No, I do not." Ronnie was adamant. "Sometimes, when I run faster than he does, I beat him talking, but not always," he insisted.

"Alright, boys, I think I heard Mamaw's buggy coming into the barn," Will instructed them. "Go on out and tell her what your mother told you."

Racing to the barn's door, Ronnie was one step ahead of Randy, but he stopped and said nothing. Randy immediately blurted out, "Momma wants you to come and have supper with us and tell us about Papaw Harry. Will you come and eat with us?"

"Sure, I will. Hi Ronnie, how are you?" she smiled.

"I'm fine, Mamaw. Momma and Daddy are goin' down to North Carolina to see Mamaw Presley and Papaw John. We get to stay here with you," he couldn't contain himself.

Randy interjected. "You were supposed to let me tell her. You cheated."

"I did not. You told Mamaw about coming to supper. I didn't say nothing."

"You didn't say anything, Ronnie. It's not nothing," she corrected him.

"Yep, that's what I said. Not nothing," Ronnie insisted.

Alice just shook her head and smiled as they walked toward the house.

As Alice entered the house, Lenora and Will rose to greet her. "Good evening, Momma," Lenora hugged her. "How is Papa today?"

Alice smiled and hugged Will. "Harry is in much better spirits today. He's been up walking the halls of the hospital. He said it felt good to be able to get out of the bed for a while. The doctor thinks two or three more days before he can come home."

"I understand you and Will are planning a trip to North Carolina?" she asked with a puzzled look on her face.

As he gave the boys a sidelong disapproving look, Will replied, "We did discuss the possibility of that, but it's all contingent on a lot of other things. We'll tell you our thoughts while we have supper."

Alice listened closely as Will explained his ideas. Lenora occasionally interjected her thoughts as Will spoke. When he mentioned the idea of bringing the furloughed employees back to work, Alice smiled broadly.

When Lenora mentioned the idea of helping the families in Falls Church with food products, Alice got excited. "That's precisely what Jesus told us to do," she exclaimed. "I think we could do that in conjunction with the church. I'm certain the Rector will approve, and the ladies of the church can have an opportunity to assist us."

"How will we increase our production to the level needed to service all these extra customers? Harry won't be able to do that for several more months."

"That's what we were talking about when we mentioned the trip to Roaring Fork," Will explained. "Pete, one of my younger brothers, is a possible part of our plan.

"He has a new wife, and she becomes another person dependent on the farm for a living. Their business has suffered just as ours has. Pete has been a farmer for his entire life and knows how to do it.

"I believe he would relish the idea of directing a two-pronged money-making operation. The extra revenue we can produce would provide him with a good living and make more money for Parker's Farm and Parker's Jobbing.

"I'm not sure that he and Lillian would even consider moving to Falls Church, but a face-to-face meeting is necessary for this kind of decision.

"Of course, we'll discuss it with Harry when he is physically able to make serious decisions. I would not proceed without his wholehearted approval.

"I'll depend on you, Alice, to tell me when he's ready. When it's time to visit with John Hall, I want Harry to accompany me," Will finished.

"That is an ambitious program you just outlined, young man, but I can see how Lenora became so enamored of you. Harry called you a *raconteur,* and you certainly are that, too," she smiled. "We'll see what happens when Harry comes home."

Chapter Seven

HARRY COMES HOME

On Friday, January 5th, Harry was released from the District of Columbia General Hospital. Will and Alice arrived at the medical facility before 7:30 am. Lenora had stayed at home to get the children off to school.

"Good morning Harry." Will spoke as they entered the room his father-in-law occupied. "Are you ready to go home?"

"I'm way past ready. I was ready Monday. I'm eager now," he smiled.

Alice hugged him, then kissed him lightly on the lips. "And I am eager to have you at home," she gave him a loving look. "Everybody is eager to have you at home, even little Mimi. She asked me last night when you were coming home. When I told her in the morning, she squealed with delight. She said I wanna see my Papaw."

"The doctor hasn't been here yet, so I guess we have to wait for him to examine me one more time,"

"What's his name, Harry?" Will asked.

"Doctor David Watson, he's a fine cardiologist. The nurses say he's the best one in the hospital. They say he's the best-looking one, too," Harry grinned.

When the doctor entered Harry's room, Will rose to greet him, and Alice smiled. "Doctor Watson, this is my wife, Alice, and my son-in-law, Will Presley."

"It's nice to meet you, folks," he smiled and nodded. "Mr. Parker is progressing very well and is ready to go home. He has suffered severe damage to his heart and must restrict his activity for a few months.

"He needs to stay active, but on a limited basis. No heavy lifting, no physical labor." Looking at Harry, he said, "Get out of the house occasionally to walk but let someone else maintain your farm for at least several months. Perhaps your son-in-law can handle those duties."

Alice spoke up, "Will has other responsibilities at the Capitol. He's our Virginia Senator. We have some other ideas that we'll discuss with Harry when we get home."

Harry looked up at his wife with a puzzled expression.

"Can we get your things together and head home?" she asked Harry.

Looking at the doctor, Harry asked, "Is it alright, Doc? Can we go?"

"Yes, of course, Mr. Parker. I'll sign the discharge papers to release you."

Harry boarded the carriage with some assistance from Will. Alice sat behind Harry.

As they left the hospital grounds, Harry asked, "What are these other mysterious ideas I heard mentioned? I'm only gone a short time, and the family starts plotting," he asked, half-joking.

Will decided to introduce the subject gently. "It's the beginning of a new year, and that is always a good time to start charting a course for the next twelve months. When we get you home and fed properly by Alice, we will explore a few possibilities."

Harry's curiosity was temporarily stifled as he was met with three eager grandchildren waiting for him at the front door. "Oh, Papaw, we've missed you so much," Mimi exclaimed as she grabbed Harry's leg. "Come sit with me."

"Take it easy on Papaw," Alice advised. He still needs a little rest to get all better.

Ronnie and Randy were elbowing each other to see who could get the closest to Harry first. Both spoke at once, "You always sit with Mimi. It's our time to be with you. We've missed you the most."

"That's not fair," Mimi started crying.

Lenora separated her brood and said, "There will be time enough for everyone to sit with Papaw. Let's have some supper first and let him rest for a while."

"Alright, Presley, come on in here and let's talk. Alice and Lenora can finish cooking supper."

"Harry, I sat at my Senate desk on Tuesday and looked at some things we need to accomplish this year. Our goals should include getting our furloughed employees back to work, doing something to ease our neighbors' pain here in Falls Church who are out of work due to this depression and helping our former freedmen deal with Jim Crow.

"At present, we're not getting enough orders from the War Department to rehire our employees. So, if we had more customers, we could produce more products and provide jobs for our people."

"Where would we get more customers?" Harry asked.

"John Hall has been selling beef to retail stores all over this part of the country for many years. We could sell pork, vegetables, and fruit to these same customers.

"You and I can talk to John and tell him what we have in mind. We are not competing with him because we'll sell different products."

"Don't you think these stores already have suppliers for this kind of groceries?"

"I'm sure they do, but not nearly as many as they used to have. A lot of these producers have gone out of business. We've managed to hold on because of our War Department business. Although it's not as large as it was, it's still a steady business, and we get paid on time.

"John can advise us which customers are doing reasonably well with their business during this depression. I will make contacts with them and ask for their business. As a Virginia Senator, I assume that folks will be receptive to talking to me.

"Many of our employees are customers of these stores, too. If they go back to work, they can buy from the stores.

"It's simple economics. If people have jobs, they have money to spend, and the economy starts to hum again. It must start somewhere."

"Now you heard Doctor Watson today. I am going to be unable to work much for several months. All this extra production is going to take a lot more work on the farm," Harry insisted.

"Which brings me to my next point, Harry. I have a younger brother named Pete down in North Carolina. He has just taken on a new bride, and they are still on Paw's farm at Roaring Fork.

"Another brother, Billy Bob, actually it's William Robert, but we call him Billy Bob, runs the farm. Pete works for him, but he might be interested in moving to Falls Church to run the farm here.

"He's been a farmer his entire life and knows how to do it. If he moved here, he could oversee things. Naturally, he would work under your supervision. Even recovering from a heart attack, you could make decisions and give Pete directions."

"I have never wholly turned things over to anybody to run my farm. Several employees over the years have been given responsibility but never complete control.

"And I don't know your brother. Is he reliable? Can I trust him? Will he even consider moving to Falls Church?"

"I can answer in the affirmative on the first two questions. Pete was raised as was I in a Christian home to be honest and trustworthy. We worked hard to make a living on a farm, and we were God-fearing Methodists. My stepfather is a Methodist minister.

"To answer your third question, I honestly don't know if he would move to Falls Church. I will need to make a trip to Roaring Fork to discuss it with him and Lillian, his wife."

"There are a lot of ifs here, Presley," Harry shook his head. "We don't know how John Hall will react when we ask for his help. We don't know if your brother will make a move, and we don't know if we can acquire these new customers."

"Yes, that's all true, Harry, but my Paw used to say, you don't know lessen you ask. We've got a lot of questions and a lot of asking to do. The big question I have for you is, do you want to proceed?"

"I need to think about it for a little while. What does Alice think? Lenora too?"

"I believe that all of us are waiting for your reaction. You take as much time as you need to make your decision. You are the ultimate decider because this is your farm.

"I just want to do something to help us through this depression. It's been almost four years now, and people are hurting."

Will was quiet for a moment, thinking that he might have overwhelmed Harry with too many important decisions when he was still recovering.

"Harry, I would like to give you some time to talk with Alice alone and then sleep on the general idea. Let's get back together tomorrow for a preliminary plan if you are comfortable with proceeding."

Chapter Eight

DECISONS, DECISIONS

As he neared the Hall's Manor, Will saw Jim Hall arriving just ahead of him. Jim looked up and saw Will, so he waited before entering the house.

"Good afternoon Senator Presley. I didn't know you were coming by today," Jim greeted him.

"Well, I asked John this morning if he was available today. He told me you would be here, too. I have some things to discuss with the two of you."

John heard them talking and opened the door. "Come in, gentlemen. It's too cold to be standing outside. Come on into the parlor, and we'll chat.

"Can I get you a cup of coffee or a shot of bourbon?"

"I'm not much for drinking bourbon, John," Will shook his head. "My Paw had a problem with it, so I try to avoid it. Just get me some coffee, please."

"Get me a shot of bourbon, Dad," Jim suggested. "It's been a hard week for me in D.C."

Speaking to his wife, John said, "Honey, would you bring a cup of coffee for Senator Presley and a glass of bourbon for Jim and me?"

"Yes, of course, I will. Hello, Senator, and here's my little Jimmy," she said as she hugged her son.

Jim smiled and hugged his Mother. "She always makes a fuss over me when I come by," he grinned. Looking at Will, he said softly, "I do like the attention, though."

"Be seated, gentlemen, and tell me what's on your mind," John added.

"I've got two or three things, John," Will began. "First off, I've got some ideas about expanding our operation at Parker's Farm. Because the War Department has cut back on our orders, it has become necessary to furlough several employees. If we could find some new customers, we could bring them back to work."

"Yes, I see," John stroked his chin. "What can I do about that?"

"You have retail customers who buy beef from you. If we could sell pork and vegetables and fruit in season, we could increase our products' demand.

"We would not compete with you because we sell different products. If you introduce me to some of your customers, I will have instant credibility and quickly build a customer base.

"Harry is still unable to assume a full workload, but I have a brother in North Carolina who might be persuaded to move here and help with the extra work at the farm. Lenora and I will make a trip to North Carolina soon to discuss it with him."

Listening intently, John looked at his son. "What do you think of that, Jim.?"

"I like the idea that the Senator wants to take action to improve the economy here in our community. It won't affect our business, and it will help him." He grinned and said, "He'll owe us a favor."

"Alright, Presley, I'll write a letter of introduction and give you a list of our customers, but I think most of these people know you already. Many of them probably voted for you."

"Thanks, John, I'm much obliged to you," Will was gracious.

Jim spoke up, "What else you got on your mind, Will? You said you had two or three things."

"Jim, I'm sure you remember having lunch with Jeremiah Jones the other day. Jim nodded, and he continued, " I am deeply disturbed by this Jim Crow thing by which our black friends are being mistreated."

Looking at his father, Jim related Jones's story of being denied service in a restaurant near the Capitol in D.C.

John sighed and said, "I've seen those situations, too. Discrimination against our black brothers is deeply ingrained in these ex-Confederates here in Virginia.

"It's just gonna take some time for these folks to forget the war."

"John, the Fourteenth Amendment gave freedmen full citizenship rights in the United States. It just ain't right the way they are being treated," Will was adamant.

"Now, Senator, we have the Reconstruction Act of 1867 and the Fourteenth Amendment of 1868," Jim insisted. "Legislatively, that's all we can do. It's up to the Justice Department to enforce the law, not the Legislature."

"I do understand what you're saying, Jim, but it just seems that we should do something."

John spoke, "Jim, did I hear you say that you expressed indignation to the owner of the restaurant who turned you away?" Jim nodded, and John continued. "You can say what's on your mind when the occasion arises.

Also, you can introduce Jeremiah to your congressional colleagues and include him in social events.

"When you get to know someone as an individual, you tend to warm up to them. There are other freedmen in the Legislature, and you can befriend them, too. Be patient and take it one at a time."

"Thank you, John. You remind me very much of my Paw. I was a young man when he died in an accident, and I miss his sage advice."

"Well, I'm flattered that you equate me with your father. I'm happy to stand in for him," John smiled.

"One other thing, gentlemen," Will said apologetically. "My wife thinks that we, as a nation, should try to do something about the suffering that's going on among our working citizens. People are dying of starvation, lack of shelter, and lack of medical care. These are all things that we can take for granted, but many, many people are suffering."

John stroked his chin before he spoke. "Are you suggesting that the federal government provide direct assistance to these people?"

"Yeah, something like that," Will nodded.

Jim joined the conversation. "Senator, don't you remember back in April '74 when Congress passed a bill to add 400 million greenbacks to the economy and 100 million to the overall money supply? Grant vetoed it because he said it would create an inflationary cycle.

"I don't believe Congress will even consider providing direct aid to individuals now, even though Grant is not our President."

John interjected, "And who knows how the Presidential Electoral College will work out. We could end up with Rutherford Hayes as our President - a man who lost both the popular vote and the disputed electoral votes down South.

"I think it will be best to shy away from that idea for now. I can understand Lenora's concern, but we must concentrate on what is achievable in Congress. That's my opinion."

"I want to offer my sincere thanks to both of you for your advice and time today. I think I have a better understanding about how to proceed with everything," Will was gracious.

"Before you go, Presley, I'll get a list of my customers for you to take with you. Give my regards to Harry," John replied.

Jim shook Will's hand and said, "I'll see you around the Capitol, Senator. Maybe we'll have lunch with Jeremiah again one day soon."

As he rode back toward Parker's Farm, Will thought, *"Lenora ain't gonna like this."*

Chapter Nine

THE PLAN

Realizing how many movable parts there would be in his embryonic plan for Parker's Farm, Will recruited Lenora's assistance in organizing the steps required to move forward.

"I believe we should think about making a trip to talk face-to-face with Pete and his wife," Lenora suggested. We cannot write anything in stone, but we need to find out whether there is any interest on their part.

"We would be asking them to leave behind everything they know and enter an unfamiliar environment. That cannot be very comforting to anyone. Remember how anxious we were when we moved to Memphis to take on a new responsibility?"

"It is even worse for them. At least you and I had some experience working in different environments. I had left my childhood home and made a new life for myself. Pete and Lillian were born and raised in Roaring Fork. They have never been anywhere else."

Will shook his head and wondered if he was crazy to consider such a proposition.

"On the other hand, they might welcome an opportunity to move away from the farm and become independent," Will thought.

"Remember how I suggested you introduce our marriage and potential move with the Freedman's Bureau to your parents?"

"Yes, you used your natural charm to paint a rosy picture of what we would be doing. You made us sound like pioneers for freedom and justice," she smiled. "Daddy even told you that you had the gift of gab and ability to sell anything."

"I'm guessing I got that from my Maw and Paw. They encouraged all of us kids to believe in ourselves and to dream big. If Paw hadn't held onto that positive attitude, he would have never made the trip alone from England with no money and only limited prospects. Somehow he could envision a life with a wonderful wife, a brood of children, and becoming a landowner.

"If Maw hadn't kept her dream of being a teacher alive by starting with her husband and children, she would never have become a respected lead teacher in Graham.

"So there's no reason we can't dream about building Parker's Farm into a larger business, and in the process, help our families and friends improve their lives."

"That off-the-cuff speech is precisely the reason you have succeeded as a politician, Will. It's the reason you convinced me to marry you and move many miles away from my home to pursue a dream. It is why you continue to be able to persuade others to follow your lead.

"I believe you will be able to make all of this happen, but you might have to give others a little time to digest the ideas. Daddy and Pete may not be as adventurous as you are. So let's, take this one step at a time."

"I indeed, chose the right person to be my wife and partner, Lenora. You listen to all my rantings and give me much-needed feedback.

"It would be best if we could meet with Pete and Lillian alone for the first discussion, but the logistics of that are complicated," Will thought. "If we drive to the farm in Roaring Fork, Billy Bob and Martha will probably want to know what's going on and possibly confuse Pete's thinking."

Lenora asked, "What if we had your Mother and John contact Pete asking him and Lillian to meet us at First Methodist on the day we arrive? Of course, we will need to give Sally and John a brief idea of the meeting's purpose."

Will considered her suggestion and asked, "How will we get the message to Maw and John? A letter will take too long."

"We could send a carefully worded wire to the newspaper office, the General Store, or wherever you feel would be most appropriate and discreet. You and I can practice saying the most we can in the fewest words. On second thought, I might be better at that task," Lenora laughed and winked at Will.

"I thought you liked to hear me talk," he frowned but with a half-crooked smile. "Let's hear your concise yet profound communication skills."

"How about something like this?

> To John and Sally Henderson, Graham, North Carolina
> Please ask Pete and Lillian to join us in town at the church 4:00 Saturday. Important proposal for their future. Keep private. We will arrive 3:00 by carriage. All is well."

"My goodness, Lenora, you have a gift for intrigue, but that might work. Tomorrow, I will speak with your Father and get permission to have a preliminary discussion with Pete. If he is agreeable, I will send that wire from the Capitol first thing Monday."

After Church on Sunday afternoon, Will met with Harry to continue their considerations for the future.

"How are you feeling today, Harry?"

"I am somewhat weak, but being back home with Alice feeding and nursing me, I'm improving rapidly," Harry smiled and patted his wife's hand. "I have been thinking about your proposition and your vision of what our future could be, Will."

Will thought about Lenora's advice and decided it was best to listen without adding anything.

"I appreciate that you have been thinking about our future, and I did not intend to sound negative when you offered your ideas. It is just that I have operated the farm on my own for so many years, and I am reluctant to turn over management to anyone else.

"My recent medical setback clarifies that I will be limited in any activities requiring physical labor; however, my mental abilities have not been affected. Consequently, I would be open to hiring someone who would report directly to me in the foreman's role. If your brother is interested in that job, I will welcome further exploration. So you have my agreement to talk with him and ask him to visit us before making a decision."

"Thank you, Harry. Thank you very, very much," Will smiled and shook hands with his father-in-law. "I agree that it is wise for everyone concerned to ease into any changes. Your daughter has inherited your calm consideration of situations and a talent for the process. She suggested that she and I meet personally with Pete and his wife to introduce the possibility of their relocation."

"That's my girl," Harry responded proudly.

"Tomorrow, I plan to send a wire to Pastor John requesting he set a meeting for us. If all goes well, Lenora and I will travel to Graham the following Saturday, meet with them, and return Sunday. I hope you and Alice will agree to let the children stay with you while we are gone."

Alice overheard this request from the kitchen and popped in to say, "We would not think of having our babies stay anywhere else."

Monday morning, Will sent his wire to the Graham Gazette office. Within an hour after that, the message was delivered to Pastor Henderson at the church.

"Listen to this, Sally," he said, reading the wire to his wife. "What do you think this is all about?

"I don't have any idea, but I am certainly glad they ended with all is well," she answered.

"I think we should ask a few questions before we talk with Pete," John insisted. "I will send a return wire to get a few details."

"Good idea, John. I have some planning to do if they are staying with us," Sally pondered.

When Will received a return wire on Tuesday, he responded in hopes of reducing the anxiety John and Sally might be feeling. The message included information that the proposal for Pete was a favorable opportunity, that reservations at the Palmer House were being made for himself and Lenora, and that they invited John and Sally to join him and Pete and Lillian for dinner at Palmer House following the initial discussion.

On Wednesday, John and Sally rode their carriage the ten-mile trip to Roaring Fork. To distract Martha, Billy Bob, and Willadeen, Sally gathered her children in the big house to catch up on family news. John asked Pete to come to the Roaring Fork Church with him on the pretense of evaluating some structural damages.

"What do you think he has in mind, Preacher?" Pete asked upon hearing of the requested meeting.

"I don't have the details, Pete, but it must be important, and it needs to be kept private from the rest of the family for now. Will insisted that the meeting would be with you and Lillian only. We also get to have dinner together at the Palmer House."

"Wow, Lil and me neva had a chance to do that afore," Pete sounded excited. "Now, I jist hafta explain why we're going back ta town after the weekly delivery."

"Just say you are taking your bride shopping," Henderson suggested.

On Saturday morning, Will and Lenora boarded the train in D.C. for a five-hour ride to Asheville.

"You know, Lenora, this is our second trip to Graham since I vowed I would never return, and you convinced me to go both times. You must enjoy seeing me uncomfortable," he joked.

"That's my job, Will. I know when to push you to do what needs to be done even when you resist," she smiled. "Admit it; you know you want to see your Mother and John again."

"Yes, even a brief visit with them will be worth the trip," he agreed.

Arriving mid-afternoon at John and Sally Henderson's home, the Presleys were tired but exhilarated by the warm greetings received from Sally and John and Pete and Lillian.

Will received an embrace from the sister-in-law he barely knew. "Lillian, you have grown into a beautiful woman, and I can see that you are making my little brother a happy man," he said while holding her hands and smiling at her with his crooked grin until she blushed.

"Come on inside," John motioned. "We have a few hours before we need to go to the Palmer House."

As they sat around the Henderson fireplace, Will explained the Parker Farm history and its potential for the future. He talked about an opportunity to be part of a growing business. At last, he came to the proposition. "Pete, would you and Lillian be willing to visit us at the farm to become familiar with the operation?"

Lillian looked at Pete with some trepidation. "How far is the Parker Farm from 'ere, Will?"

Lenora sensed Lillian's uneasiness and took her hand. "It is the better part of a day's trip by rail and carriage, but it is not bad. You will need to begin with a carriage ride to Asheville, where you can board the train to Washington, D.C. We will meet you there and bring you to our house where you will stay during your visit. We can probably arrange for you to have a tour of the capital city before you leave. Think of it as an adventure."

Will added, "We will organize the travel connections for you. There will be no cost to you except your time, and we will enjoy having you with us. Once you get oriented to the area and have time to think about the opportunity, the decisions are all yours."

Pete finally spoke. "My head's spinning. How long afore I gotta answer?"

"We will be leaving before noon tomorrow, so you have all evening and the next morning to ask any questions you may have. Remember, we are only talking about a visit at this time. You do not have to commit until you have all the information you need."

"It's kind of ye to thank of us, but ye know we've neva bin outta Roaring Fork sept fer goin' ta town ever Satadee. We'd be like a fish outta water in a big city," Pete said, lowering his head.

"You would be a lot better off than I was when I left home with no place to go and no prospects. You would have a family. You would have a comfortable home. You would have a type of work that is familiar to you. You would have a chance to advance to a different level than you ever will staying here and answering to Billy Bob."

Lillian looked at Pete and said, "It'd be somethin' we neva thought a doing. What could it hurt ta go for a visit?"

"Let's get ready to go to the Palmer House. Lenora and I need to check-in, and then we can enjoy some of their fine cooking while we catch up with what's going on in my old hometown," Will directed.

As they entered the Palmer House foyer, Will remembered how his father, J.W. Presley, told the story of his first day in Graham.

"Paw said Mr. Graham let him stay here overnight while he got all his supplies ready to set up in Roaring Fork. Although awed by the grandeur of the hotel, he was even more overwhelmed by the beautiful young woman he met at the General Store," he added, watching Sally blush.

"Even compared to the lavish hotels of our capital city, this is still quite magnificent," Will observed. "And they know how to cook here, too. Just look at the cornbread."

"Don't they 'ave no cornbread in Washington?" Pete acted surprised.

"Oh, they have their version of it, but they add sugar and sometimes other strange ingredients," he answered.

"Politicians are noted for taking something simple and making it complicated," Will added as everyone laughed.

Sally smiled at John, who knew she was so happy to see her two estranged sons communicating in such a pleasant way.

On Sunday morning, Will and Lenora had breakfast at the Palmer house and dressed for their trip home. They stopped at Henderson's home to say goodbye.

"I'm sorry we cannot stay for services. Thank you so much for arranging this meeting," Will said, shaking hands with John. "I think of you often, and your words still guide me."

"You are a good man, Will Presley. If you continue listening to your inner voice, you will not go far astray."

Turning to his mother, Will embraced her for a long time. "Maw, you were the backbone of our family. Paw chose the right person to make a life with, and I think I may have done the same."

"I believe you have, Son. Lenora is strong, smart, and, most of all, she loves you."

John's final farewell words let Will and Lenora know that he and Sally would encourage Pete to take a chance for a better future. "I will keep in touch with Pete and let you know how things stand."

On the second leg of their return trip, Lenora noticed an expression of sadness on her husband's face. "What are you thinking, Will?"

"It's one of those double-edged swords, I guess. While I am happy to think my brother might be joining us at the farm, I am sad to see Maw and John showing their age. This trip may have been the last time I will see them both."

"I hope that is not the case, but if it is, you made your Mother happy this weekend. It was evident in her smile as she watched you and Pete talk with each other."

Both Presleys napped intermittently on the long return train ride. They were greeted with love by their children and by Harry and Alice. "It's going to be an early morning, so I think I will call it a night," Will said as he hugged the boys and kissed little Mimi.

Tuesday morning, Will heard a knock on his office door. A young page apologized for the interruption by announcing, "Sorry to bother you,

Senator, but we thought you would want to receive this wire as soon as possible."

> Senator George Wilhelm Presley, Washington, D.C.
> Pete and Lillian are ready to accept the offer to visit the farm. Waiting for instructions and arrangements.

As promised, Will made all the arrangements for Pete and Lillian to have a rented carriage for their ride to Asheville and tickets for the train to Washington. The schedule brought his brother and sister-in-law to the Capital Depot on Friday afternoon, allowing Will to pick them up and take them to the Parker Farm as he left work for the week."

"Welcome to the big city, Baby Brother," Will said as he hugged Pete and Lillian. "How was the trip?"

"Long, but kinda fun ridin' while sittin' in a cozy seat lookin' at tha trees 'n' tha hills go by so fast," Lillian answered. Pete just smiled at his wife, feeling pleased that she had enjoyed this adventure.

"We'll be home in an hour," Will told them. "Lenora will have a nice supper ready for us, and you can settle in for the night. Tomorrow, you will meet the Parkers and get acquainted with the activities on the farm."

Lenora greeted her in-laws warmly and helped them unload their travel bags in the bedroom where they would stay during the visit.

The children were excited to have new visitors and insisted on showing them around. Mimi grabbed Lillian's hand, saying, "Come on, you're going to stay in my room. It's the prettiest one."

Ronnie and Randy insisted that Pete look at their room. "We have the best toys and no girly stuff. Daddy says you are his brother. We are brothers too, but everyone calls us twins."

Pete and Lillian laughed and relaxed into the family atmosphere.

Following breakfast, Will told Pete it was time to walk over to the Parker House and meet Harry and Alice. "You don't have to be nervous, Pete; they are the nicest people you will ever meet.

"Harry is recovering from a problem with his heart and is limited physically, but he is healthy of mind and still in charge. He is interested in adding a supervisor to his team, and he is willing to train the right person. He wants a trustworthy person who will share his dedication to producing quality products and treating all people fairly."

"Sounds like a man I'd like ta meet," Pete responded. "You know Paw taught us all ta do good work 'n' ta be honest 'n fair in all our dealin's wit everbidy."

Alice opened the door and invited Will and Pete to join Harry by the fire. "You must be Pete," she said with a hug. "We've heard a lot about Will's younger brother."

"Hope it was sumthin' good," Pete mumbled with his head lowered.

"Of course it was," Harry answered from across the room. "Come in here where I can get a good look at you, boy. I do see a family resemblance, but you may be better looking than Will," he laughed.

Alice brought the men each a mug of coffee and left them to discuss the work. Harry gave Pete a condensed history of his farm, including his contract with the War Department. He talked openly about the poor economic conditions currently affecting people at all levels. He turned to Will to elaborate on his vision of growing the business into a jobbing company and helping the local community in the process.

Pete listened intently and said at one point, "The plan's excitin' 'n I'd be proud ta be part a hit, ifen you'd 'ave me. I ain't as educated as my big brutha, 'n' I cain't give no speeches, but I'm a hard worker, I git along wit most folks, 'n] I can learn ta handle whateva part a tha job ye trust me wit."

"I like your attitude, Pete. I will ask Will to take you around the farm, introduce you to my crews, and get a feel for where we are now. For now, I cannot go with you, but I can answer any questions that remain in your mind after you get the lay of the land."

As they walked the first half of the Parker Farm, Pete was impressed. "It's a purty place, Will. The land's flatter than back home but nice 'n' green even in tha winter. I'd like ta see hit in tha spring."

"If you and Harry can agree, you will see it in all four seasons, Pete. We are in what is referred to as the Tidewater section of Virginia. I am sure you noticed how the land began to flatten as you left the Blue Ridge mountains. There are many farms in this area, providing a varied selection of vegetables and fruits. One of our neighbors has a cattle farm. Of course, tobacco is also an important cash crop, just like back home, but timber is not as prevalent."

"Hit's so nice ta be talkin' wit ye like brothas agin, Will. Hit made me sorta sick havin' ta thank of ye as a traitor."

"Let's try to put all that behind us, Pete. The damned war tore up just about everything in the country, including family relationships. I've been trying to find ways to put things back together since I left the war.

"Some injuries will never heal, but we have no choice other than to move forward with hope and hard work. At least that's the best plan I can make for the future of my family and for the people I represent."

"Gosh, Will, ye're so smart 'n' talk so profess'nal 'n' all. I'm not shore I kin fit in wit tha likes of ye an tha Parkers."

"How do you think I learned to talk like this, Pete. After all, we grew up in the same family listening to Maw and Paw. Maw taught us to read and write, but we copied Paw's way of talking.

"I learned very early that my mountain accent was a liability to me, and I set out to do something about it. I paid very close attention to the way

Lenora and her family spoke. I listened to the military generals who were in charge of my various jobs.

"I kept asking questions and reading to learn as much as possible about our history, our government, and the social order. At first, every word out of my mouth was spoken with hesitation. Gradually, it became more natural for me to speak proper English; however, I still have a slight mountain accent. Fortunately, many of my constituents find it charming," Will flashed his crooked grin.

"If you come to Parker's Farm, you will be talking mostly with the crews, and I doubt that they will care how you speak, although you might get a bit of teasing," Will chuckled.

"Lil 'n me's gotta talk this ova. It's a big decision. What ifen Mr. Parker decides it's a mistake afta we move all tha way up 'ere from home? I'm a little scared bout hit, Will."

"Would it help if Harry agreed to give you a trial run? Maybe you could stay a few weeks to get oriented and begin to take on some responsibility. That way, both you and Harry could have a chance to get an idea of how the relationship might work."

"Yep, that's a good idee, Will. Ye're tha smartest brotha I got, but don't be a-tellin' Billy Bob I said hit."

Will smiled and could feel Pete was starting to relax and warm up to the proposition. "When we get back to the house, you go in and let Lillian know what you are thinking. I will go back to Harry's place and discuss the trial period idea."

Harry agreed with Will's suggestion and offered Pete a four-week orientation period with pay. Will sent a wire to John explaining that Pete and Lillian would be staying for a month. Then he drafted a letter to Billy Bob and the rest of the family to let them know what was happening.

Lillian was happy to spend more time with Lenora and the children but worried about insufficient clothing for an extended stay. Lenora eased her worries and assured her that she had extra dresses that should fit her nicely. "We'll have a chance to get to know each other better, Lillian. You can help me entertain the children."

Will smiled more than usual during the next few weeks thinking. "*Harry may be right; I can sell most anything I believe in if I do it with a soft touch and a grin. My plan is starting to work.*"

Chapter Ten

WORKING THE PLAN

February 14, Valentine's Day, was a sunny but chilly Wednesday morning at the farm. The Presley family finished breakfast and prepared to face their daily routines.

Will quietly approached Lenora, who was clearing the table. With a tap on her shoulder, he spun her around and leaned in for a kiss. "You are just as pretty today with your hands in the sink as the first day I saw you at the Surratt Boarding House almost fourteen years ago."

Why Will Presley, what got into you today?" she smiled.

"It is Valentine's Day, you know, the special day set aside to pay tribute to the one you love."

Pete and Lillian were watching this unexpected display of affection with approving eyes while the twins giggled, and Mimi said, "Am I your Valentine, too, Daddy?"

"Yes, Mimi, you are my Princess, but Mama is my Queen."

Boarding his carriage for the trip into the city, Will waved at his extended family and wished them all a Happy Valentine's Day.

Harry knocked on the Presley front door, surprising everyone.

"Daddy, what are you doing walking over here in the cold?" Lenora asked anxiously.

"Calm down, Girl; it's been six weeks since I was discharged from the hospital. I've followed all the doctor's instructions, and it is time for me to begin getting a little exercise. Are you going to ask me in or make me stand out here in the cold?"

"I want to talk with Pete before he starts work today. How about getting me a cup of coffee."

"Of course, Daddy, sit down by the fire. Pete and Lillian are both in the gathering room," Lenora said, feeling chastised.

"Good morning, folks. I just realized that we are approaching the four-week trial period and thought it was time to discuss the future.

"What are you thinking, Pete? I should also ask, what is Lillian thinking?"

Lillian looked at Pete for an answer.

"Mr. Parker, I 'preciate what ye dun fer us an I kin see a big future fer tha farm 'n fer a jobbing business. I like tha folks ye got workin' fer ye. Theys all good men. Ifen ye thank I kin do what ye want, I'd be eva so happy to be part of yer plans. I thank Lil an I kin make a fair home 'ere, but we got a lotta work ta do to fit in 'n ta find our place," Pete responded, trying to use his words carefully.

"I am delighted to hear you say those things, Pete. Just like your brother, I can see that you are also a good man. Anything you don't already know, we can teach you. Knowledge can be acquired. Skills can be mastered. I believe that character and attitude are the most critical assets a man can possess," Harry opined.

Changing his focus to Lillian, Harry asked, "May I assume that you agree with your husband, Miss Lillian?"

Lillian stuttered a little before responding. "Yes, Sir, I thank this is an op'atunity we'd neva 'ave back home. I already love Lenora'n tha children. I am dreamin' a addin' sum our own youngins 'ere on tha Parker Farm."

"It's all settled then," Harry said, shaking hands with Pete. "You will start as a foreman taking direction from me. We will give you time to get comfortable with each part of the job before adding more responsibility. We'll bring back the furloughed men one or two at a time as the need arises. Eventually, we will need to hire additional workers, and you will be overseeing all of them."

Pete was smiling from ear to ear, and Lillian was hanging on to his arm. Lenora almost cried as she said, "Will was right again. Today is, indeed, a very happy Valentine's Day."

"Do you know the origin of Valentine'Day?" Harry asked.

Pete looked at Lillian and shrugged his shoulders. "No, Sir, I don't thank we do."

"Like many of our special days, it is said to have had its beginning in Greek and Roman history as well as some pagan rituals.

"There are stories about two different Priests, both named Valentine and later called St. Valentine.

"Emperor Claudius II had prosecuted one after he refused to worship the Roman gods.

"The other went against the emperor's orders and secretly married young couples. Emperor Gothicus executed him on February 14, around 269 A.D. Since he died for the sin of arranging marriages, his death is remembered as a day of love.

"The holiday also has origins in the Roman festival of Lupercalia, held in mid-February which celebrated the coming of spring, including fertility rites," Harry told his rapt audience.

"How do ye know all that, Mr. Parker?" Lillian asked in a shy voice while Pete sat dumbfounded.

"I read a lot in the cold weather. Reading has always been an education and a sanctuary for me. During my recovery, it has been much-needed comfort."

"I don't know whether I believe any of that; however, mid-February for us farmers usually brings the end of winter and the beginning of the planting season. In other words, Pete, it is time to get off our backsides and get to work," Harry laughed and slapped Pete on the back.

"Where do ye want me ta start?" Pete asked.

"I would suggest that we make a list of what can be done now before planting season begins. Decide how many workers will be needed. Contact the furloughed employees and let them know when to report, meet with each group and clarify what they need to do between now and the end of March.

"After you get the men started, you and Lillian need to make a trip back home, get the personal items you need, talk with your Mother and family about your plans, and return here as soon as possible."

"Slow down, Mr. Parker, I'm a-gonna have ta write sum of this down.

"My brothers and me had a yearly routine, mostly a plantin' 'n loggin'. Course, we had to carry the timba ta town eva week. We planted and harvested tobacco fer sale, but the food garden wuz tended by the girls. We did hafta kill a hog eva fall. It wuz tha same eva year. We didn't havta thank bout hit. It wuz jist did the same thangs ova an ova.

"Now it looks like I gotta make a plan an show otha folks what ta do. That's a whole new way a thankin' fer me. Ye is gonna hafta hep me till I git used ta hit."

"That's what I've been telling you, Pete. You have a chance to change your life by becoming a leader of men. I'll certainly help you at every step, but you need to make a commitment to learning and to stepping out of your role as a follower. I have confidence that you can grow into this responsibility if you decide that is what you want."

"Thank ye, Mr. Parker. Ye're so kind ta give me an opp'tunity to improve life fer me 'n' Lil."

"Another thing that will help you to get started is the fact that we still have five experienced men working on the farm. They have all been with me for a long time and are familiar with our usual planting cycle. Henry is the natural leader of the five. When we had an attack from the Klan, Henry's brother, Marvin, was killed. Henry was severely injured but, thankfully, recovered. Alvin and Simon, another set of brothers, are very reliable workers. Elijah and Raymond, also brothers, have a brother, Zeke, who might be interested if we need more help. The last three are black boys and trusted members of our crew."

"Yes, Sir, I believe I've met all five, and they seem ta know what theys doing alright. Do ye thank theys gonna ave a problem takin' orders from me?"

"When they realize that your job is going to be something different from what they have been doing, I think they will continue to be team players. They are fond of your brother, Will, because he treats everyone with respect. At Parker Farm, we have always valued our workers and treated them accordingly. I feel certain that you will continue that tradition."

"Oh, yes. The Presleys learned early from Maw and Paw that we ain't better than nobody else, and nobody's better than us. We are all God's Children.

I'm going to ask you to have the five of them come up to the house to discuss our future. We will fill them in on our plan for growth."

It was an unusual occasion for the crews to be called away from their work for a meeting. "I'm sure hoping we're not being furloughed too," Alvin said to Henry.

Mr. Parker thanked the men for the work they have been doing and began to lay out the farm's possible growth plans. He explained the concept of becoming a jobbing company and how it would necessitate increased production and require additional crew members if successful. He described Pete's role in the expansion.

"In the short run," Harry added, "It will be business as usual. I am counting on each of you to help Pete become familiar with our methods for preparing the planting areas, seeding or transplanting, fertilizing, weeding, and harvesting.

"Pete grew up farming and logging but with different crops and in more mountainous terrain. Once he understands our current process, he will be able to oversee the increase and addition to our annual production."

"Pete's an alright guy, but do you think he could drop some of that mountain twang? Don't want him scaring the sows before breeding season," Elijah teased, winking and grinning at Pete.

"I'm aimin' ta work on 'at," Pete smiled.

Pete looked at Henry and asked, "Kin you walk wit me out ta the fields and give me tha gen'ral idee of what ye would be doin' this time a year?"

"Sure thing, Pete. In late February and early March, we are usually getting the ground ready for planting, breaking up clods, removing dead brush, and that sort of thing. We decide how many root vegetables to put out. There is also work to be done with the final apple harvest. On a farm, there's always work to do," Henry advised.

"Lil and me's gotta make a trip back home ta pack our belongings and say goodbye ta tha family. It should only take a few days, but it's prob'ly best ta do hit now 'stead a when the new work is startin'. Kin I ask ye to add Raymond's brotha, Zeke, to the crew an get the men started on the usual work while I'm gone?"

"That will be no problem, Pete. Is there anything extra that I need to tell them before you return?"

"Ye might tell 'em to make all tha plantin' areas a bit bigger this year cause we's hoping fer sum new customers."

"They will be excited to hear about the plans for growth since that will make their source of income more reliable," Henry assured Pete.

Chapter Eleven

THE ROBBER BARONS

"Hey, Miss Lenora, that shore wuz a fine meal ye cooked fer us tanite," Pete said as he rose from the dining table. " 'at Virginia ham ye baked was mighty tasty. Somehow it wuz diff'runt from what we had in North Ca'lina."

"Well, you probably had salt-cured ham down South. Up here in Virginia, we mostly cure ham by smoking," she smiled.

"How do ye smoke a ham? Lillian was puzzled.

Explaining, Lenora said, "We have a smoke-house down behind the pig lot. At the hog-killing time in the Fall, we take the meat, including the hams, and hang it in the smoke-house.

"Then, we put some hickory wood in the building and build a fire. We keep the flame low and mainly make a lot of smoke to fill the place. The smoke dries the moisture from the meat and keeps it from spoiling.

"Salt does the same thing as far as drying out the meat, but it leaves a salty taste. Smoking leaves a smoky taste in it. That's why it tastes different."

"Well, I seen men smoke 'backer, but I neva seen nobody smoke a ham," Lillian giggled.

"I declare, Lillian, you're a funny girl, playing dumb like that," Will chuckled.

'Oh, did ye thank she wuz jist playin'? Pete joked as Lillian playfully smacked his arm.

"You men go on into the parlor while Lillian and I clean up the kitchen," Lenora suggested.

"Come on, Pete, we're keeping these ladies from their work. Let's go and sit a spell," Will replied.

"I am as interested in news, local or national, as the next person; however, I get impatient with the long build-up to the main point. Will is known for elaboration. He thinks it enhances the story. Just give me the basics unless I ask for more," Lenora chuckled and winked.

Lillian snickered for a moment, then looked to her sister-in-law for advice. "Kin I ask ye something?"

"You can ask me anything, Lil; we are the same as sisters now."

"I've been havin' some signs that make me wonder ifen I might be in the family way. It's been three months since I've had my regular visit, and my stomach is uneasy most mornings."

"Oh, I am so happy for you, Lil. Pete will be beside himself, and all of us will welcome another Presley baby into our fold. I will take you to town to see our doctor next week. Maybe he can confirm what you are thinking.

"Is it alright for me to tell Will that we might need to build another house for you and Pete? I'll ask him not to say a word to Pete until you have had an opportunity to tell him, but he needs time to plan the work."

"Yes, I guess that will be alright. I don't want to cause you, Will, or the Parkers any trouble. We already owe you so much. Adding another little one does change everything. How will I continue to do my part of the work ifen 've got a baby on my hip?"

"Now, don't you start making up problems, Lil. We will all work together as a family. A new baby is not trouble; it is a blessing," Lenora smiled, embracing her sister.

As they got comfortable with a mug of cider, the brothers resumed their discussion.

"I been hearin' tha farm boys talkin' 'bout sum Robber Barons. Who 'er 'ese bad guys?" Pete wondered.

Chuckling, Will answered, "That's what some people are calling a group of about twenty or so super-rich guys. They're men who have gained a monopoly on some businesses and squeezed out any competition. Many working people believe that they have gotten rich while their workers have barely survived.

"I've heard some folks refer to them as *snollygosters,* too," Will grinned.

"What's a *snollygoster?*" Pete was puzzled. "I aint neva heerd that word afore."

Smiling, Will replied, "It's a slang word meaning someone who has wholly deserted any ethical standards in pursuit of making money and winning every time."

"There is some talk that laborers might try to organize and force these big businessmen to pay more fair wages."

"How kin they do that?" Pete was puzzled.

"They believe that if they withhold their labor, a business won't be able to operate without them," Will explained.

"I always wondered that 'bout Mr. Graham down in North Ca'lina," Pete added. "Course I neva heerd nobody say nuthin' like that," his eyes widened as he spoke.

"According to Paw, Mr. Graham was always fair with him and willing to help him when he needed it. These Robber Barons have big companies with thousands of employees.

"Because a lot of people are out of work, they are cutting wages for the employees. They seem to think that their employees will have to be content with lower wages, or they'll hire other people who'll be happy just to have a job and will work cheaper."

"Why do ye thank Mr. Graham didn't try ta do 'at ta tha men who worked fer him?" Pete asked.

"Maw used to say that Charles Graham believed in what he called *enlightened self-interest,*" Will answered him.

"It seemed to work well for him and the people who worked for him.

"I assume the Robber Barons don't understand the concept. Since they have gotten rich without doing that, they won't change unless they are forced into it by their employees. They control the money that the workers depend on to feed their families."

"Then ther ain't no way fer the workers to force 'em ta change, is ther?"

"In Europe, workers have instituted what they call a *sit-down strike;* they stand outside the entrance to the business and refuse to do their assigned jobs. Fights have occurred as outsiders have attempted to assume these jobs, but, in many cases, it has been successful."

"Have ye 'n' Harry eva had yer workers ta complain about wages?" Pete asked.

"Not yet, but we pay our employees very well and appreciate and respect them," Will explained.

"Who 'er 'ese big biz'ness men who ther' callin' Robber Barons?" Pete wondered.

| John D. Rockefeller | Cornelius Vanderbilt | Andrew Carnegie | J Pierpont Morgan |

The "Robber Barons"

"Well, the main one is J.P. Morgan, a big-time banker in New York City. He loaned money to almost all railroad companies, and when they started going bankrupt, he called his friend Cornelius Vanderbilt.

"Vanderbilt operated a steamship business on the Great Lakes, hauling freight from Chicago to New York. He took over many of those railroads and doubled his freight hauling business. Vanderbilt repaid very quickly the loans Morgan had made, and both men prospered."

"What'sa wrong with that? Pete questioned.

"It's not illegal, but it allowed Vanderbilt to monopolize the freight business."

"That's two of 'em, but ye said ther's a bunch of 'em," Pete was curious.

"A man named Andrew Carnegie owns a steel mill outside of Pittsburg. Railroads use lots of steel for rail lines and rail cars and engines. Vanderbilt bought all his steel from Carnegie, so his steel company monopolized the steel industry.

"John D. Rockefeller started an enterprise called Standard Oil Company in 1870. He had been in the oil refining business for several years, working for other companies.

"J.P. Morgan introduced him to Carnegie, who bought a lot of fuel oil for his steel business. Carnegie's steam-operated machines in his mills began to replace coal as their primary fuel to make steam. Oil is cheaper and cleaner-burning than coal.

"Vanderbilt's steam-engine trains switched to fuel oil, too. That was another big boost for Rockefeller.

"Consequently, as these men monopolize their businesses, they control wages and have a lot of influence on our economy and the politicians."

Pete nodded his understanding and said, " So, 'ese rich fellers 'er runnin' the country-not our leaders? Is 'at what yer sayin'?"

"That's what lots of folks think. Lenora calls them Plutocrats, yet some folks call them Robber Barons," Will grimaced slightly.

"Well, I wuz jist a wonderin'," Pete said.

Before turning in for the evening, Lenora asked Will to come for a walk with her. She pledged him to secrecy as she relayed the possible good news of another family member joining the Presley clan in late summer.

Will was happy for his brother. "It will change his life forever, just like my boys and Mimi changed mine, and that is a good thing.

"I will talk with Harry, and we will start planning the design, site, and work schedule. Don't worry; we will have them a place of their own before the blessed event."

Chapter Twelve

LABOR UNIONS

Lenora and Lillian joined the men in the parlor. As they were seating themselves, Lillian said, "I heard you two talkin' 'bout Robber Barons. But I've heard folks talkin' 'bout labor unions. What's that all about?"

Will answered, "I shared with Pete a little information about them, but if you sincerely want to know more, I can tell you. I've done some research on them.

"The greedy, 'Robber Barons' use unfair business practices and exploit their workers. This exploitation led to riots, strikes, and the emergence of labor unions. In an attempt to improve the wages and working conditions of American workers, the movement began.

"The Robber Barons became wealthy and successful due to the economic system of free enterprise that operates in the United States. Significant business operations are essentially free of state control or federal regulations.

"This free enterprise system, combined with the idea of *Laissez-Fair'economics* relies on supply and demand to regulate prices and wages. This system is excellent for the Industrialists, whose riches and power enable them to exercise a powerful influence over the government. Still, it's terrible news for the workers who lack any form of representation.

Urban Mansion

"The labor union movement is fueled by the emergence of two distinct classes, the rich and the poor. The people of America adhere to the ideals of the War of Independence and the American Constitution, which fosters fairness, liberty, democracy, social equality, order, justice, fraternity, and independence. Working folks believe their rights are denied by the powerful industrialists' unethical, corrupt, and unchecked actions. The men who started the labor union movement were motivated by improving working conditions and wages. This cause moved many people.

"The unions saw conflict between the industrialists and the workers due to their opposing beliefs and views. The Robber Barons believe in the right to run their businesses as they see fit and employ working practices to increase productivity and maximize profits.

"Believing that labor is a commodity, and wages should be predicated on supply and demand, the right to hire and fire at will, and the right to set working hours and working conditions becomes their prerogative.

"The opposing viewpoint is that workers are not just a commodity, and they deserve the right to have a say in their working conditions, their health and safety, the hours they work, and their rates of pay. The labor union movement is based on these conflicts of interest.

Factory machines eradicated the need for many skilled workers, and work was repetitive, boring, and monotonous and gave no sense of satisfaction or pride in work.

"The mechanization of industries provided new, heavy machines that lacked safety devices causing high numbers of injuries. Injured workers receive no compensation and no wages when they are unable to work.

"Many industries, like the mining industry, are hazardous. Other jobs are also harmful, with workers breathing toxic fumes.

"The Panic of 1873 continues to be a severe economic crisis that has caused a hard-hitting depression. Wages have been reduced while working hours increased. These workers are paid less for more work".

"Well, it's easy for me to see why they need to have labor unions. They must have somebody to stand up for their rights and speak for them," Lenora offered her opinion. "I'm happy that we treat our employees like they are part of the family. Of course, Pete and Lillian are members of our family."

"Yes, but so are Henry, Alvin, Simon, Raymond, 'n Lije," Will added.

"Will, I've heard some people talking about *Molly Maguire*. Who is she?" Lenore asked.

Chuckling, Will answered, "*Molly Maguires* is a name they call a group of Irishmen who are active in labor disputes in the Pennsylvania coal mines. They are a secretive bunch who don't reveal who they are. That enables them to carry out strong reactions to things they disagree with at their workplace.

"The group started in the Old Country and came here when the Irish Immigration began in the 1850s. In some parts of the country, folks called *Ribbonmen,* but the Molly Maguires name was used primarily for the rural country cousins and the *Ribbonmen* for the more urban city folk.

"Convicted in court for some violence in Pennsylvania coal mines, many Mollies were hanged by the federal government."

"Yeah, I heard about the hanging and wondered why they were hung," Lenora added.

Chapter Thirteen

THE PRODUCE SHED

At breakfast, Will said, "Pete, let's you and me go over and talk with Harry. I've got some ideas about building a shed to sell our fruits and vegetables to our new customers when we start the jobbing business."

"Alright big brother, I'm ready when you are," Pete replied.

"Good morning, Alice," Will greeted his mother-in-law when she answered his knock on the door. "Is Harry up and about yet?"

"Good morning, Will and you too, Pete," she smiled. "Yes, Harry is sitting in the parlor drinking his second cup of coffee. I'm sure he'll be glad to see you, men."

Rising as he heard Will's voice, Harry spoke," Come on in here, men. Good morning to both of you. What's up so early in the morning?"

"It is early, but I have some appointments at the Capitol today, and I want to run something by you.

"Down in Asheville at the farmer's market where we sold our tobacco crop in the Fall, they had a shed where farmers sold fruits and vegetables. Paw used to go there every year at Christmas time and buy fruit for us kids.

"It was about one hundred feet long and about twenty feet deep. It had a covered roof on top and sides covered with boards enclosing it. But the front was open. It had a canvas that would roll up in the daytime then roll down at night to cover up what was inside.

"They had built shelving that looked like ascending stairsteps—leaving space between sets of shelves so folks could walk around them. There were about four sets of shelves.

"If we had a shed like this, we could set up baskets full of vegetables and fruits so storekeepers could buy them and load their wagons. I would guess they'd want to buy about three times a week to have fresh produce."

"Do you think storekeepers would come here to buy? I always had to deliver to the War Department," Harry observed.

"We can make that clear to them when we first start," Will answered. "If we have to deliver to them, it'll be more expensive for us. We'll need to have delivery drivers and extra wagons to maintain. Our prices will, by necessity, be higher."

"Will storekeepers leave their shops to buy produce? I believe they will be reluctant to do that," Harry offered.

"We'll suggest they come early in the morning before their stores open. If they get here by 4:30 or 5:00 a. m., they can then return to their stores with fresh produce by 8:00 a.m.

"I will know more about that when I start contacting merchants. If our competition is delivering, we might need to rethink our plan, but we might convince our customers we can keep our prices lower if they can pick up."

"Spoken like a true salesman, Presley," Harry smiled. "That gift of gab, also, is what makes a good politician."

"I will start contacting the customers on the list John Hall gave us. We need to have a general idea of our customer base before planting season. It'll help us gauge our need for employees, too.

"Once we get the planting done, we'll build the shed. It should go up quickly and easily, with just a roof and three sides."

Alice was standing at the doorway to the parlor, listening intently. As Will finished speaking, she entered the conversation. "I feel a whole lot better about this enterprise now, Will. I believe you have a good solid, workable plan.

"Lenora was right; you are a smart man."

"Yeah, Maw used to say that about Paw," Pete interjected. "Guess Will took after Paw quite a bit."

Grinning sheepishly, Will said, "Guess all of us boys took after our Paw, didn't we, Pete?"

"Yeah, I reckon so," Pete scratched his head. "But I always thought ye older boys wuz more like him, ye and Buck and Johnny."

"Right, Paw worked more with us in the logging. You younger boys were working tobacco. Billy Bob helped us some in the logging, but Paw wanted you younger ones to stay out of the woods because it was too dangerous."

"I heerd Maw tellin' him that one day," Pete answered. "Maw worried 'bout all of us boys a-workin' in tha woods."

"Do ye reckon she knowed Paw wuz gonna have a accident, Will? She seemed ta know a lot of stuff wuz gonna happen."

"Some people call that women's intuition," Alice remarked. "Sometimes, you just get a feeling of impending doom. I've experienced it, but I don't have any explanation for it."

"Will, do you think we'll need another smokehouse for pork?" Harry asked.

"I'm not certain about that, but by Fall, when we kill hogs, we'll have a better feel for that. We need to raise more hogs first," Will calculated.

"Do you think they'll want to pick up their pork, too?" Harry was interested.

"Maybe, but it won't need to be more than once every week or two. Pork is cured and won't spoil so quickly like produce will. We'll schedule pork to be picked up on a different day than vegetables and fruit if they pick it up.

"That way, we can spread the workload, produce on Monday, Wednesday, and Friday, pork on Thursday."

"You have given this whole idea a lot of thought, Will; I'm impressed with your thoroughness. The more we talk, the more I like the whole concept. I'm getting excited."

"We hafta stay updated on the situation we're facing. Things change, and we *must* change with them. One of my colleagues in the Senate calls it staying in tune with the times.

"We're gonna be alright, Harry. And, too, I want to be ready to step down from the Senate if the Legislature doesn't reappoint me in '80.

"Oh, are you wanting to leave the Senate, Will?" Alice was surprised.

"No, not really, but with the State Assembly dominated by Democrats now, I'm not certain they'll want to retain me. The party in power controls these political jobs. You gotta always be thinking ahead."

"Well, if you ask me, I think you've been an outstanding Senator," Alice commented as she patted his arm.

Pete had a question for Harry. "How quick kin we git more hogs a growin' 'n makin' meat? It seems ta me we gotta have more of' 'em if we sell more customers."

"That's a good question, Pete," Harry answered. "We have primarily white English pigs. They can produce 10 to 12 piglets per litter. There are mainly two seasons per year they will breed-Spring and Fall, but they are capable of breeding year-round."

"Ye mean they kin easy make 20 to 24 babies a year?" Pete was amazed. "How long afore they git big enuff for eatin'?"

"We usually try to get them to 300 or 400 pounds. It takes about a year. But we typically kill hogs in colder weather, so the meat doesn't spoil before getting it cured. Sometime around Thanksgiving or just before. It depends on the weather.

"A young sow can begin breeding at about 7 to 8 months, so we can cycle the older ones (about 6 or 7 years) out and use them for meat," Harry explained.

"So what you're saying is that we can move quickly as the demand grows for our meat?" Will suggested.

"Yes, we can. And we can plant many of our vegetables twice per year. As well, we can stagger the plantings each time so that we don't need to harvest them all at once." Harry continued.

"Hey, man, this here farmin's a lot more harder than I wuz thanking'," Pete interjected. I got lots of stuff ta learn."

"Now, don't worry about it, Pete. Harry is here to guide you if you have questions," Alice assured him.

Will added, "And I suggest you and Harry talk for a spell every morning to layout your plans for the day, at least for the first year or so. After you get some experience on this farm, you will be a good foreman here."

"And don't forget, Pete, you've got experienced people working for you. Many of the men we are calling to come back to work know a lot about farming. Don't be afraid to ask questions of them," Harry advised.

Looking at Will, Harry said, "I like your ideas about Parker Jobbing and the way you propose to display and market our products. Now, we just need to implement the plan. Make it work, my son."

"Will do, Harry. I'll begin this weekend contacting our prospective customers." Will smiled and waved goodbye as he and Pete left.

Chapter Fourteen

NEW CUSTOMERS

"Hey, Pete, bright and early in the morning, you and I are gonna make some visits to the storekeepers on this list that John Hall gave us. These are folks who buy beef from him."

"Where's 'ese stores located, Will?" Pete asked.

"Most of them are right here in Falls Church and Fairfax. That's where we'll start. It's close to home, and it will be easy for them to come to us and pick up.

"But as we grow, we can branch out into Alexandria and Leesburg and Warrenton and Manassas. We need to grow carefully to ensure our resources can handle it."

"Yep, it's kinda scary thankin' about all this extra work, but I reckon Paw hadda start little when it wuz jist him 'n' Vernon. When all us boys growed up 'n' wuz able to he'p 'im we dun more loggin' 'n' planted a bigger 'backer patch."

"Now you've got the idea, Pete," Will assured him.

"Will, I'm gonna let you do most a tha talkin' when we see 'ese storekeepers, I don't talk like y'all up here in Virginia. I noticed folks lookin' at me kinda funny when I talk."

"I know what you mean, Pete. When I first came here, nobody would hire me because of my accent. It took a while, but I learned to talk like these people just by listening to them. When you and I learned to speak, we heard Paw and Vernon and the boys at the sawmill.

"Our black farmworkers still retain their accents, but they don't talk as much to customers as you will.

"Are you about ready to go see some customers, Pete?" Will asked as he rose from the breakfast table.

"Yep, just let me finish drinkin' this last sip o' coffee 'n' I'll be ready. Are we takin' tha buggy 'er tha wagon?"

"We'll take the one-horse buggy. We're gonna stay pretty close to home today. Roy Ailor's store is our first stop. He's not more than a mile or so from here."

"Oh yeah, me and Lil' rode down ther one day. He's a nice man. Kinda heavy-set and bald like Lil's daddy. He was real friendly and all, you know.

"Said he'd worked on the railroad but got let go when they went outta biz'ness. His wife and nephew, Leon, run tha store when he hadda work on the railroad," Pete related.

"Alice trades with them a lot. She gets flour and meal and sugar and coffee, things we don't raise here on our farm," Will informed him.

As they pulled up in front of Ailor's store, Pete was nervous. "Ain't neva been no salesman afore, Will. You'll hafta do all tha talkin'."

"Just relax and be yourself, Pete. You don't hafta impress Roy. He's just a workin' man like you are. He puts his pants on one leg at a time.

"Hello, Roy," Will smiled and extended his hand. "Have you got a few minutes to chat?"

"Good morning, Senator, you too, Pete. What are you fellows up to today? I'm happy to see you."

Pete smiled and shook hands with Ailor. "I wuzn't shore you'd remember me, Mr. Ailor."

"Of course, I remember you, Pete. You came in here with your wife just a few days ago. It's good to see you again."

Will joined the conversation. "We want to talk some business with you, Roy. I know you are familiar with our operation supplying fruits and vegetables and pork to the War Department.

"Since the war ended, they aren't buying as much from us, and we had to furlough several employees. This depression has hurt all of us business people. I'm guessing you have been affected too," Will replied.

"Yes, of course, we have. You are aware that I lost my job with the railroad, so that's why I'm here today. Ruby has been working at home. She's planting a garden this year. Everybody's scrambling, I guess."

Will nodded in agreement. "We want to try to do some things to help our business. If we can find storekeepers like you to buy from us, we can bring back our furloughed workers. When they have jobs and money to spend, it helps other businesses in the area."

"You are exactly right, Senator. Many of your employees were customers of mine, and we saw a decrease when they were laid off. What are you going to sell to grocery store owners?"

Will spoke slowly and deliberately. "Just the same produce and meat we have always sold, but more of it.

"I know you have other sources you have been buying from, but we are close by and your neighbors and friends. If we have more outlets, we can grow more and provide jobs for our people.

"We are planning a shed to display the produce. You can bring your wagon and pick up fresh vegetables three times per week. It's closer for you to buy from us."

"Yes, yes it is," Ailor was getting excited. "Leon has been going to a wholesale market in D.C. once a week. Sometimes the stuff spoils before we can sell it. Buying it closer to home, we can get smaller amounts and buy more often.."

"That is what my pitch was going to be, Roy. Would you like to work for me?" Will teased.

Smiling, he shook his head no but said, "I like your ideas. It seems that everybody in Washington has been concerned with all the chaos out West - Jesse James and Sitting Bull and Black Hills Gold. We need to be aware of the needs of our folks right here at home," Ailor was emphatic.

"I agree with you, Roy. Sometimes we get tunnel vision and only see the headlines of the newspapers. That's why Harry and I are trying to make changes in our operation. Pete has moved here to work with us and will help with the expansion."

"Count me in, Senator. I believe you're on the right track with your business," Ailor shook Will's hand. "Now I've got some things to get done in the store. Thanks for stopping by."

Pete waved as they started out the door. "Good to see you again, Mr. Ailor. Guess I'll be seeing you at our place this Spring."

"Yes, Pete, it's good to see you again, too. Give my regards to your Missus," Ailor nodded.

"See Pete, how easy that was. You just have to be yourself and don't try to make folks think you're somebody that you're not."

Climbing into the buggy, Pete was delighted. "Wher' we a-goin' next, Will? I thank we 'er gonna git a lot more customers."

Chuckling, Will said, "Yes, I think we are on to something here, Pete. We'll see Bill Padgett next. He has a general store about five miles out in the country. His customers are mainly farmers themselves, so he might not buy a lot of vegetables or pork,"

"Then why 'er we even foolin' with hin fer?" Pete asked.

"Well, we've got apples and pears to sell. Our orchards are still producing even now into February. He might not be able to get very much fruit this time of year. I want to ask him about grapes too. I've been thinking about adding some vines to our mix of fruit.

"You never know, we might start making wine on the farm," Will suggested with tongue in cheek.

"Next thang you'll be tellin' me is ye 'er gonna make corn whiskey like Paw used ta make," Pete grinned.

"I suspect Harry and Alice, maybe even Lenora would object to that idea. I'm just kidding about wine and whiskey, but we might want to grow some grapes.

"There's Padgett's General Store up ahead there. From the looks of his hitching post, I don't think he's busy today. I hope he'll have time to chat with us," Will observed.

"Good morning, Mr. Padgett. I'm Will Presley from Parker's Farm. Have you got a few minutes to chat with Pete and me?"

"Good morning to you, Senator Presley. I've always got time to talk with our elected officials. What's goin' on in D.C.?"

"We have lots of problems out West with the railroads, train robberies, Indian unrest, and a gold rush in the Black Hills of South Dakota. But I am more concerned about our situation right here in Fairfax County.

"Hundreds of people are unemployed, and folks are struggling to survive.

"At Parker's Farm, we have supplied the War Department for many years, but our business has waned with the war ending. We have found it necessary to lay off most of our workers.

"In trying to devise a solution to our dilemma, Harry and I have decided to open a jobbing business to supply our products to grocery and general stores. Do you buy vegetables or fruits from any local wholesalers?"

"Yes, and no," he grinned. "Most of our customers grow their vegetables on their farms, but we do buy some things they don't grow. There is a big produce market in D.C. I go over there about once per week to pick up a few things."

"We grow a variety of vegetables in our place and plan to expand our selection. Also, our orchards produce several different varieties of apples and pears. Plans are being made for adding some grapevines. Your feedback could help us decide what selection of vegetables we might add, the things you buy, which your customers don't grow for themselves."

"That sounds interesting, Senator. I certainly am interested in buying locally as much as possible. When do you plan to open your jobbing operation for business?"

"We plan to begin doing wholesale business by May 1st. We're building a shed to store and display baskets of produce. We'll plant our usual assortment of vegetables but add more rows of each. As customers tell us what they want to buy from us, we'll add those.

" Our orchards are now producing again at full capacity. As you know, we got burned out about ten years ago, but we replanted and have now made our way back to where we were before the fire."

"I remember that. Didn't the Klan set fire to your orchards?"

"Yes, they did, and it takes a long time to re-establish them. We added some new varieties of apples and pears, too. It's a better assortment than we had before. I am very proud of our fruit trees. We can be a great source for you on that at least, Mr. Padgett,"

"Call me, Bill, Senator. That's not so formal."

"I will, Bill, if you'll call me Will," he chuckled at his joke.

Laughing, Padgett said, "Alright, Senator, I'll tell Mike, my son, about your operation. He's the one who makes the weekly trip to D.C. for produce. Let us know when you're ready to do business."

"Thank you, Bill. I'll be back to see you about May 1st," Will waved goodbye.

"Alright, Pete, I want to make one more stop, then we'll head back to the farm."

"Wher 'er we a-goin' next, Will?" Pete questioned.

"Over in Fairfax is a man who goes to our church. His name is Fred Turner. He and his wife run a small grocery there. Fred and Harry grew up together and were classmates in school. Fred is a jolly little feller who laughs and makes jokes a lot. You'll like him."

As Will and Pete arrived at Turner's store, Fred was walking into the building. He stopped and spoke to his arriving visitors. "To what do we owe the honor of this visit, Senator?" Turner smiled.

"I wanted to introduce you to my brother, Pete, who just moved here from North Carolina. We're getting ready to start a new business and need more help.

"Pete and his bride haven't been married long and were eager to try a new job."

"A new business, huh? Not many people are starting new things since this depression's dragged on for so long. What are you and Harry up to now? By the way, how is Harry since the heart attack?"

"Harry is doing fairly well, considering everything. He's taking it slowly and minding the doctor's orders. Pete is going to be helping Harry with the farm. The doctor has told Harry that strenuous work is out of the question for a while."

"Well, hurry up and tell me what you two boys got up your sleeve. Curiosity is killing me," Turner laughed.

"We're establishing a business we're calling Parker's Jobbing. We want to sell fresh produce to groceries and general stores in our area."

"Aren't you folks selling your stuff to the War Department anymore? Harry's been doing that for a long time."

"Yeah, we're still gonna do that, but they aren't buying much since the war's over. A lot of our workers are furloughed, and we want to bring them back to work."

Turner spoke, "I've been buying from a farmer out in the county, who brings it to me twice a week. I'd hate to quit buying from him, but I might buy some things he doesn't raise. Have y'all still got the apple orchards?"

"Yes, we do. Also, we plan to add some different vegetables to our mix, radishes, onions, green peppers, and maybe some melons in the summer."

"Are you gonna deliver your stuff?"

"Not planning on it. We can keep our prices lower if we don't have to deliver. Our place is close enough to yours that you can come by early in the morning and pick it up in your wagon. You can look it over real good and pick the baskets you want."

"So, Pete, are you really claiming kin to the Senator?" Turner grinned.

"Yep, I reckon so, but it wuzn't my fault. You'd hafta blame my Paw," Pete laughed.

Turning back to Will, Turner said, "Let me know when you got things ready to sell. I'll check it out. Tell my old friend, Harry, I was asking about him."

Waving as they left, Will replied, " I'll come back about the first of May. That's when we hope to be in business."

Driving back to the farm, Pete asked, "What'd ye thank 'bout how it went today?"

"I believe we're on to a good thing. We were well-received by our neighbors, and that's a start. As we acquire more customers, we'll all be better off. Harry should be satisfied with our results so far.

Chapter Fifteen

GEORGE ARMSTRONG CUSTER

When Will walked into the front door of the Parker home, Harry looked up and spoke. "Presley, sit down here and let's chat. I've got some questions. I think you can answer."

"Sure, Harry. I don't know if I have any answers for you, but I'll try."

"I was just reading about General George Custer and Little Big Horn River in South Dakota. His whole unit got wiped out in that battle. Why was he even out there, anyway? I haven't been to the War Department in a while. I don't know what's going on."

"Well, first off, Custer was a Union general during the Civil War. He graduated from West Point in July of 1861, just after the war started.

"The class of cadets he was a part of was supposed to graduate in 1862, but when the war broke out, the War Department shortened the training period from five years to four.

"Several of Custer's classmates bombed out, and many more left to join the Confederate army, leaving only 24 cadets in the class. Custer was ranked 24th."

George Armstrong Custer

"Do you mean he was last in his class?" Harry was incredulous.

Chuckling, Will nodded. "Major Jack Williams, my boss, when I worked at Fort Whipple, knew him at West Point. Williams said Custer was a flamboyant character. He had long, flowing, blonde hair and wore a red tie. He decorated his uniform with extra buttons, and his belt had a large buckle."

"Did he get by with that at West Point?" Harry asked.

"Not at West Point, but when he was given a unit to command, he did.

"Starting as a messenger for General McDowell in the First Manassas Battle, he quickly transferred to the cavalry and distinguished himself in the Peninsula Campaign with McClellan and Burnside.

"Leading his men in a charge, he was always out front risking his life. Many officers frowned on that, but Custer led from the front. Most of the time, he removed his hat, so his men could see him leading them

"He was different and determined to make a name for himself.

"I met him for the first time at Antietam when he was a captain. His cavalry unit couldn't get across the river on Burnsides's bridge. A bunch of snipers on Marye's Heights kept shooting them as they tried to cross one by one."

"Isn't that where you got a medal for routing those snipers? – the medal of valor?"

Choking up, Will nodded. "There were some boys from Graham on that hill shooting our men.

"Custer stayed with Burnside as a cavalry officer while I was in the infantry. We fought together at Chancellorsville and Gettysburg. By then, Custer was a Lieutenant Colonel.

"After the war, the Lakota tribe of Indians created an uproar over the railroad invading their native land. Their leader was Chief Sitting Bull, along with a young warrior named Crazy Horse.

"Grant negotiated a treaty and gave a large body of land to the tribe. I heard it was about the size of the whole state of Ohio. They moved north to allow the railroad to continue toward the West.

"Before long, gold was discovered in the Black Hills – right smack in the middle of Indian Territory. Prospectors were moving out there and disturbing the Indians again.

"Custer was sent to confirm that the gold there was plentiful. Black Hills gold would be a boon to the federal government and help alleviate the effects of the depression.

"Grant offered six million dollars to buy back the land from Sitting Bull. (This was the modern-day equivalent of one hundred million dollars.) Indignantly, Sitting Bull refused to accept Grant's offer.

"What happened when Sitting Bull said no to Grant?" Harry was listening intently.

"The President ordered Custer to lead a force of about 1500 men and forcibly remove the tribe."

Harry asked, "When did all of this take place? I didn't hear anything about it."

" It happened last summer around the end of June, I think. Grant kept it quiet. He didn't want his political enemies to know about it.

"Custer was eager to make a name for himself because he wanted to run for President of the United States.

"Finding Sitting Bull's tribe camped on the banks of the Little Big Horn River, Custer divided his forces into three groups of 500 men. Ordering one to attack from the rear and one from the West, he led the third group himself.

"With his golden locks flying in the wind to enable his men to see him, he was an easy target for the Indians. His entire unit of 500 men was killed, including Custer himself.

"When the other two units arrived, Sitting Bull and his tribe had vanished.

"When the news got back to Washington, Grant was furious. He called General William Sherman in for a consultation, and they devised a sinister plan. Knowing that the Lakota tribe depended on the buffalo to survive, Sherman proposed a bounty for dead buffalo.

"Sharpshooters headed West in droves, and the slaughter began. From an estimated level of six to seven million, the herd dwindled to about three hundred.

"A cowboy who came to be called Buffalo Bill is purported to have killed more than 4,200 by himself. He had a contract to provide meat to the Kansas-Union Pacific Railroad workers. In addition to being paid for the buffalo flesh, he collected the United States government's bounty money.

"What happened to Sitting Bull and the Lakota nation?" Harry worried.

"Sitting Bull was forced to move his tribe further north into Canada. Buffalo was more plentiful there, but the colder winters took their toll on the tribe. Many of the weaker ones died."

"Now, I understand why Grant wanted to keep it quiet. That would have been politically damaging," Harry dropped his head. "It is embarrassing how these Native Americans were taken advantage of by our leaders."

Chapter Sixteen

THE COMPROMISE

Walking into the Capitol Building's rotunda, Will spotted two of his friends, Jim Hall and Jeremiah Jones. They were talking with a group of six other men. Seeing Will, Hall waved for him to join the group.

"Come on over here, Senator. I want you to meet some of our colleagues in the House. All of these men are Congressmen:

" Max Rosenbaum, from New York, John David Vincent, from Ohio, Tim Russell from Pennsylvania, from South Carolina, Louis Grisham, Joe Scarlett, from Florida, and Hugo Longley, Louisiana.

"So what're the latest happenings in the Presidential situation? Is the House of Representatives prepared to decide our next President?" Will was curious.

"Senatah, we 'r gettin' clo'suh ta de cidin' that isshew," Longley drawled in his Louisiana accent. It mightn't hafta go ta the 'hole House. It kindly looks like we 'r gonna work it out amongst 'er selves."

"Hey, that sounds great," Will was relieved.

"I don't like it," Jeremiah was adamant. His voice rising, he said, "If you turn them Rebs loose from the military governors down there, they'll go right back to treating black folks like they did before the war.

"We ain't gonna be no slaves for white folks no more. Those days are long gone. Black codes that kept us, virtual slaves, ain't gonna cut it, gentlemen. Listen to me now. There will be big trouble again if you proceed with this plan."

"Now, Jones, you are assuming an awful lot there," Vincent tried to assure Jeremiah. "These are honorable men who are telling you what will work. Besides, we will get our President in the White House. That's a big win for us."

"Hold on here, gentlemen. Am I to understand that you six men will decide the outcome of our Presidential election?" Will was amazed. "How can you do that? Isn't that unconstitutional ?"

"Senator, I am aware that you haven't been around Washington very long," Rosenbaum added. "Politics is all about compromising to get things done," he said smugly.

Will, looking to Hall, said, "Go back to the beginning and tell me the whole story. I'm not certain I understand what you're talking about."

All eyes turned to Hall. "Senator, these men represent the campaign staffs of Hayes and Tilden. They are willing to allow Tilden's electoral votes in their states to be counted for Hayes in exchange for removing the military governors from their three states. That action will give Hayes 186 electoral votes and leave Tilden with 185. It only takes one electoral vote to win. It's just as simple as that."

"Yeah, Senator, tha wahr's been ova for nigh onto twelve yeahrs now. We 'r tarred o' havin' these Union ahrmy officers tellin' us whut we can 'n cain't do. Get 'em outta our way and let us be," Grisham drawled in his South Carolina twang. "Y'all can have tha White House. Just get Union soldiers outta tha South."

"I'm not a Constitutional scholar, but it doesn't sound right to me," Will shook his head.

"You leave it to us, Senator," Rosenbaum chuckled. "We'll get it done."

Will turned to leave, and Hall and Jones followed him. The three men sat down on a bench, and Jones began to speak, "Jim Crow is gonna get a lot worse now. I have kin folks down in South Carolina who say the soldiers ensure their safety. There still are some lynchings going on. People will be terrified when those soldiers and the governor leave."

"From what I understand, Electoral Votes can be cast at the discretion of the Electors. Usually, they vote for the popular vote winner, but the Constitution does not require it," Hall explained. "At least we will have a resolution of this impasse."

"I am concerned that it's not the best resolution, but I can't control that situation. We have a whole list of other problems to work on. If we can do anything in the Senate, Jeremiah, you keep me informed," Will rose to leave.

"I certainly will, Senator," Jones assured him.

"And so will I, Senator," Hall added.

When Will arrived at home, Lenora noticed that he seemed bothered. "What's wrong, Will? You seem concerned about something. Do you want to share it with me?"

"Yes, my sweet lady. I talked to Jim Hall and Jeremiah Jones today. They conversed with some other Congressmen from the Presidential campaigns, discussing a plan for solving the impasse. I'm not too fond of their solution, but I am helpless to do anything. After dinner, I'd like to walk over and chat with Harry. Your mother always looks forward to seeing the children."

"Lillian might consent to sit with the children. I'd like to hear about this conversation, too."

As they prepared dinner, Lenora mentioned to Lillian that she and Will wanted to talk with her father about the Presidential deadlock's proposed solution. "Would you sit with the kids while we walk over there?"

"I'm happy to sit with 'em, Missy. One thang I miss about Roarin' Fork is playin' with Martha's and Willadeen's young'uns. Pete likes yer two boys, too. I thank he's excited about us having some young'uns."

When Will knocked on Parker's front door, Alice answered it promptly. "Come into this house, children. To what do we owe this wonderful surprise?"

"Will and I want to talk to Daddy. Is he busy with something?"

"He's not busy at all, just sitting in the parlor having his after-dinner cigar. Harry, Lenora, and Will are here," she called to him.

"Good evening, Harry. If you have a few minutes to spare, we'd like to chat with you."

"Sure, you young folks, come on in here and sit. What's on your mind?"

"Daddy, didn't the doctor tell you not to smoke?" Lenora frowned.

"Now, Princess, don't you be fretting your pretty little head about Daddy. I'm a big boy and make my own decisions. A man has to have a few small pleasures in this life."

"Presley, what have you got on your mind?" Harry changed the subject.

"A compromise has been proposed for solving the deadlocked Electoral College dispute, and I want to hear your opinion on the subject," Will was solemn.

"Samuel Tilden's supporters suggest they will cast all the electoral votes in South Carolina, Florida, and Louisiana for Hayes in exchange for a promise to remove the federal troops and the military governor from those states. They are the only remaining ones to maintain military rule.

"That action will give Rutherford Hayes 186 electoral votes and the White House office. But it effectively ends the Reconstruction effort."

"Will, this is the end of Ulysses Grant's term, and maybe it's time to move on to other things. Hayes is a Republican, and we will retain the power on that end. Democrats are now in control of Congress, but at least Hayes has veto power over any radical items the Democrats might legislate."

"Daddy, that action will overturn the vote of the people. Tilden is a Democrat, but he got the majority of the votes. It doesn't seem right to me," Lenora complained.

Alice joined the conversation, "Will, is there anything you as a Senator can interject into the issue?"

"I'm not a Constitutional lawyer, but I don't believe a Senator has a vote on this kind of issue, Alice. I thought that Harry would have some ideas about it," Will explained.

"There is not any action you can take that would change the outcome of this deal," Harry dropped his head. "It isn't right, but it'll probably happen."

Inaugurated on Monday, March 5, 1877, Rutherford B Hayes became the 19th President of the United States of America. He served only one four-year term in office.

Chapter Seventeen

THE WRONG HEROES

"Mama, Mama, make Ronnie and Randy stop chasing me," Mimi cried.

Lenora ran up the stairs, where she saw Mimi trying to hide under a bed. "What is going on up here?" she asked.

"Boys, don't be running away while I'm talking to you," Lenora demanded. "Sit down and be quiet until I ask you to explain why you are scaring your sister. First, I want to hear from Mimi. Why were you running, honey?"

"They told me to hold up my hands and give them all my toys. I asked them to leave me alone, but they started chasing me with sticks, pretending to shoot guns. I got scared, Mama."

Lenora looked at Ronnie and Randy for an explanation.

"We were playing train robbery. I was Jessie James, and Randy was my brother, Frank."

"He always takes the best parts," Randy grumbled.

"Don't you know that Jessie James is a bad man, boys?"

"But Mama, he always gets away with it. Nobody can catch him," Ronnie said with hands on his hips.

"They got in trouble at school today, too," Mimi told Lenora with a grin.

Jesse James

"Let's hear the whole story, boys. Randy, what happened at school?"

"We were playing the same game outside during recess," Randy responded with a sheepish smile. Some of the girls complained to Miss McAlister and said we were playing too rough. She sent us both to the shed for an hour."

"They call that shed the Naughty Room," Mimi added.

"That shed couldn't hold me. I'm Jesse James!" Ronnie bragged.

"Well, I can hold you!" Lenora scolded. "You are both to stay in your room until your father comes home. He will want to have a serious talk with the two of you. Come on, Mimi, we are going to have some fun of our own."

Randy looked worried, but Ronnie was still bragging about how he broke out of the shed. "That teacher is no match for Jesse James."

"I told you we would get in trouble if we kept showing off," Randy was remorseful.

Lenora was preparing supper with Mimi at her heels when Will came in the door.

"Daddy, Daddy, Ronnie, and Randy did a bad thing today. Mama told them to stay in their room until you got home."

"I'll take it from here, Mimi. Your father is tired. Go set the table and give him time to relax," Lenora directed.

"Lillian, would you please watch the pots and make sure nothing burns? I need to speak with Will."

"Shore, Len. I'll be happy ta take keer of it."

"How was your day, darling?" Lenora asked, hanging Will's coat up for him.

"Oh, the usual political game. How can I convince you that I am right and you are wrong? Can we make a deal? That sort of thing.

"What was Mimi trying to tell me?"

"Your eleven-year-old twins have become enamored of Jesse James. I guess they have heard other boys talking about his outlaw pursuits. In their minds, he is a hero who performs dramatic feats and always manages to elude capture.

"They had to be disciplined by Miss McAlister today for rough play during recess. When they got home this afternoon, they continued by terrorizing Mimi, pretending to be Jesse and Frank James on one of their train robberies."

"Why don't you call them down to supper? We will sit together at the table as usual. I will ask them about their day to allow the natural conversation to develop," Will suggested.

Mimi overheard her father's plan and was not happy. "Aren't you going to punish them, Daddy? Are you going to let them eat supper like nothing is wrong?"

"Princess, you can help me handle this by being very quiet and listening. I'm sorry they scared you, but I know they love you."

Ronnie and Randy followed their mother down the stairs to the dining table. Randy said, "Hi Daddy," with his eyes on the floor. Ronnie followed with, "We were tired of sitting in our room."

"How was school today, boys?" Will asked, passing the biscuits.

"Pretty good until recess," Ronnie answered with not a slight touch of remorse.

"Oh, that's strange," Will quizzed. "Most students like recess the best."

Ronnie continued, seemingly unaware that he was digging his hole deeper. "Miss McAlister doesn't know what fun is. Randy and I were having a great time playing like we were the James Gang."

"How do you know so much about the James Gang, Ronnie?"

Randy shook his head in hopes that Ronnie would stop making things worse.

"Everybody's talking about them. Plus, there's always a copy of the Washington newspaper in the classroom. We try to keep up with what's going on in the world. Miss McAlister says she wants us to be informed," Ronnie said as if to justify his behavior as being educational.

"Nice try, Son, but I doubt that the James Gang is at the top of Miss McAlister's list of critical national news."

"But Jessie is more interesting than most of those old men in the paper."

"Are you aware that Jessie James has killed innocent people for no reason and that he has stolen from poor working-class folks who have done him no wrong?" Will asked in a calm voice while sipping his stew.

Ronnie and Randy were staring at the table without making a sound, wishing they could disappear from the eyes of their parents. Mimi was enjoying their discomfort.

In an unsure voice, Ronnie asked, "Isn't Jessie just fighting back because his family got hurt? I thought he was standing up for poor people. Lots of folks think he is a hero."

"It is essential to know the whole story before making anyone your hero, boys. Some tales you may hear are just stories, with the bad parts ignored.

"My father told us that he learned the hard way not to take anything at face value."

Will held the rapt attention of all three children, but paused to give them a chance to respond or ask a question.

Mimi spoke first. "What's face value, Daddy?"

"In simple terms, it means that things are not always what they seem. On closer inspection, a bright shiny stone may not be a precious jewel.

"As a young man, my father left his home in Ireland, and attempted to start over in London. He was tricked into buying a sick horse that died immediately, and then he was jailed for failure to pay for the dead horse.

"After his release from jail, he took a chance to start over again in America. He was lied to during the long voyage, and a thief aboard the ship stole his money.

"He believed what the shipping agent told him and signed a contract of indenture. Upon arriving in North Carolina, he learned that only part of what the agent had told him was genuine. He would have to work much longer to pay off his debt and own less land than promised.

"Although he was disappointed, he worked hard. He married your other grandmother, Sally. They raised nine children and bought more land before he died in a logging accident.

"He did not steal from others. He did not use the excuse to hurt other people because of his family's mistreatment. J.W. and Sally Presley were my first heroes.

"Pastor John Henderson was my next hero. He taught us that all people are children of God and that we should treat everyone the way we wished them to treat us."

"Why are you telling us this story? Randy asked.

"I am telling you these stories because I want you to be careful in choosing your heroes. I hope you will take the time to get all the facts before you decide what is right.

"For example, what ill did Jessie James or his family suffer that justifies his rage of stealing and killing?"

"People say his family lost everything in the war," Ronnie offered. "They talk about a *lost cause*. What does that mean?"

"If you will help your mother clear the table, we can move into the gathering room for the rest of this conversation."

As the family sat by the fire, Will began to tell his children about the Civil War. He told them about the argument over slavery, the attempt to divide the country, the senseless loss of life, and property destruction.

Lenora smiled as she listened to her husband's eloquent description of the most horrible events. She noted how he could tell the story in terms the children could understand.

The boys asked Will about his part in the war. He shared what he could while withholding the worst agonies that he could not forget.

"I had to leave home because I could not fight for a cause I did not feel was just. When no other options were available, I joined the Union Army for one tour. Ever since leaving, I have been attempting to make things right again.

"The *lost cause* refers to a system that existed in the southern states and was lost when the south lost the war. That included the system that allowed white people to own black people."

"People can't own other people, can they?" Randy looked confused.

"No, they cannot. The war decided that. But some people have not accepted the truth; therefore, they call the result of the war the *lost cause*."

"What does all that have to do with Jessie James," Ronnie was getting impatient.

Will raised his voice slightly to say, "I am trying to tell you there is a reason that your flashy hero feels entitled to do the things he does, but it is not an excuse.

"As I understand it, the James brothers were Confederate soldiers in the Civil War. When the war ended, they came home to devastation, as did many others. At that point, they had a choice of what to do with the rest of their lives. I think they took the wrong road, a road that harms many innocent people and the road that will eventually lead to their downfall.

"My Paw used to say *somethings you just have to learn by living,* but I am trying to protect you from realizing that the result of violence is more violence.

"There is nothing wrong with playing games of chase and tag. All young people do that. What is wrong is frightening other people by pretending to do them harm.

"I hope that you will make good choices when you come to forks in the road or times of decision.

"I also hope that you will find good people in your life to look up to as heroes."

"You are my hero, Daddy," Mimi smiled, curling up on Will's lap.

Randy said, "I'm sorry we scared you, Mimi."

"Me too," Ronnie said with a look of shame.

"It's alright," Mimi responded. "I still love both of you."

"On that note, let's have some apple pie," Lenora suggested looking at Will with pride.

Chapter Eighteen

PARKER JOBBING BEGINS

"Hey, Pete, today is the 23rd of April. I'd like to open the produce shed for storekeepers next Monday. That'll be April 30th. Can you have things ready by then?"

"Yep, I think so. We've got bushel baskets and a few peck baskets. We can pick carrots, radishes, turnips, potatoes, sweet potatoes, spinach, lettuce, cabbage, kale, beets, onions, early peas, and the first crop of green beans. Tomatoes, corn, green bell peppers won't be ready until about the 1st of June."

"How much pork do you have in the smokehouse?" Will asked.

"We've got 14 hams, 12 sides of meat, and I guess 150 pounds of sausage. We're kinda low on bacon cuts cause Mr. Harry and Miss Alice like it, and your boys do too."

"Yeah, our boys saw us making sausage one time, and they haven't eaten any of it since," Will chuckled.

"When I was a boy, I didn't think I'd like sausage either, but when I smelled it cookin', I changed my mind," Pete grinned.

"Alright, we'll start with two rows of each of the items you've got ready to pick. Put everything in bushel baskets to start. If anybody wants just a peck or two of something, we can fill those from the bushel baskets. I'm hoping they'll buy full bushels, but we can accommodate the ones who won't, I reckon," Will was smiling.

"I'll go back on Friday to see the three customers we saw before. There are three more on our list, so I'll see them on Saturday. You probably need to stay here and ensure everything gets finished and displayed by Saturday evening.

"Get Raymond and Elijah to night-watch Saturday and Sunday nights. I'll make sure they've got rifles. Tell them we'll pay extra for their night duty.

"Zeke and Alvin can alternate weekends with them. They probably need extra money too," Will instructed.

"How come the black boys get all of the extra pay jobs? It don't seem right to me," Pete objected.

"Raymond, Elijah, and Zeke all have a passel of young'uns like Maw and Paw had. It takes more to feed a bunch of children. But you can alternate some other boys in there if any of them want to work extra hours at night.

"I don't expect that this will be a permanent arrangement. Later on, we can build some folding doors and put padlocks on them. Our men need to make some extra pay for a while to help them get caught up on things. They've been out of work for a while."

"Do you think Mr. Harry'd wanna come out and watch us set up the display?" Pete asked Will. "I think Harry's advice could help us make it look better, and he probably would like to be involved in the start-up of this new business."

"Yeah, that's a good idea, Pete. I'll tell Harry that you suggested it. He's still walking with a cane, but he won't have to lift anything. You younger men can do the lifting and hard work."

"Yep, Mr. Harry can just be the boss-man. Do you remember when Paw wanted just to be the boss?" Pete remembered.

Breathing a sigh, Will remembered very well. That was when the accident happened. "Yes, I remember it all too well. That was one of the saddest days of my life. When we had to tell Maw that tree fell on him, I felt so much sorrow for her," as tears filled his eyes.

Friday, April 27, 1877

As they sat down to eat breakfast, Will said, "O.K. Pete, I'm heading out to see Roy Ailor, Bill Padgett, and Fred Turner today. Go over and ask Harry to accompany you to the shed as you set up our display.

"I'll be back at about four o'clock this afternoon. Keep part of the crew filling baskets as they pick the vegetables from the garden. Two men should be able to put it on the shelves when they're ready. Harry can put prices on the filled baskets as you display them. He knows what the prices are in today's market."

After breakfast, Pete knocked on the door of the Parker home. When Alice opened the door, Pete smiled and said, "Mornin' Miss Alice, has Mr. Harry finished breakfast yet?"

"Yes, he has, Pete. Won't you come in the house?"

PARKER JOBBING BEGINS   89

"Yes ma'am, I'd jist like to talk to Mr. Harry fer a second, If he's available."

"Sure, Pete. I'll go get him for you."

"Good morning, Pete. What's going on with you this morning?" Harry asked as he extended his hand.

"Will thought ye might wanna go down ta tha shed 'n' he'p us set up tha display of baskets. Said ye could tell us tha prices 'n' show us how to set 'em up."

Alice spoke, "Now, Harry, you don't need to be lifting any baskets. You know what the doctor said."

"Alice, the young man, didn't ask me to lift any baskets. He just wants me to suggest prices for the vegetables. I need to get out of the house and get involved in our new business."

Pete volunteered, "Miss Alice, we can carry tha front porch rocker to tha shed, 'n' Mr. Harry kin set down, 'n' watch us. He sets on the porch a lot anyway."

Chuckling, Harry replied. "See there, Alice, problem solved. Come on, Pete, put the rocker in the buggy."

Four O'clock

As he approached the shed in his buggy, Will was surprised and somewhat amused to see Harry sitting in a rocking chair supervising the workers. "Hey Harry, that looks like a great job. How'd you get that assignment?"

"Pete, our foreman, gave it to me. It was the only way Alice would approve of me getting involved."

"And it sure has been nice havin' him to he'p us," Pete volunteered. "We wouldn't a knowed where to start sorting this stuff out 'n' displayin' it."

"Looks like you've about got the shelves full. How much more are you gonna pick today?" Will looked at Harry.

"I thought we should have an extra bushel of each item ready in case some customer wants more than we think," Harry responded. "We can line it up behind the shelves and add it in when we get space."

"Good thinking, Harry. I believe we're gonna get a good start on Monday. Roy Ailor said he'd be here at 5:30. Bill Padgett is coming early too. Fred Turner will open his store before he comes, but he begins at 6:00.

"I'm going to see Jim Lanning, Arthur Ely, and Bill Turbeville in the morning. Do you think we can handle them on Monday, too, or should we ask them to come Tuesday?" Will asked as he looked at Harry, then at Pete.

"I think we can handle all of them on Monday without making them wait too long," Pete offered. "They can pick what they want 'n' our boys can load 'em up. Can you help us, Mr. Harry?"

"If you'll get my rocker back down here," Harry grinned.

"Yep, when we git a wagon loaded, Mr. Harry kin write down what they got 'n' they kin pay him. That way, we kin go on to another customer 'n' git them loaded. Dependin' on when tha customers git here, we kin probably be done by dinner time or maybe 1:00.

"Being as how these men 'er comin' in at 5:00, we'd still git a good day's work outta them," Pete figured on his fingers.

"Hey, Presley, in the morning, stop by and see Claude Brown. He has a meat market about a half-mile on down the road from Roy Ailor's place. Brown buys beef from John Hall, but I don't know his source for pork. He might be interested in buying from us. He attends church over at Falls Church, where we worship, and we are close by here, too."

"Alright, I'll see him as I head out – my first stop," Will acknowledged.

Saturday Morning

"Good morning, Mr. Brown," Will spoke as he entered the meat market.

"Well, hello, Senator, what brings you out this way on a Saturday morning?" Brown asked.

"Harry asked me to stop in and tell you about our new business. We are starting to sell vegetables, fruit, and pork to storekeepers in our area. We keep quite a bit of cured pork in the smokehouse, including bacon and sausage if you are interested. I'm certain you already have a source, but we are close by and convenient for you."

Aren't you boys selling to the War Department anymore?" Brown was surprised.

"Oh, yes. Mr. Brown," Will assured him. "But since the war ended, they haven't bought as much, and we had to furlough some employees. This depression has affected all of us, but we want to bring our people back to work. By selling our produce to storekeepers, we can afford to re-employ them. We have to do something to work ourselves out of this economic disaster we're in."

"I see, Senator, but please call me Claude. Mr. Brown is so formal."

Smiling, he replied, "My mama taught me to respect people and use titles. Still, I feel more comfortable using first names. Will you call me Will?" he smiled, his usual reaction when he used Will twice in a sentence.

"Yes, Will, but, as you said, I've been buying pork from a local farmer. He only butchers hogs once per year, in late fall, so he starts to run out by spring. Do you folks have a good supply?"

"At this point, our smokehouses are full, but we expect our grocery store operators to buy some sausage and bacon."

"When are you opening for business," he seemed interested.

"First thing Monday morning. Roy Ailor is coming in at 5:30, and we are looking for several others on Monday."

"I can probably come on Tuesday morning. I can arrange for my wife to tend the shop while I'm gone. Will somebody be available to show me around?"

"I feel sure that Harry would be glad to do that since he asked me to invite you to come in. I'll tell him. What time do you expect to arrive?"

"Not very early. I'll want to help my wife get the shop open before I leave. Let's say bout 9:00. Harry should be out and about by then."

"Thank you, Claude; I'll tell Harry to look for you on Tuesday."

Except for Arthur Ely, the other storekeepers promised to come early on Monday morning to look at the product offerings for sale. Ely explained that Monday morning was his allotted time to re-stock his store shelves but that he should arrive by noon. He teased Will by saying, "Are you going to buy me lunch?"

Will grinned and nodded his assent. "Can you eat a ham sandwich with pickle slices on it?"

"Since you put it that way, I might get there by 11:30," he smiled.

"I'll tell Alice to have it ready for you," Will promised.

When he arrived back at the farm, Harry was sitting on the front porch in his rocker. Will stopped and walked over to chat with Harry.

"How did it go today, Senator?" Harry delighted in saying Senator when addressing his son-in-law.

"Everybody I talked with seemed excited about our new venture. All agreed to check us out. I promised Ely that I'd have a ham sandwich for him. He's not coming until about noon."

"Great, it sounds like you are quite a good salesman, Presley. I'm proud of you," Harry patted him on the back.

"How good a salesman I am is yet to be determined. If our customers buy everything we offer them, then I'll accept the moniker of a good salesman."

"By the way, I asked Pete to get the coal-oil lanterns from the barn and hang them in the shed. It won't be daylight when our first customers arrive. We'll need some light."

"Good idea, Harry. I didn't think of that."

"I told Pete to hang them in the center of the shed on the roof trusses. I think it'll light up the place very well."

"I am eager to see how it goes on Monday. If it works, we'll be helping a lot of people. At least we're doing our part to combat the depression," Will was pensive.

"Claude Brown is coming on Tuesday. We might have to make some more sausage and cut some more sides of bacon. He is primarily interested in those two items from us. If our grocery store operators buy much, they could buy us out. Can we make more on Monday afternoon?"

"Yes. Henry Rolen can do that. He makes most of the sausage and cuts the sides of bacon. I'll check it and ask Henry to do it if necessary."

"Harry, it might be better to allow Pete to ask Henry. He's the foreman," Will cautioned.

"Yes, you're right, Presley. I usually give the orders, but I know I must learn to delegate. Pete is the foreman; he should talk to Henry.

"You have talked with all our prospective customers, Presley. How much do you think we can sell to these folks?"

Speaking slowly, Will replied, "I am cautiously optimistic. I know we grow high-quality fruits and vegetables. Our pigs are well-proportioned with fat and lean. It will be easier for the folks with whom we have talked to buy here locally.

"I am convinced we must start slowly, then gradually increase our customer base. We'll learn as we go and make the necessary adjustments. But, I do believe this will be a successful venture and that we can contribute to our community as a result of it."

"We'll get a good feel for it on Monday and Tuesday. I am eager to see how it goes," Harry replied. "Thanks for your planning and hard work, Presley. I'm happy my daughter chose you as her husband."

Chapter Nineteen

OPENING DAY

"Let's go, Pete, it's 5:00, and Roy Ailor will be here at 5:30. We need to let the night-watchmen go home, and we need to get the coal-oil lanterns lit."

"Alright, brother, I'm ready," Pete smiled eagerly. "Let's go."

Just as Pete lit the last lantern, Harry drove up in his buggy. Looking up, Pete said, "Good Mornin' Mr. Harry, I see you got yer rocker with ye. Are you ready to go to work," he grinned.

"Yeah, Pete, got everything I need to do a full day's work," Harry said with tongue-in-cheek.

"Is that Roy's wagon I hear approaching," Will wondered aloud.

Just then, Roy spoke. "Mornin' men. It looks like you fellows have everything ready to go. Let's see what you got."

"Mornin' Roy,' Harry greeted him. "I haven't seen you in a while. Thanks for coming."

"Yes, I guess the heart attack kinda slowed you down some," Roy smiled wryly.

"I like what you folks are trying to do here. If you can get more store-keepers to shop locally, it'll help all of us."

Henry, Alvin, Simon, and Zeke arrived just five minutes before 5:30, prepared to load the baskets Ailor chose to buy.

"Alright, boys, it looks like Harry has some good prices here, and your produce is exceptional. Give me a bushel of potatoes, onions, radishes, sweet potatoes, beets, cabbage, lettuce, and green beans. I'll start with one bushel of each. Can I come back on Wednesday to get more if I need to?"

"Of course, Roy," Will looked pleased. "You can come back Friday, too; we'll be here."

Alvin and Simon loaded the baskets for Ailor while Henry filled the empty spaces left at the front of the rows.

"Before you go, Roy, walk over to the garden with me. I want to show you something. We are growing three varieties of tomatoes. I believe we are the only people in this area who'll have them."

"Harry, aren't those things poison? I've heard that people are afraid to eat them. Where'd those things come from?"

"No, of course not. When first taken to Europe, they were used as decorative plants and thought to be *wolf peach.* Once, a plant was used to poison wolves but later found to be delicious to humans and practical in various ways.

"Last year at the Exposition in Philadelphia, we discovered a man named Heinz, who had a factory in Pittsburg. Mr. Heinz made a sauce out of tomatoes which he called ketchup. Alice and Lenora loved it.

"I'm planning to contact him and carry the product here at Parker Jobbing. Alice thinks it's great on potatoes and almost any cut of meat. I want to have some things that my competition doesn't sell."

"Well, you convinced me. When will these tomatoes be available?"

"We expect our first crop to be ripe about the 1st of June. There are three different varieties, one small, one medium-sized, and one large. The smaller ones will be ready; first, I think."

As Ailor returned to his wagon, Bill Padgett and Fred Turner arrived almost simultaneously. When they alit from the wagons, Padgett and Turner spoke to Ailor. "Looks like you got a wagon load, Roy," Padgett observed.

"Yeah, Harry and the Senator have a nice selection of everything, and it's priced right," Ailor replied.

"How much did Harry pay you to say that?" Turner teased. "You'd make him a real good salesman."

"Get Harry to tell you about them new tomatoes he's growin' over in the garden. They are exciting."

"Aren't those things poison?" Turner was skeptical.

"Harry doesn't think so. He'll tell you about it before you leave."

Will greeted the two arrivals and showed them the display of vegetables. "We have some pork in the smokehouses, too," he informed them. "If you need sausage or sides of bacon or hams or side meat, we have an ample supply."

As Will was speaking, Jim Lanning and Bill Turbeville drove up in their wagons. Harry smiled broadly and greeted each one. Will shook hands all around and welcomed his customers. "Help yourself, gentlemen. Just tell the boys here what you want, and they'll load it into your wagon."

As he finished paying for the produce he bought, Turner said, "I like your new operation here, Harry. It will be very convenient for me and help me keep fresh vegetables and fruit in my store. How many days per week will you be open?"

"We are planning to be open Monday through Friday, but we can adjust that as necessary. My suggestion is to come here two or three times per week and buy what you can sell in two or three days.

"We can replenish our picked items every day in the afternoon when our customers have already been here. Keeping fresh products in your store will keep your customers coming more often and increase your business."

"I think you're right, Harry," Turner smiled. "Now, tell me about those tomatoes."

"Alright, let's get Padgett, Turbeville, and Lanning to walk over to the garden with us. This is a fascinating new item, and I'm excited about it."

When Harry finished his pitch on the tomatoes, he told them that tomatoes would be available by the 1st of June. "I think we will, for a short time, be the only folks around here who have them for sale. Let's take advantage of it to increase our business and be a step ahead of our competition. For this first year, I will give you men an exclusive on tomatoes. I won't sell to any other stores in this local area. After this year, I'll open up and try to sell them in a wider area. I believe this will be an item in great demand when folks become aware of them."

Turner spoke, "I want some of the first crop to ripen," he enthusiastically proclaimed.

"Me too," Lanning chimed in.

"I want to try them, too," Padgett added.

"Alright, men, we'll be open here at 5:30 on Monday through Friday. Come by any morning that you need more produce, vegetables, fruit, or pork meat.

At 11:15, Alice walked down to the shed carrying a basket. "I have a ham sandwich for Arthur Ely. It has pickle slices on it, just like Will ordered it. I brought some milk, too."

Will smiled and thanked Alice. "Thank you, Alice. I hope Arthur shows up soon."

Just as he spoke, he heard a wagon approaching. "I believe that's Mr. Ely now," Pete informed them. "He's a tall man who is easy to spot in a crowd."

"Hello, Mr. Ely," Will greeted the new arrival. "Glad you could make it today."

"The promise of a ham sandwich is what got me here today, Senator." Ely grinned. "And the chance of seeing this pretty lady, Miss Alice."

"Aww, Arthur, you always say the right words to an old lady. Thank you for your flattering comments."

"Don't forget, Arthur, this pretty lady's husband is here, and he knows how to use a shotgun," Harry teased.

"Put down the shotgun, Harry. I'll just take the sandwich the Senator promised me," Ely laughed out loud.

"Alright, Mr. Ely," Will smiled. "Pick out what you want to buy today, and I'll ask our men to load it for you. While we're loading it, Harry wants to tell you about a new product we are offering."

Ely was somewhat skeptical about the tomatoes but promised to buy a peck when they were ready.

"Can I get some sausage and bacon, Pete?" Ely inquired.

"Sure thing, Mr. Ely. How much of each do you want?" Pete asked.

"About ten pounds each. I'm coming back on Friday. Can I get more, then, if I need it?"

As Ely drove away, Harry asked Pete, "How much sausage and bacon do you have left to sell?"

"Looks like about 90 pounds of sausage and twenty-five pounds of bacon, Mr. Harry."

"Well, I usually take about 50 pounds of sausage and 50 pounds of bacon to the War Department on Friday. Claude Brown from the Meat Market will be here in the morning at about 9:00. Pete, you and Henry better make about 100 pounds of sausage and cut 100 pounds of bacon this afternoon. Send the rest of the men home so that the night watchmen can get some sleep before they come back tonight.

"Schedule everybody to arrive by 8:00 in the morning. We need to pick more vegetables to sell on Wednesday."

"Yes, Sir Mr. Harry. We can do that.'Er ye happy with tha way thangs went taday?" Parker nodded and smiled at him.

Will climbed into the buggy with his father-in-law after placing the rocker in the back. "Well, Harry, what do you think of our first day in business as Parker Jobbing?"

"I am pleased with our start. I do believe you are on to something with this business. It just might be the impetus we have needed. My only regret is that I am limited in my activity. Still, Pete and our other employees adapted well to the changes we made. Good job, Son," Harry was proud of Will.

Chapter Twenty

THE SOUTH LEGISLATES SEGREGATION

Will was in a cheerful mood as he arrived home from his workday at the Capitol Building. There was something about the beginning of summer in Northern Virginia that rejuvenated his spirit.

Whistling as he entered the front door of the Presley home, Mimi, racing to meet him, yelled, "Daddy's home, Daddy's home," and raised her arms to hug him.

Reacting to Mimi's excitement, Lenora came from the kitchen to greet him, too. "Welcome home, my darling. Did you have a good day?"

"Yes, I did. People all over the Capitol were smiling and feeling good about the beautiful Summer weather we've had for the last few days."

"Will, I hate to spoil your uplifted mood, but I received an unsettling letter today from Charlotte Hill down in Knoxville. If you want to take a few minutes before supper, I'll read it to you," she sighed.

"Alright, let's sit down in the parlor," he frowned.

Opening the letter, Lenora began to read:

> Dear Lenora,
> I hope this letter finds you and your family in good health. Teddy and Orville, our two boys, have been attending public schools here in Knoxville. When they both started school, I returned to teaching. Norville has been working in a textile mill as a maintenance man, and he loves it. You know how he always enjoyed working with his hands.

Everything was going well for us but we are distressed that our State has not updated the laws. Our boys cannot understand why they cannot attend classes with all of their friends. Black children are still forced to attend separate schools from white children. It just breaks my heart. We do not know how to explain these unfair laws to Teddy and Orville.

Because Tennessee was the first state to ratify the Fourteenth and Fifteenth amendments, Norville and I were shocked.

After fighting in a bloody war to force the abolition of slavery and working for the education of black children, we were dismayed that Tennessee seemed to be living in the antebellum days.

Our legislators have also reverted to laws against associating with blacks in social or church settings. People are calling it mixing and mingling. Bias and bigotry are rampant in Tennessee. Blacks are not welcomed in public facilities like restaurants or hotels and even on streetcars. Is the Virginia legislature doing the same things?

During Reconstruction, we talked about the black codes. Now they are being called Jim Crow laws, but it's all the same things. Blacks are treated as second-class citizens.

Will is a Senator. Can't he do something about this kind of conduct? Norville asked me to write to you because we are so concerned about returning to the old ways.

We hope to hear from you soon and are eager to visit you in our nation's capital.

We miss you.

Charlotte and Norville Hill

"Will, are you aware of Jim Crow laws in Virginia?" Lenora wondered.

"Yes. Some of the state's legislators are moving that way now. Martial law is no longer viable anywhere in the South. Returning to Home Rule has allowed most of them to reestablish the old laws against black folks.

"What does that mean for the black people we know, Will?" I'm worried about some of our workers here on the farm."

"As long as they work for Harry, they will not face any discrimination in employment, but that's probably the only way we can protect them. Their children will not be welcomed in public schools. They are not even officially permitted to have white friends.

"Just as my friend, Congressman Jeremiah Jones, they can be denied service in restaurants, stores, public transportation, and even the right to congregate with white people for church or social occasions." Will shook his head.

"I don't understand this. The fourteenth amendment was supposed to guarantee that all people born in the United States would have the same citizenship rights," Lenora demanded angrily.

"That was certainly the intention, Lenora, but remember what I told you I feared after the ratification of the fourteenth and fifteenth amendments?

"Without continuous enforcement, all we have are nice words on paper."

"Who is supposed to enforce those rights?"

Will explained that the return of Home Rule left most legislation to the individual states.

"I am learning that the dispute about legislative power at the state level versus the federal level has been ongoing from the founding of our country. Since the war, the south has been even more sensitive about protecting their state powers."

"So all the fighting and working to make things more *just* was for nothing?" Lenora cried.

"It does feel that way sometimes, Lenora, but at least we did manage to get those rights encoded in the Constitution. Individual rights cannot be changed without another amendment. Our work now must involve selecting the right people to represent us at the state and federal levels."

Lenora was crying harder. "That means that only men have an opportunity to vote for change. I can barely stand thinking that I will never have a voice in our state and country's important issues and that Mimi may be just as powerless. Mary Agnes was right. The campaign for women's suffrage is an ongoing fight, and I want to be part of that fight."

"Don't cry, Lenora. You are not powerless."

"How can you say that, Will? All I do every day is take care of our children, cook, and clean. I'm not complaining because I want to be a good mother and homemaker, but I do not influence the bigger world."

"I guess I would feel the same way if I were in your situation, but you are wrong about having influence.

"You have been a significant influence on me since we first met. You have encouraged me to try things I never thought I could do. When I became an elected official, you prodded me to take a stand for justice.

"Women have a remarkable ability to influence the men in their lives who do currently have voting rights. I know the time will come when women will have voting rights, but you can use the power of influence to work toward the needed changes until that beautiful day.

"Women can use that influence to positively affect their husbands, fathers, brothers, uncles, and of course, their sons."

"Thank you, Will. I appreciate your saying that I have had something to do with your thinking. What bothers me is that I feel so out of the loop.

"When I worked at the War Department, I knew what was going on and felt free to express my opinion. When we went to Memphis to work for the Freedman's Bureau, I felt a sense of accomplishment seeing the schools built and the children learning. I miss that feeling."

Lillian was listening to this conversation and said, "Lenora, I'd be happy ta help ye wit the chil'ren ifen ye want to do sumthan' in the community."

Will spoke up. "That is a generous offer, Lil, and a possible solution.

"Lenora, you could organize a group of women in our surrounding area who would be of like mind about several causes.

"If you want to promote women's suffrage, you might enlist help from Mary Agnes. If finding and supporting the state office candidates to oppose the Jim Crow laws, I'm sure my friend Jeremiah would be happy to assist you."

Lenora's imagination began to race. "I should begin with the ladies at church," she suggested. "Some of them have voiced their support for change. Many of them have husbands who are prominent in our area. We could build on that base of open-minded thinkers and then move out to other cities. I have lots of ideas about posters and newsletters," she rattled on.

"Oh, thank you so much, Lil. I wouldn't take advantage of your generosity, especially with you getting so close to having one of your own, but that would give me a chance to meet and talk with other women. I would feel that I was starting to contribute to something bigger."

As she began supper preparations, Will heard Lenora singing to herself.

The next day, Lenora approached Lillian, "Would you mind sitting with the children sometime next week to allow me to meet with some ladies from the church?"

"Why, Lenora, I told ye I'd be happy to help with whatever you need. You and Will have been so good to us, and I love your children just like mine. I'll be glad to start supper ifen ye need to be out of the house in the afternoon. Just tell me what you want me to do, and I'll do it fer sure. I'm a big girl and I can handle it."

On Sunday, after services, Lenora spoke with the Rector's wife, Cora. "Excuse me, Mrs. Stevenson, may I speak with you for a moment."

"Certainly, dear, how is the lovely Lenora today?"

"I am feeling very well, thank you; however, I have been thinking about the difficult times many of our neighbors are having with the recession and wonder if we could form a committee to plan how our church might help. With Father Richard's consent, I would love to be responsible for getting such an effort started," Lenora proposed.

"It would not be like Richard to turn down a volunteer, but I will ask him this afternoon and get back to you. By the way, please call me Cora. We are all friends here."

To her surprise, The Reverend Richard Stevenson and his wife arrived at Lenora's front door the next day.

"May we come in, Lenora?" The Rector asked, taking her hand and smiling.

"Please do, Father Richard and Cora. I would like you to meet my sister-in-law, Lillian Presley. She and her husband Pete, Will's brother, have moved here to help run the farm."

"Greetings, Miss Lillian. We are glad to have you join our community and our church if you feel so inclined."

"Pete and me have been to your services, and they are very nice but a bit fancier than we wuz used to in North Carolina. Our churches were mostly Methodist," Lillian responded.

"You will find that we are not that different," the Rector informed her. "You might say we are almost kissing cousins," he laughed and shook Lillian's hand.

"We are here to discuss your idea," Cora interjected. "I shared your suggestion with Richard, and he insisted we hear more."

The Rector asked, "Please expand on your concerns and how you propose the church might get involved."

Lenora took a deep breath and began. "My concerns are centered around three areas of inequality. I have heard that I expect too much, too fast. I have been advised to be patient. It has been suggested that some things are beyond my ability to change.

"Will and I spent the first few years of our marriage working in the Reconstruction effort and in the campaign to pass the fourteenth and fifteenth amendments. We wanted to ensure that the people freed from slavery had the same opportunities guaranteed to all United States citizens.

"Briefly, we thought we had been part of a successful campaign. Now I learn that the southern states are reversing much of the gains through local Jim Crow laws.

"I was passionate about the women's suffrage movement but again have been told to wait.

"Most currently, I am concerned about increased poverty as a result of the depression.

"To answer your first question, I am concerned about equal rights for black people, equal rights for women, and equal rights for all poor people.

"Your second question about how our church can be involved is just as difficult to answer. Despite what you may think, I am not naïve. I know one church in one town in one state cannot solve these problems. What I want to find out is whether we, as a group of Christians, can at least make an effort to ease some of the local issues," Lenora gulped and stopped talking.

"Why Mrs. Presley, I think you should give the homily at next week's services," the Rector responded.

Lenora blushed and said, "I don't mean to cause trouble, Father. I cannot sit still when I know that so many of our neighbors are beset with problems if I can do anything to help. Isn't that what Jesus told us to do?"

"Yes, Lenora, Matthew 25 instructs us to take care of those in need. That is how we can show God's love. There is no question that the church should be involved in reaching out to our less fortunate neighbors.

"We can individually do our part; however, we can make a more considerable impact if we combine our efforts. I think you would find that most of our parishioners are eager to be helpful; however, they need a leader to motivate them. That might just be you, Lenora," the Rector smiled.

As Cora was listening, she offered a suggestion. "Perhaps, I can arrange a luncheon meeting of our most active ladies and give you the stage to present the issues. Some of them may have ideas."

"Thank you both so much for being open to doing something new. I am so excited that my head is spinning," Lenora almost giggled.

Lillian took advantage of the moment to assert her potential role as Personal Assistant to a woman with a mission. "May I offer you a piece of Lenora's wonderful apple pie, Rev. and Mrs. Stevenson?"

Chapter Twenty-one

LENORA TAKES CHARGE

Cora did what she promised and scheduled a luncheon meeting at the church for the following Saturday. The guest list included ten wives of prominent members. Mrs. John Hall greeted Lenora with, "I understand that our Senator's wife has a message for us today."

"Today, I'm just plain Lenora, Marian. Hopefully, the fine ladies of Falls Church will have creative ideas about how we can demonstrate our Christian love to our neighbors and friends during these difficult times."

Following a light lunch, Cora stood to get the attention of the group and introduced Lenora. "I feel confident that most of you know Lenora Presley, but you may not have heard her speak. Today she would like to share her concerns and seek your suggestions about several persistent problems that haunt our community. Please welcome her."

Nervously, Lenora rose and gathered her thoughts.

"Ladies, first, I want to thank you for being here today and for listening to me rattle on, as I tend to do." Snickering was heard from some, smiles and puzzled looks from others.

"I was raised right here in Falls Church, so I feel a solid connection to whatever is going on in my backyard.

"Working at the War Department, I gained a broader interest in what was happening in all parts of our country. I dreaded the War and still grieve over the tragic resultant division and destruction.

"When the war ended, I felt a need to do something to help put things back together. That is probably magical thinking; nevertheless, I joined my husband, Will, in a campaign to provide opportunities to newly freedmen. Assigned to a post in Memphis, Tennessee, we became employees of the Freeman's Bureau.

"It was only one year of my life, but what I saw and heard during that year permanently changed my thinking.

"This wonderful country that we are blessed to have as our home is still a work in process. As I understand our Founders' intentions, we, the people, are empowered to ensure that the work toward a more perfect union continues.

"What empowers us is our collective votes, our influence, and our actions.

"I am saddened to see that the gains made through the terrible civil war and the unfinished reconstruction projects have been reversed by new Jim Crow laws in the south and even here in our area.

"It is disappointing to me that women were excluded in the voting rights legislation.

"It is heartbreaking to see families unable to feed their children amid this terrible depression."

Sensing that she had the attention of her audience, Lenora knew they were waiting for her to make the point.

"I guess you are wondering why I am telling you things that you already know. My goal is to seek your help in addressing at least one of the three areas of inequality.

"These problems are overwhelming, and it is easy to think they are beyond our abilities to affect. It is easy to believe that our lack of voting rights renders us impotent to change anything."

She heard some rumblings among the ladies and saw a few nods of agreement.

"I had become discouraged about all of these problems and my lack of involvement in any change efforts. My wise husband reminded me of what we women do have. We influence all the men in our lives in small things every day.

"How many of you have influenced the way your husbands eat, dress, and talk?" She heard laughter.

"How many of your husbands, sons, brothers and even fathers are better men because of you?" All hands were raised.

"I realize that securing equal rights for our black neighbors may seem too difficult a task to undertake.

"Sadly, I also realize that securing women's suffrage will continue to be a fight for many years to come.

"I am not expecting you to leave all of your household responsibilities to become activists in the public arena. Thankfully there are those heroes who devote their entire lives to such goals.

"What I am proposing is that you don't have to walk a protest line, carry a sign, or wave a flag to make a difference. It is possible for us as a group right here, right now, to make a difference in the lives of some local families.

"We can pool our efforts and organize our resources to provide much-needed food, clothing, heating supplies, medical care, and friendship.

"We can not only go to church; we can be the church in our area. We can follow the words of our Lord and render love in tangible forms to the least of these."

"How do we start?" A lady in pink shouted.

Cora spoke up, "We start by getting ourselves organized. We make a list of needs and divide ourselves into sub-committees, each having a leader.

Chapter Twenty-two

THE GREAT RAILROAD STRIKE

On Monday morning, July 16, 1877, Will sat at his desk in the Senate Office Building. He reviewed some sales figures for Parker Jobbing and felt good about the new venture's progress.

A knock on his door interrupted his perusal of the business sales. "Senator Presley," his office assistant stuck her head in and said, "You have two visitors to see you. Representatives Hall and Jones are here. Can you see them now?"

"Show them in and get us all a cup of coffee. Come in, gentlemen. To what do I owe this surprise?"

Both men smiled briefly and shook his hand. "We heard some bad news this morning and wanted to hear your opinion of the situation," Jeremiah Jones informed him.

"Yeah, Presley, it looks like we've got more problems coming our way," Jim Hall added.

"What's going on that seems so dire at this moment?" Will was surprised.

"Railroad workers in Martinsburg, West Virginia went out on a sit-down strike this past Saturday, and it seems it might spread to some other cities," Hall said.

"Why are they striking?" Will asked.

"Baltimore and Ohio cut their wages three times this year. They are having trouble keeping food on the table. B & O is the country's largest railroad company, and they have operations in New York, Pennsylvania, and Maryland," Jones was worried.

"I'm so distraught because I remember the Paris Commune of 1871. People were murdered, and buildings and property were burned to the ground. It was a war," Jones remembered.

"Yeah, I heard about that, but I never thought it would happen here," Will mused.

"Many of these workers are struggling to survive and feed their families," Hall added. "Survival leads desperate people to take desperate actions.

"That's what happened in Paris. The National Guard was ordered to quell the residents who were trying to improve their living standards."

"We've heard rumors already that the railroad companies will ask the state governors and maybe even the federal government to send troops to fight the rebellion," Hall continued.

"What alternatives do we as legislators have to intervene in this situation?" Will asked Hall, the Yale lawyer.

"None whatsoever," Hall replied. "We might exert some influence on the President and ask him not to send U.S. troops, but we have no authority over the governors of West Virginia, Maryland, or Pennsylvania."

"People are saying that the railroad companies are organizing local militias to come and forcibly control these desperate people. Some people are calling them *goons*. I suppose that means bad guys," Jones said.

"It seems to me that the B&O railroad should be able to pay their workers a living wage. Since the Depression has forced many smaller companies to file for bankruptcy, B&O has taken much of its business. Then, too, they have acquired most of their equipment at bargain prices.

"If they are buying all these companies, why can't they pay their workers better wages?" Will asked rhetorically.

"It seems that when they buy these small companies, they fire all the workers. These people then become desperate for jobs, so by cutting wages for their other workers, they can leverage the lower wages."

"Do you mean they tell workers they must work for lower wages, or they will hire the other folks who have no jobs?"

"That's the way monopolies work. If you control all the business, you can dictate the terms for everybody concerned," Hall observed.

"That does not seem to me to be the proper way to operate a business," Will replied as he furrowed his brow.

"Isn't there anything we can do about this situation, Jim?" Will asked his lawyer friend.

"At the current time, there are no laws that allow us to take any kind of action. People have proposed anti-monopoly laws, but, so far, we have none."

Jeremiah Jones spoke, "The outbursts are spreading, too. In Maryland, B&O's headquarters, they were forced to call in two National Guard units. Railroad workers, local townspeople, and business owners who sympathized with the laborers opposed the Guard units and pinned them down."

"President Hayes sent some regular U.S. army troops in to aid the Guardsmen. It took a couple of days, but the army prevailed."

"I certainly hope this doesn't precipitate another Civil War," Will worried.

"It might not start a war, but it will make things worse for the working man who has a railroad job. Many of those folks are black, and for the first time in their lives, they've had good-paying jobs," Jeremiah replied.

"Well, it won't do anything to aid the economy as it struggles in this Depression. It's only going to exacerbate the situation," Will observed.

"Parker Jobbing is doing a small part to provide jobs for a few people, but this railroad strike just makes things worse."

"What do you expect workers to do, Senator. They can't just sit back and watch their families go hungry. They must fight back," Jones said emphatically.

Looking at Hall, Will asked, "What are the chances that we can pass some legislation to prevent these big companies from snatching up all these smaller businesses?"

"Yeah, and can the federal government do anything to help these starving people whose jobs are now gone?" Jones asked.

"President Grant was opposed to the government getting involved in welfare programs," Hall related. "He was very strongly a capitalist. He felt that the churches should tend to the poor and the hungry."

"Jim, I'm not certain if you are aware of what Lenora and Alice are planning for Falls Church, but they want to provide some food and clothing for those in need in our community. It will be on a minimal basis, not anything near what the state or federal government could do," Will informed his two friends.

"My father has friends who are in management at B&O. They have discussed an Employee Relief Fund to provide death benefits and healthcare for employees, but no action has taken place," Hall reported to his friends.

"Hopefully, they will implement those ideas soon," Will said, "That would go a long way to resolve this strike."

July 21, 1877

Strikers in other cities began to fight for their cause. Pittsburg, Pennsylvania, became the site for the worst violence of the strike.

Thomas Alexander Scott was the head of the Pennsylvania Railroad. Someone described him as the first of the Robber Barons. He suggested that *the strikers should be given a diet of rifle lead, and see how they liked that kind of bread.*

Because local law enforcement refused to use violence on their friends and neighbors, Pennsylvania Governor John Hartranft called in the National Guard Infantry Regiment to subdue the strikers.

On July 21st, Guard members bayonetted and fired on the rock-throwing strikers. Twenty strikers died, and twenty-nine were wounded.

Strikers, though, were not deterred by the violence from the National Guard. On the contrary, they became infuriated. Opposing the actions of the Guard, strikers forced them to take refuge in a railroad roundhouse.

The strikers burned thirty buildings, and 104 locomotives, and 1,245 freight and passenger cars were destroyed.

On July 22nd, the Guard shot their way out of the roundhouse, killing 20 more strikers as they left the city. After more than a month of fighting and destruction, President Hayes sent in federal troops as he had done in West Virginia and Maryland and finally ended the strike.

In Philadelphia, three hundred miles to the east, strikers battled Guardsmen and set fires that burned much of the Center City. Governor Hartranft called on President Hayes, and once again, federal troops were needed to quell the riots. Similar activity spread to Reading and Scranton, and federal troops were necessary.

July 25, 1877

Further north in New York, other strikers organized protests. Groups in Albany, Syracuse, and Buffalo made their presence known.

In Albany, at the Van Woert Street crossing, a group of strikers gathered, awaiting the arrival of a scheduled train. When it stopped, they began to pelt the cars and the train personnel with stones, rocks, and pieces of wood.

The militia was called in to defend the railroad, but the protest continued into the second night. Then, the mayor of Albany rescinded the militia and used the police department to stop the altercations.

In all three of the involved cities, workers from various trades, coal miners, small business owners, and townspeople sided with the railroad workers. Resentment of the railroad companies and the power they wielded on the local economy was the driving force.

Illinois

On July 24th, a mob of unemployed workers stopped all rail traffic in Chicago. Both Baltimore and Ohio, and Illinois Central were affected and paralyzed.

Demonstrators in Bloomington, Aurora, Urbana, Peoria, and Decatur shut down other rail yards across the state.

Sympathetic coal miners in Carbondale, Braidwood, LaSalle, and Springfield went on strike as well. They were citing poor working conditions and low wages. A group calling itself The Working Man's Party organized demonstrations that drew crowds of 20,000 people.

Mayor Monroe Heath of Chicago organized an unofficial group of 5,000 men to help restore order. Partly successful, they soon were joined by the Illinois National Guard and U.S. military troops mobilized by the Governor. Finally, the restoration of peace came.

The Chicago Times headline blared the following day:
Terror Reigns,
The Streets of Chicago Given Over to Thieves and Cutthroats.

When peace was restored, 20 men and boys were killed. None were police or troops. Dozens more were wounded, and the loss of property was estimated to be millions of dollars.

Missouri

On July 21st, in East Saint Louis, Illinois, a central freight rail hub, all traffic was halted, and the city remained in control of the strikers.

The Saint Louis Working Men's Party led 500 men across the Missouri River in solidarity with the 1000 rail workers on strike.

This action was a catalyst for labor unrest spreading across the United States. The eight-hour workday and child labor were the unifying issues that motivated these laborers.

President Hayes sent federal troops from city to city, and at long last, 45 days after it started, the Great Railroad Strike ended.

Strikers in Pittsburg burned 39 buildings, more than 60 passenger cars, and almost 1400 freight cars. All told, the carnage amounted to a short, forty-five-day war with no apparent winner. Reforms for workers were born in the aftermath of the widespread strike.

Chapter Twenty-three

THE INTRUDER

Arriving home early on Friday afternoon, August 3rd, Will noticed Harry and Alice sitting on the front porch. He waved and called out, "I'll be right back. I want to put my horse and buggy in the barn."

Smiling as he returned, Will noticed that Alice and Harry had a troubled look on their faces. "Is something wrong?" he looked first at Harry, then at Alice.

"Alice was reading an article in the Washington newspaper about the big railroad strike that just ended. It's troubling to think about all those killed and wounded and the property destroyed.

"Another all-out war could have started right here. Many things need to change in our country," Harry worried.

Alice replied, "We are developing two separate groups of people in the United States – rich and poor. The rich are extremely rich, and the poor are very poor.

"We are trying to do some things to help a few folks here in Falls Church, but it's just such a small group. I wish there were some way to do it on a national scale," she shook her head.

"Several weeks ago, Jim Hall, Jeremiah Jones, and I had this same conversation at the Capitol. Hall doesn't think there's any chance the federal government would get involved in this kind of project.

"There is a group who call themselves *The Salvation Army*, who minister to poor people. A Methodist minister named William Boothe and his wife, Catherine established the London group in 1865. They are reaching out to other European countries, but not the USA at this point," Will related.

Unexpectedly, they heard shouts coming from the Shed. "What you doin', boy?" Elijah yelled. "You come back here with dat stuff."

Hurrying to the back of the house, Will and Harry saw Elijah holding a teenaged boy's arm. "Dis boy had hisself a big bag of taters, onions, beets, tomatoes, and green beans. He wuz helpin' hisself ta 'er stuff." Elijah explained.

Lenora, Alice, Ronnie, Randy, and Mimi joined the group to see what the commotion was about.

Realizing the boy was very close to her two's age, Lenora walked over and patted her hand on the child's shoulder. "Would you like to tell us why you are here taking our food without permission, young man?"

"We's hungry, Ma'am. Ain't had nuthin' ta eat in two days."

"Who are We, honey?" Alice softly asked him.

"My Momma, my two brudders, 'n my two sistas, Ma'am. We's all a fam'ly."

"Where do you and your family live, child?" Lenora asked with tears in her eyes.

"We's been campin' down by da crick that runs to da riva."

"Why you been campin' boy?" Elijah asked. "Ain't you got no house ta live in?"

"No Suh, de landlord kick us out. Momma didn' have no money ta pay 'im wit. My Poppa lost his job wit da railroad. He say dey let all da Jim Crows go first."

"Boy, you black, but you ain't no Jim Crow. Who tol' you dat?" Elijah was agitated.

"My Poppa say dat's whut da foreman say when he tol' 'em not ta come back ta work no mo."

"Where's your Poppa, now, Son?" Harry asked him.

"He say he wuz goin' ta Pittsburg ta try 'n git a job. We ain't heerd nuttin' from 'im in 'bout five 'er six weeks. Da landlord tol' us ta move outta his house 'bout two weeks ago. We's been campin' eva since."

After returning from the weekly trip to the War Department, Pete and Henry drove up in the wagon and joined the group. Harry spoke to Pete, "Can you use another helper to work the vegetable garden right now?"

Pete nodded and said, "Yes, Sir Mr. Harry. Everything is ready to pick now, and we need to add another late planting on several things. Who ye got in mind?"

"This young man right here has a bag of vegetables he needs to pay for. Can you start him on Monday?" Harry asked.

"Yeah, I reckon so. Me and Will both worked a garden back home in North Ca'lina afore we wuz as big as this boy," Pete said.

"Mr. Harry, kin me 'n you talk in private fer a minnet?" Elijah asked.

"Sure, Lije, walk over here with me." Walking a few steps from the group, Harry stopped and said, "What have you got in mind, 'Lije?"

"If I'se kin borrows a wagon, I'se take dat boy to his Momma and git dem otha young'uns. I'se takes 'em home wit me 'n let dem stay wit us fer a while 'til dey kin finds another place. If we pay dis boy fer workin' here, dey kin pays rent someplace 'n not hafta camp outside."

"Alright, 'Lije, but if your wife objects, let me know, and we'll work out something else," Harry answered.

Harry explained to the rest of the group what Elijah planned to do. The boy and Elijah got in the wagon that Pete and Henry had driven to town.

As they started to leave, Will spoke to Pete and Henry. "Go to the smokehouse and get some ham, bacon, and sausage for Elijah to take to these folks. They will need to eat at his house for a few days. The boy's already got a bag of vegetables."

As the group walked back to the house, Lenora spoke, "I've got an idea that might help these folks and some others here in Falls Church. Let's sit on the front porch and talk for a while before supper."

"Of course, Princess, you know I relish the idea of talking with you," Harry grinned.

Harry, Alice, Will, Lenora, and Pete sat on the porch. Lenora sent the children into the house under the watchful eyes of Lillian.

When they were all seated, Lenora spoke. "We could hire some women to can our vegetables. We can label them as Parker Farms Products and sell the canned goods to our retail store customers and the War Department. Then we could provide jobs for more people and increase our business volume of sales.

"It would also give us more items to distribute in the Church's effort to feed hungry people. Matthew 25:40 says, Inasmuch as ye have done it unto one of the least of these, my brethren, ye have done it unto me."

Smiling, Alice replied, "What a wonderful idea, Len. I love it, but what would it involve on our part to get it started?"

"We would need a kitchen and stove for cooking and heating, jars with sealing lids, and some big pots in which to cook. Mason jars are available from the farm supply store.

"We'll need some employees to prepare the vegetables for cooking and canning," Will added. "Maybe the mother of the young man we just hired to work here will be available to work for us."

Pete listened carefully and replied, "Lillian might be interested in working in the cannery. She did some of that back home before we got married, and Martha was doing some canning at Roarin' Fork."

"Well, it sounds very doable to me," Harry interjected. "At first, I was skeptical, but since we have experienced people, I like the idea."

"The first thing we need to do is build a big kitchen out away from the house," Pete was speaking softly. "I've done some buildin' afore. All we need is a big open space with room for four or five cookstoves."

"I am excited to think we can make such a big difference in the lives of many more people," Alice gushed.

"And we can make a lot more money," Harry winked at Lenora. " Let's do it, Presley," he looked at Will.

"Harry, you talked me into it. Henry and Pete can start buildin' next week," Will replied.

Saturday Morning

After checking the shed shelves' stock, Pete looked up and heard the wagon entering the garden area. Elijah and the young black boy alit and spoke to Pete.

"Good mawnin', Mista Pete," Elijah smiled.

"Who's yer sidekick there 'Lije?" Pete grinned.

"This heah's Jackson Jefferson, but dey jist calls 'im Jackie. He wanted ta come ta work taday. I tol' 'im he cud wait 'til Mondee, but he comes on anyhow."

"Well, I'm glad tha boy wants ta work. We quit at noon, so it's a short day, but a good one ta start 'im," Pete took off his hat and scratched his head.

"Here's what we need ta pick this mornin', Lije. Jackie kin he'p you fill baskets ta put on display fer Mondee. We need four bushel of corn, two green beans, two potatoes, three tomatoes, two onions, four lettuce, and two cabbage. Kin ye git alla that done by noon?"

"Yep, I thank so," Lije nodded. "Is Zeke 'n Alvin comin' in?"

"Yeah, but I thought I'd git them ta slice some ham 'n bacon 'n make sausage. I know we sent some home with you ta feed yer comp'ny. Figgered we'd need some more Mondee when Roy Ailor gits here."

Harry came out from the house and saw Jackie with his arms folded and his head down. "Good morning, young man. Are you ready to go to work?"

"Yes, Suh, Mista Parker. "Lije say it'd be alright."

"I don't believe they told me your name, son," Harry said.

I'se Jackie Jefferson, Suh."

"How old are you, Jackie? What grade are you in at school?"

"I'se 14 last month, 'n just finish tha 8th grade. We be outta school in summer time 'n I'se kin work all day.

Zeke and Alvin arrived almost simultaneously and saw the newly hired hand. "Looks like we git some more he'p 'round here. This boy gonna he'p us?" Alvin wondered.

"Yep, I reckon so," Pete smiled. "Me 'n Will worked a garden afore we wuz this boy's age."

"Alright, men, let's go to work. Alvin, you 'n Zeke go to tha smokehouse, cut some meat, and make sausage fer Mondee. Me 'n Lije 'n Jackie'll pick vegetables. Let's git 'er done afore dinner time, men."

Looking over the filled and neatly arranged shelves of vegetables, Pete was satisfied with the display. Walking to the smokehouse to check on the meat cutters, he spoke. "That otta be enough fer Mondee felleas. It ain't quite dinner time yit, but I thank we kin call it a day. Y'all kin head on home 'n see yer fam'ly a while this Sat'adee.

"Lije, you 'n Jackie kin head on home. Tha boy put in a good day's work. I'm proud of ye, son," Pete complimented him.

As Lije and Jackie left, Harry and Will walked to the shed to meet Pete. "How'd it go today, Pete?" Will asked.

"Went real good. We got the display refilled and some more meat cut. We're ready ta do biz'ness Mondee mornin'."

"Yeah, it looks good, Pete," Harry said. "How'd the new boy do?"

"He's a good worker. Stayed right with me 'n Lije 'n picked as much as either one of us did. We got done quicker 'n usual by havin' tha boy's he'p. If we start tha cannin' business, we gonna need him to he'p. This summer and afta school's out in tha Fall he kin work all day."

"Alright, Pete, when you and Henry finish the delivery to the War Department on Monday, stop by the lumber yard and buy what you need to build the kitchen. We have a charge account there," Harry directed.

"Yes, Sir, Mr. Parker. Will do," Pete nodded.

Chapter Twenty-four

CANNERY BEGINS

When he returned to the farm after the Monday delivery to the War Department, Pete was surprised to see Jackie working with Lije. "Hey Kid, ain't you in school today?"

"Yes, Suh, Mista Pete, but I'se gets out at 2:00. Mista Lije say I'se kin come ta work afta school. I'se gets here at 3:00."

"Yep, Pete, tha boy wants ta pay fer tha stuff he got offa tha shelves on Friday. We need tha extra he'p since you 'n' Henry gonna build a factory ova ther," Lije explained.

"Yer right, Lije," Pete acknowledged. "I'm glad tha boy wants ta work 'n' pay his debts."

Lije continued, "By da way, Mista Ailor was here dis mawnin' fer his pickup. He say he got a house fer rent close ta his store. He know Jackie's daddy, Johnny Jefferson. Dey work together at da railroad afore dey both got laid off from work.

"He say Johnny was a porter 'n' a good worker. If de boy got a job 'n' kin pay de rent, he let 'em move in his house 'til Johnny gits back."

Just as Lije finished, Will joined the group. "Did I hear you say Roy Ailor wants to rent a house to the Jefferson family?" Will asked.

"Yep, that's what he said," Pete acknowledged.

"I'll stop in and see Roy in the morning. When I get home tomorrow, we'll tell Bessie they've got a place of their own," Will told them.

"Let's walk over to Harry and Alice's after dinner tonight," Will suggested to Lenora. "I want to talk to him about helping Bessie and the Jefferson kids rent a house from Roy Ailor. Lije said Roy has a rental house close to his store. I think it'd be a good spot for them to live."

"Oh, yes. I agree," she smiled. "It's within walking distance of our farm and would be convenient for Jackie to get here after school."

"Uh-huh, and if Bessie wants to work in the canning business, she can get here easily, too,' he observed.

After Dinner

Will knocked on the door at the Parker House and waited for Alice to greet them. She opened the door and smiled. "Well, lookee who's here. Come in, children, I'll get Harry. You two go on into the parlor."

When Harry entered the room usually reserved for guests, he smiled, hugged his daughter, and shook hands with his son-in-law. "What a nice surprise. To what do we owe the pleasure of your company?"

"Oh, Daddy, how you do go on," Lenora grinned.

Alice just shook her head and smiled. "She's still your little Princess, isn't she?"

Will began the conversation. "Harry, Lije told me Roy Ailor was here today, and he has a rental house close to his store."

"Uh-Huh, I talked with him this morning, and I had the same thought you're about to suggest to me," Harry nodded.

"Alice and I talked about helping the Jeffersons move in there. It will be convenient for the boy to work for us."

"But I suspect they have no money to pay the first month's rent. Maybe we can arrange an advance on future earnings and let the boy work to pay us back."

"You're a mind reader, Harry," Will grinned. "That's what I had in mind for this family."

"It makes me feel good that we're doing something to help people in need," Alice nodded her head, "It's the Christian thing to do."

At precisely 7:00 a.m., Will arrived at Roy Ailor's store. Roy was arranging baskets of produce along the front area and refilling them for the day's customers.

"Good morning, Senator; nice to see you out so early."

"On my way to the Capitol, but I need to chat with you for a minute."

"Sure, Senator, you talk while I finish filling this display."

"We are eager to help the Jefferson family with their need for housing, and we understand you have a place to rent."

"Yeah, I told the boys at your place what we got here. Now, it ain't no fancy place, but it's better 'n' campin' on the river."

"How much ya want for it, Roy?"

"Senator, I'd hafta have ten dollars a month. How much 'er you gonna pay Johnny's boy?"

"We'll pay him what we pay everybody else, about seven dollars a week. That's twenty-eight dollars a month."

"Yeah, he can afford to pay ten dollars, but I need him to pay upfront. Renters sometimes move out owing you money if you don't do it that way," Roy shook his head.

"Alright, Harry and I thought that might be the case. We'll give him an advance to pay the first month and deduct it from his wages over four weeks. We won't let them go without something to eat."

Will reached into his pocket and fished out a ten-dollar bill. "That'll get them started. I'm going back to the house and tell Lije to take a wagon home tonight. Pete and I can help them move to the place.

"I am much obliged to you, Roy. If they give you any problems, tell me about it, and I'll try to straighten it out with you."

"Maybe Johnny will be back home soon. I don't believe he'll get a job in Philly. Pennsylvania Railroad has people furloughed just like B&O has. Would you hire him on your farm?"

"We can probably use him somewhere. We're going into the canning business. Several of our customers have asked us about providing them canned produce for the winter. If she's interested, we can use Bessie, too."

"Wow, if them folks get three in the fam'ly workin', they'll be in high cotton, so to speak," he grinned.

When he returned to Parker's Farm, Will found Lije in the corn patch. "I arranged for the Jeffersons to move into Roy's rental house today. When you go home this afternoon, take a wagon and load their belongings. Pete and I will meet you at Roy's place and help unload."

"Yes, Suh Mista Will. Bessie's otha young'uns kin he'p too. Lucy's jist a li'l more'n a year younger 'n' Jackie. Dem otha two boys, Eddie 'n' Jimmy is 'bout eleven 'n' nine, 'n' li'l Susie is almost seven. Dey kin he'p us load 'n' unload too."

"Yeah, I figured that, but I wanna talk to Bessie 'bout workin' in the cannery. Roy seems to think that Johnny won't get a job in Philly and will want to return home. We could probably use him in the cannery too." Pete walked up to join the conversation. "Sounds like we gonna staff this cannery afore we git 'er built," he grinned. "I like the idea of getting' tha whole fam'ly involved. It'd be good if they got something to hold the whole bunch a them together."

Pete and Henry worked all day on the cannery building and finished the foundation. Lenora walked out to check on their progress. "Hey Pete, could you use the twins to help you here? I want them to learn to work.," she asked.

"Uh-huh, I reckon so, Len," Pete smiled. "You can't start 'em too young."

Henry added, "They can do a lotta things that'll save us time and steps, Miss Lenora. Fetching nails and boards fer us, and holding boards while we saw. It'll be good fer 'em."

"Alright, tomorrow after school, I'll send them out here. You can feel free to discipline them and keep them working."

When Will arrived home from work, Ronnie and Randy ran to greet him. "Daddy, Daddy, can Randy and me go with you to help Jeffersons move into their new house?" Ronnie begged.

Pete, joining the group, spoke to Will, "Len wants these boys to learn to work."

"Uh-huh, I like the idea, too. Did you boys help Uncle Pete and Henry on the new building today?"

"Yes, Daddy, 'n' I did more work than Randy did," Ronnie bragged.

"Huh-uh Daddy, he *did not*. He just runs faster than I do and gets there first," Randy explained.

"Pete, come on and let's get it done. Lije'll be looking for us," Will urged him.

As Pete drove the short distance to Ailor's rental house, Ronnie and Randy wrestled in the back of the wagon. "Now, you boys behave back there. One of you is liable to fall off and hurt yourself," Will scolded them.

"I see Lije and that Jim Crow kid who works at the farm," Ronnie exclaimed as they neared their destination.

"There's a whole bunch of Jim Crows carrying stuff into the house," Randy added.

"Where'd you boys get that Jim Crow word?" Will frowned.

"At school, that's what everybody calls them," Ronnie said adamantly.

"Huh-uh, some people call them Niggers," Randy corrected him.

"I don't want to hear either of those words used again," Will demanded strongly. "You must respect other people and treat them the way you want them to treat you. It's written in The Book," he explained.

"Everybody else does it, Daddy, but I heard a teacher call them darkies because they're black," Randy informed him.

"Well, all three of those are ugly names, and I don't want to hear it ever again," he affirmed.

Pete stopped the wagon and jumped to the ground. "Come on, boys; we hafta he'p Lije git this stuff unloaded."

Will went into the house to meet Bessie Jefferson. "Good afternoon, Mrs. Jefferson. I'm Will Presley."

"Yas Suh, Senator, I knows who you are. I sho' 'preciate y'all he'ppin' me wit these kids. It's hard sleepin' on de ground."

"Yes, Ma'am, it certainly is. Have you heard from Mr. Jefferson lately?" Will asked.

"Yas, Suh, I got a letter somebody wrote for him last week. A lady who lives close to de camp read it to me. Johnny say he comin' home soon as he kin catch a train comin' dis way."

"That's good news, Mrs. Jefferson. Maybe Johnny can find a job here."

"I'se sho' thankful ta de Good Lawd you give Jackie dat job. Me 'n' dem kids all prayed ever night the Lawd would take keer of us," she was sobbing.

Bessie, may I call you Bessie?" he asked politely.

"Oh, yas, Suh, Senator, I'se jist plain ol' Bessie," she lowered her eyes.

"Would you like to have a job? We are building a cannery to preserve vegetables and fruit for the wintertime. We plan on doing it in large batches and sell it to our store customers. Is that of any interest to you?"

"Oh, Mista Will, I would love ta do dat. I done some canning on de plantation. My Lucy could watch my little young'uns 'til I'se gets home."

"That's great, Bessie, but we're not finished with the building yet. When everything is ready, we'll notify you. I suggest that you discuss it with Johnny when he gets home. The approval of your husband is important," Will said.

Pete stuck his head in the door. "Got it all unloaded, Will. Does Mrs. Jefferson need us to place anything for her?"

"No, me 'n' de kids kin do dat, Mista Pete. I'se much obliged ta ye good folks. I'se looking forward to a new job in dat cannery, Mista Will. You be sho' 'n' let me know when it's all finished."

"We certainly will, Bessie. Come on, Pete and you boys. We need to get home before dark."

Chapter Twenty-five

FIRST BATCH

With wood fires burning in all five cookstoves, the kitchen was steaming. The August heat searing into the windows of the building intensified the oppressive air.

Lenora, Lillian, and Bessie, Jackie's mother, were sweating profusely, so Lenora suggested a break. "Let's sit down and have some cold tea and rest for a while. When we finish this last batch of green beans, we'll call it a day."

"Thank you, Lenora. This baby's been kicking the fool outta me today. I needed to sit fer a spell," Lillian said, wiping the sweat from her brow.

A tall, slender black woman with dark skin and a big smile, Bessie Jackson seemed happy despite her recent past difficulty. She was a devout believer in God and prayed often-many times, aloud.

"How many jars a dem green beans has we made, Miss Lenora?" Bessie inquired.

Lillian walked over to the shelf, where jars of beans were cooling, and counted them. "Looks like we got twenty-eight on the shelf. I believe there's twelve more still cookin' and sealin' on the stove. That's a good start, I'ma-thinkin'.

"Lenora, do you think we're gonna need some more help here?" Lillian questioned.

"Yes, we need someone to prepare the vegetables to be cooked. We also need a backup for you, Lil. That baby's going to be coming in just a few weeks. Bessie, do you know anyone who wants a job?"

"Well, Miss Lenora, Alma Rogers might wanna work wit us. She's Zeke Washington's woman."

"Oh, I didn't know Zeke was married. It would be nice to have his wife working with us."

"Well, I ain't sho' she wanna work, Missy. She got three kids, 'n' she ain't his wife. She's a white woman, 'n' dey won't let 'em git married. Jim Crow laws say mixin' 'n' minglin' amongst white 'n' blacks is agin de law."

"That don't seem right ta me," Lillian interjected. "Preacher Henderson back home always said we're all God's children black or white."

"I'se jist tellin' ye what de law say, Missy," Bessie dropped her eyes.

Lenora spoke, "A State Code states that white persons who marry negroes will be jailed for at least one year and fined a minimum of $100. Those who perform such ceremonies face fines of $200, of which one-half will go to the informer.

"Another Statute states that white people who intermarry with a colored person will be imprisoned for between two and five years. Ministers who performed such ceremonies will be subject to a fine of $200, of which the informer received half. "White and colored persons going out of the state to marry shall be punished as if married in the state."

"Can't Will do something about that, Lenora? He's a Senator." Lillian questioned.

"That's a state law, not federal, Lillian. Will doesn't have any authority over state laws."

"But I bet he knows some state people who could do something about it, don't he?" Lillian continued.

"He has friends in the Virginia Legislature, and he could broach the subject with them, but I'm not confident it would do any good. Many of these Representatives are church-going folks but still southern Confederates in their thinking. I'll mention it to him at dinner tonight.

"Bessie, you ask Alma if she is interested in working at the cannery. If she is, bring her with you as soon as she can make arrangements for child care while she works," Lenora ordered.

At the dinner table that evening, Lenora gave Will an accounting of the first day of production in the cannery. "We need at least one more person to help us now, and maybe more as the business grows. When fresh vegetables are not available this fall and winter, we'll sell more canned goods.

"We'll have apples and pears from the orchard up until February. Apple butter, jelly, and jam can be made through much of the winter. It will be possible to keep the cannery employees on payroll almost year-round," Lenora was excited.

"Sounds good to me. You've had a good day and a great start," Will smiled.

Lenora hesitated, then spoke, "Did you know Zeke has a family?" she asked.

"I heard Lije say something about his woman and kids, but I don't know anything about her."

"Her name is Alma, and she's a white woman who bore three kids to Zeke."

"How'd you know so much about her," Will was curious.

"I asked Bessie if she knew anybody who wanted a job. She told Lillian and me about Alma Rogers, Zeke's woman. They can't get married because of a Jim Crow law in Virginia."

Will nodded his head and rubbed his chin.

"Can you do anything about that? It doesn't seem fair to me," she was annoyed.

"That's a state law, and I have no jurisdiction, Len; you know that."

"Yes, I do know, but it just isn't right that folks are not allowed to love each other just because of the color of their skin," she exclaimed.

"Anyway, Bessie thinks she might want to work in the cannery, and she is going to ask her tonight."

"Now Len, be careful. We don't want to stir up trouble for ourselves. The Klan is still active in these parts."

"Yes, I'm aware of that, but we need some help, and she needs a job. It's not like we're gonna advertise it. We'll do it discreetly."

"Alright, all I'm sayin' is that people talk and things become known before you know it," Will cautioned. "I'll make sure that Pete and all our farmhands keep their rifles close by in case we encounter troublemakers or Klansmen.

"Do you think we should discuss this with Harry and Alice, Len? After all, the cannery bears their name."

"Of course we should. We'll walk over after dinner and visit. The boys and Mimi can tag along with us. I'm sure Mama and Daddy would like to see them."

As they approached the porch at the Parker house, Harry and Alice were sitting in the swing singing a hymn from the church. Alice, in her small soprano voice, was almost drowned out by Harry's booming baritone vocals.

Ronnie and Randy ran onto the porch as Alice exclaimed, "Well lookee who's here Mamaw's little men. And here's little Mimi too, Mamaw's baby girl."

Not to be left out, Harry said, "And Papaw's Little Princess. Come and give us a hug, children."

Harry looked at Will, then Lenora, and said, "Glad you came over tonight. How'd things go today, Len?"

"Very well, I think. We canned forty quarts of green beans, and we'll do tomatoes tomorrow.

"We need some more help. Bessie did a good job, and Lillian worked hard in some oppressive heat. Bessie said that Zeke's woman might want a job,"

Alice smiled broadly, "Isn't that wonderful. I like the idea of families working for us. It is so much easier to work with people you know."

Will spoke, "I haven't met her, but it is my understanding she's a white woman. That could create problems for us with the Klan. They're still active around here."

"She's not his wife, Mama. The Virginia Jim Crow laws prevent them from getting a legal marriage," Lenora informed them. "They do have three children, two girls and a boy."

"What is she going to do about child care?" Alice wondered. "She can't just go off and leave them unattended."

Answering, Lenora replied, "Bessie suggested that some of her neighbors could attend to them. The area where they live contains mostly colored families, and her children play with them anyway."

Harry jumped into the conversation. "Sometimes, you just have to do the right thing, even if it's unpopular. I believe the right thing is not to oppose mixed marriages unfairly. Many white men have fathered children with black women who were not their wives. Somehow they think it's different when the situation is reversed."

"I am not debating whether it is fair or unfair," Will was adamant. "I'm just saying it could be dangerous if the Klan becomes aware of it."

"I told Bessie to bring her in for an interview if she's interested in working, but I didn't commit to hiring her. If it's a bad idea, I will thank her for coming in, and then she can go back home when Bessie finishes for the day. I'll give her some vegetables for coming in today to compensate for her time."

"I think that's a good plan, Len" Will smiled. "You are as smart as you are pretty."

"Oh, how you do go on, Will Presley," Lenora blushed.

The Next Morning

At 7:00, Bessie came bouncing into the cannery kitchen with a big smile on her face. "I brung Alma wit me, Missy. Here she is."

Looking up, Lenora smiled and spoke to Bessie, then to Alma. "It's nice to meet you, Alma. Come on in, and let's talk. Have a seat over here at the table with me."

What Lenora saw from Alma disturbed her. Alma dropped her eyes but let a smile break the solemn expression that told a resignation story to her lowly lot in life.

Alma may have been in her mid-twenties but gave the appearance of middle age. Her long brown hair had not seen a washbasin in many moons; however, there had been an apparent attempt at neatness. The prominent cheekbones and sunken cheeks hinted at poor nutrition. Her simple homemade dress had been made from a flour sack.

As Alma sat down, she began to speak slowly. "I 'preciate you givin' me a chance at gittin' a job, Miss Lenora. Me 'n' Zeke has ta live in a one-room shack wit dirt floors 'n' big cracks in tha wall. Our kids has a li'l bed, but it ain't big enough fer all three of 'em, so tha boy has ta sleep wit us.

"Zeke was real happy when Bessie tol' us you was wantin' some more he'p. I'ma good worker 'n' need a job."

Lillian looked at Lenora with tears in her eyes but said nothing. Finally, Lenora spoke, "I want to give you a chance to do this job for us because I can see you need it. Zeke has been an excellent addition to our work crew, and Lije has been with us for several years. We'll pay you the same wages that Lillian and Bessie earn for their work. If that's satisfactory, you can start to work today.

"We're canning tomatoes, so you can cut the stems and peel them for the cooking pot. I want to can four bushels today. Then, tomorrow, we'll work on corn."

At 4:00, the four-woman crew had finished 35 quarts of whole tomatoes and 10 quarts of tomato juice. "Good job today, ladies. We'll have a nice assortment of canned vegetables to show our customers by the end of this week. We'll start selling them on Monday."

"It shore has been a big he'p havin' Alma workin' with us," Lillian commented to Lenora loudly enough that all could hear.

"Thank you, Miss Lillian. It's been good gittin' ta work wit you folks," Alma responded with a smile.

When Will arrived home, Lenora was apprehensive about telling him she hired Alma. She kissed him lightly on the lips and smiled. "Well, I hired Alma today, and she did a good job. We got 35 quarts of tomatoes and 10 quarts of juice. Tomorrow we'll work on corm. By the end of the week, I hope to have a big assortment of products to sell our customers."

"Alright, Len, but don't say I didn't warn you about the Klan," Will shook his head.

"Will, she needs this job, and she is a good worker. Nobody has to know she lives with Zeke, and most of the time, our customers won't even know who she is because she'll be working in the kitchen. Lillian and Bessie like her too."

On Wednesday, Alma and Bessie shucked corn for cooking. Then after cooking, they cut the kernels off the cob. The team finished thirty-two quarts of corn and sealed them in the jars.

Lillian asked Lenora, "Have you ever pickled beets or cucumbers?"

Looking puzzled, Lenora shook her head and asked, "Pickled beets or cucumbers? No, I never heard of it."

"It's almost effortless. You have to peel beets, but just cut up the cucumbers; place them in vinegar, add salt, sugar, and spices. Martha learnt me how to do it before I left Roaring Fork. They're a perfect thing to add to a meal."

"It's great to have them in the wintertime, especially Thanksgiving and Christmas when most vegetables ain't growin' nowhere."

Lenora added, "I did see some pickled cucumbers in Roy Ailor's store. It had a label from H J Heinz, the company that makes tomato ketchup. I guess we could compete with them. Ours would be like homemade."

Will arrived home early on Friday afternoon and stopped in at the cannery. "Hello, my beautiful bride," he smiled at Lenora. Then addressing the rest of the women, he nodded politely and said, "Hi ladies. Have you had a good day?"

Lillian spoke, "We shore have Will, and a good week too. We done 40 quarts of green beans, 35 quarts of tomatoes, 10 quarts of tomato juice, 32 quarts of whole kernel corn, 20 quarts of pickled beets, and 20 quarts of pickled cucumbers. Depending on how many you sell, we might make some apple butter, jelly, and jam next week. If need be, we can put up some more vegetables," she smiled proudly, patting her ever-expanding belly.

Chapter Twenty-six

WHO IS ALMA MAE ROGERS

Lillian befriended Alma Rogers from the first day they began working together. She could sense that Alma felt inadequate around Lenora, Will, and the Parkers. This feeling was not new to Lillian.

When Pete convinced her to leave their homes in Roaring Fork and Old Yellow Creek for an opportunity many miles away from everything they knew, she was apprehensive about fitting in with a more educated and worldly group of people.

The Parkers had welcomed them into the family with open arms with no apparent reservations. Both Will and Lenora had gone out of their way to make them feel comfortable and productive. Nevertheless, there remained concerns about having received unearned benefits.

Alma's shy lack of confidence gave Lillian a new purpose. Alma was a person she could help. By helping her gain confidence, she would be assisting the Parker Family, including Will and Lenora, to achieve their goals.

At last, Lillian had a sense of purpose. She realized her lack of formal education and experience in this more urban and sophisticated society; however, she knew her way around the kitchen and simple food preparations.

Lenora noticed a change in the way Lillian was walking and the constant humming of a tune as she worked. "Lil, you seem unusually happy these days."

Sitting side by side with Alma as they shucked fresh corn, Lillian began opening a conversation with the intent of learning more about her new friend.

"Alma, tell me something about your children."

Not accustomed to being the center of any discussion, Alma stuttered a bit before offering, "Well, Miss Lillian, we have three. Our oldest girl, Nettie, just turned seven. Rosie is five, and we named her after my mother, who died almost ten years ago from consumption. Our baby boy, Charlie, is two and a half."

Lillian could not miss the love in Alma's eyes and the smile on her lips as she said each name.

"If I ain't being too nosy, how did ye and Zeke meet, Alma?"

Silently staring at the ground, Alma thought for a moment before saying anything. "It ain't a pretty story, Miss Lillian."

"Please just call me Lil, Alma; we're friends now."

"Alright, Lil and my mother always called me Alma Mae. If you promise not to think too badly of me, I'll share my story.

"When my mother became ill, I had to take over all the household work. My brothers were no help; in fact, they left home soon after she died. Our father took to drinking pretty heavy. After a while, he couldn't hold a job, so there was no money in the house. He took to beatin' me when there was no food to make for supper."

"I'm so sorry, Alma Mae. What did you do?"

"We didn't have no other family close by, so I asked our neighbors if they had any work I could do in return for some food. When my father learned I was begging, he became furious. He threatened to kill me if I done that agin. When he got even drunker, he tried to do things to me that no father should ever do to a daughter. One night, I was so scared of him, I just ran. I didn't know where I was goin' but had to get away from him."

Lillian hung on every word, not knowing what to say. Alma Mae needed to tell this story to someone, and Lillian accepted her role as a kind listener.

"I slept in the woods one night and then started walkin' towards whatever fate awaited me. After a few hours, a wagon stopped beside the road. Zeke was driving the wagon on his way to work at a local farm. He seemed very friendly and asked if he could help by taking me wherever I was going. When I started to sob and told him I had no idea where I was goin', Zeke helped me onto the wagon and drove me to his home. He needed to get to his job, so he showed me where the food was and told me to get some rest.

"That evenin', he shared his food with me and told me I could stay there until I had time to make a plan. He couldn't pay me to cook and clean, but I started doin' that in return for a place to stay and food.

"At first, I thought stayin' with Zeke would be temporary. After a few weeks, I came to depend on him and him on me. We liked each other. We could talk and laugh with each other. I felt safe with Zeke, who was kinder than any man I had ever known. The friendship became love, and now we are a family."

"That's is a sad but also a beautiful story, Alma Mae."

"We would be married, Lil, if we could. You know the law won't allow it. We could be in big trouble if someone reported us to the authorities. The Parkers took a chance when they offered me a job. Zeke and me are very thankful and don't want to do anythin' to harm this family."

"Yes, Alma Mae, we are all aware of tha unfair laws that are currently on the books in this state. We hope the regulations will someday be changed. We also know that some people like to stir up trouble, and we'll be careful not to draw attention to your relationship with Zeke. Is it alright with you if I share yer story with Senator Presley? He may not be able to do anything about tha state laws, but he knows people who might have some influence."

"Yes, Lil, you can share my story. Just don't do nothin' that will bring trouble to your family or the Parkers. I couldn't stand it if your kindness to us brought any trouble to your doorstep."

That evening, Lillian spoke with Will and Lenora. As she shared Alma Mae's story, she and Lenora both began to cry.

"It is not right!" Lenora yelled. "Why is it still true in this country that is supposed to be based on freedom and fundamental rights for all people, that some people are prevented from living out their normal lives in peace without constant harassment?"

Will shook his head and replied, "There is much more work to be done to see our stated ideals become a reality.

"It is our job to keep on pushing forward even when it feels like pushing a boulder up a steep hill. We must persist in the pursuit of what is right."

The following week, Will thought he should stop by to see Roy Ailor on his way to the office. He was interested in Roy's opinion about the canning business. Roy also had his finger on the pulse of public opinion.

It was early morning before opening hours when Will approached the store. Roy was rearranging his front porch produce display when he looked up and waved. "Good to see you, Senator."

Stepping down from the carriage, Will walked up on the porch to shake hands with his old friend. "Good to see you too, Roy. How's the retail grocery business these days?"

"Pretty good. The town is growing, and I seem to have a few new customers every month."

"That sounds very optimistic for our economy. How are our canned products being received by your customers?"

"Your stuff is selling better than I expected. Everything looks good, and we have had repeat buyers of most vegetables. Of course, your apples continue to be favorites as well.

"Now, Will, I don't trade in rumors nor gossip, but there is something you might want to be aware of concerning your workers."

"Please tell me, Roy. We have a good team of workers. I can't imagine any of them being a problem."

"It's not the worker herself that is a problem. It's who she is living with and the children they had together."

"You must be talking about Alma Mae and Zeke. They don't want to cause anyone trouble. They both do their work well and keep to themselves outside of their daily jobs."

"That may be true, Will, but you have to know that folks take exception to a white girl hooking up with a black man as if they were husband and wife. It is just not fitting. Most people will ignore them outside of a few rumors; however, there are always those men looking to make an issue of how other people live."

"If the laws were not still so discriminatory, Zeke and Alma would be married.

"They are decent people who do their best to make their way in life, take care of their family, and not be a burden to anyone. How does their living arrangement affect anyone else?"

"Don't kill the messenger, Will. I'm only warning you so that you can be prepared. You might want to think about having some protection around your operations. Don't forget about the Klan visits your family had in the past."

"Thank you, Roy. I'm not angry with you. It's just that we keep fighting the same battles. It makes it difficult to remain optimistic."

Will shared Roy's warning with Lenora that evening. She was indignant. "I dare anyone to say an ugly word to Alma Mae or Zeke. The first ignorant busy body who sticks their nose in our business will have to deal with me!"

Will laughed and grabbed his wife for a spontaneous kiss. "That's my girl."

The warning did not go unheeded. Will got permission from Harry to erect fencing around the cannery operations and to arm his leaders. He spoke with Zeke privately and gave him a rifle for their house.

After church services that Sunday, Lenora was approached by the wife of a vestry member. Mrs. Ruby Sinclair put her hand on Lenora's arm and said, "I need to speak with you outside before you leave."

"Certainly. How may I help you, Ruby?"

"Oh, you have it wrong, Lenora. I'm here to help you.

"People are talking about that loose woman you have working at your place and the half-nigger children she is raising.

"It is a disgrace to all Christian people. We cannot believe a Senator and his family would condone such behavior."

Lenora tried unsuccessfully to conceal her outrage. "Hold it right there! What I cannot believe, Mrs. Sinclair is your hypocrisy. Your husband is an elected leader in this church, and you stand here outside of the symbol of faith, denouncing all the things we claim to believe."

Shocked by Lenora's attack, Mrs. Sinclair stuttered, "What are you talking about? I was raised in this church, and no one has ever doubted my sincerity."

"Tell me, Mrs. Sinclair, where did our Lord tell us that some people are not lovable? Where did he say we should condemn our brothers and sisters because they do not live as we do.?

"Alma Mae and Zeke are not permitted by law to receive the public sanction of their marriage, but does that make their love and commitment any less blessed in the eyes of our Lord.? What I learned at home and in this church is that we are all children of God.

"I also learned that we are to love our neighbors as ourselves. What part of that simple commandment do you, a lifelong Christian, not understand?"

Mrs. Sinclair was rendered speechless. For a moment, she stood paralyzed, staring at Lenora. Then she turned abruptly with her nose in the air and retreated.

Will noticed his wife's heavy breathing as she climbed into their carriage for the ride home. "What's wrong, Len?"

She did not want to express her anger in front of Mimi, so she just said, "I had to correct one of our parishioners today, and she didn't seem real happy about it."

Because Alma and Zeke maintained a low profile in the community, there was never an uproar of protest. Personal snubs and minor threats did, however, continue for a long time.

When threatening notes appeared at their home, Alma told Lillian, who shared the information with Lenora, who advised Alma to ignore such ignorance.

When a customer at the produce stand threatened to take his business elsewhere unless something was done about the disgraceful cohabitation, ever'body is up in arms about, Pete stood up for his co-workers and friends.

Will and Lenora were both more than capable of defusing angry conversations about mixing and mingling the races, as many folks called it.

Chapter Twenty-seven

BESSIE AND JOHNNY

Ten Years Earlier

When they walked out of the courthouse in Fairfax County, the newly-wed couple was smiling broadly. Walking between them, their four-year-old son, Jackie, and two-year-old daughter, Lucy, clung to their parent's hands.

John Jefferson and Bessie Washington had worked at the Preston Plantation. Both were house servants, Bessie, a cook, and Johnny, a food server/butler for Jack Preston, a cotton grower, and exporter.

In 1856, Preston bought Johnny, a twelve-year-old boy, at an auction in D.C. Bessie was born at Preston's Plantation in 1846. He sold her parents, but she remained on the plantation and trained as a cook when she was just a young girl.

While he was a boy, Johnny was assigned to gather left-over food from the dining area and the kitchen. (The cooking building was separated a few steps from the main house to prevent fire.) The leftovers were then taken to the hovel and given to the pigs.

From an early age, Bessie worked in the kitchen and became an excellent cook, learning from the older women who mothered her and taught her the craft.

When they became teenagers, the two slaves found themselves attracted to each other, and in 1863 their first child, Jackie, was born. Two years later, Lucy joined the family.

Johnny and Bessie were given their freedom by Jack Preston when the war ended, but Jim Crow laws prevented them from marrying. Black folks were not allowed to marry, own property or businesses, or sue in a court of law. (Many states still treated freed slaves differently from white folks.)

Responding to the Massacres in Memphis and New Orleans in 1866, Congress passed the Reconstruction and Civil Rights Act of 1867. This Act bestowed the full benefits of citizenship to all persons born in the United States. Also, the law granted the right to vote to black males. (These laws later became the 14th and 15th Amendments.)

Soon after, the Jefferson couple was married with their two children standing beside them.

Johnny had rented a buggy to drive his bride and his family to the courthouse for the wedding. "Oh Johnny, it feels so fittin' to ride in this here buggy. I'se feels almost like a real laydee."

"You are my real laydee, Bessie Lee. Is it alright iffen I calls you Missus Jefferson?"

"It sho' is Mista Jefferson. I'se likes it."

"Momma, is you gonna kiss Daddy again?" Jackie asked as he grinned.

"Maybe, but he might be a kissin' me this time," she laughed out loud.

"We gonna save us up some money 'n' buy us a buggy soon, my bride. Then I'se won't have ta walk two miles to work down at de train station," Johnny said wistfully.

"Yeah, 'n' we's might even git enuff money ta buy us a house ta raise dese young'uns in," Bessie imagined.

"Uh-huh, Mista Jack he say if ya work hard 'n save yo money, ye kin git yo'self lotta thangs ye ain't had afore," Johnny remembered.

Johnny was good at his job as a porter on the Pullman passenger cars. The sleeper cars had beds that needed to be opened and made up, baggage required to be loaded when boarding and unloaded when departing. Gentlemen's shoes required shining. Johnny gave personal service with a smile.

As a house slave, Johnny knew how to do all those things. Although wages were low, good service tips added to his earnings and provided for his growing family. Life was good.

Over the next few years, Eddie, Jimmy, and Susie were born into the family. Needing a bigger house, they moved down the street into a new place their landlord built.

" I sho' wish we cud buy this here house," Bessie murmured aloud.

"Uh-huh," Johnny answered. "Maybe someday we will, my bride," he was hopeful.

Johnny's employer was the Pullman Palace Car Company, which leased their cars to railroad lines and furnished them with employees.

George Pullman believed that former house-slaves would be the best porters he could hire because they could serve the wealthy class's needs. As the Pullman company grew and added parlor cars and dining cars to their services, jobs became plentiful. Employment with Pullman became a prized opportunity.

Bessie settled into her life as a housewife and mother. Overnight trips to Cincinnati were a regular part of Johnny's routine. Soon, the children adapted to his short absences from home. An occasional trip to Chicago meant a week-long absence. Still, it meant more money for the family and became tolerable.

Providing services for wealthy and powerful people gave him the chance to become acquainted with Senators and Congressmen commuting home on weekends and during recesses. Later, Will inquired about a job for him in the Capitol. Johnny was known and well respected.

Bessie had become the head cook on the Preston Plantation. She made an extraordinary chocolate cake and a delightful apple cobbler which became the favorites of Jack Preston. And her breakfast biscuits with apple jelly were especially appreciated by the children.

Her children enjoyed and appreciated her cooking skills, too. Jackie, Eddie, and Jimmy liked their mother's fried chicken with biscuits, while the girls preferred pork chops with cornbread.

Then, unexpectedly, the Great Recession intervened.

Johnny's trips to Cincinnati began to diminish, and money was scarce. He tried to reassure Bessie that things would soon be better, but the recession continued unabated.

"Bessie, I gots bad news taday. Da boss man say all us Jim Crow porters wuz bein' cut loose from de comp'ny. Some of da white conductors got cut loose, too. Mista Roy down at da sto', he wuz one a 'dem."

"What we gonna do, Johnny? We got dese five young'uns ta feed."

"Some a da boys thinks we kin git a job in Philly. Dem New Yawk trains owned by Mista Vanderbilt goes thru Philly 'n' uses Pullman cars."

"How we gonna git dese kids ta Philly? We ain't got no money ta ride no train ova dere," Bessie was sobbing.

"Now Bessie, eva thang gonna be alright, De Good Lawd up above gonna take keer a us. I'se go down 'n' hop a freight train wit some a de otha boys. Soon as I gits a job, I'se comes back 'n git y'all.

"Don't worry, Baby; Johnny'll handle dis trouble."

The next morning before daylight, he left for Philly.

Chapter Twenty-eight

JOHNNY COMES HOME

As the sun cleared the horizon and light flooded the farm, Bessie skipped into the front door of the cannery and was bursting with joy. "Johnny come home Sat'adee mawnin'," she gushed, "Me 'n' de kids was sooo happy ta see 'im."

Lillian rushed to hug Bessie, and Lenora smiled broadly. "We're thrilled for you, Bessie." Lenora exulted. "We know you are delighted to see him."

"Yas, Ma'am, 'n' he's tickled 'bout 'er new house. He stop at Mista Ailor's sto' 'n' asked if he knowed where we wuz.

"Mista Ailor, he laugh 'n' say dey livin' in my place, Johnny, jist down tha road a piece. Dey all alright.

"Johnny, he couldn't find no job in Philly. He went ta de railroad, 'n' the hotels, 'n' the city gub'ment. Nobody got no jobs dere. He stayed in a camp 'n' slept on de ground like we wuz a doin'.

"He say dere wuz a hotel where dey throwed out left-ova food eva day. De man who throwed it out, set it in a box fer whoever got it first. Some of it had been eat on, but Johnny didn't pay it no mind. He wuz hungry.

"Dey's a lotta folks goin' hungry in dem big cities. Lotta colored folks, 'specially outta work.

"I tol' Johnny he otta stay here 'n' find a job. We need 'im at home. Me 'n' Jackie got work, so he kin take his time a findin' a job."

"Len, kin Will he'p Johnny git a gub'ment job?" Lillian questioned.

"I don't know, but I can ask. When Will gets home tonight, I'll see what he says. There might be a job working in the Capitol building. They have security people and cleaning people, plus groundskeepers."

"I'se sho' glad we met up wit you good folks here at Parker's Farm. Dat might be de best thang dat eva happen ta us."

"Alright, Ladies, let's go to work. Lillian, I think we should repeat what we canned last week to build our inventory. We can adjust it based on what our customers buy this week."

"Do you want me to get stuff ready ta cook, Miss Lenora?" Alma stammered with her eyes down.

"Yes, Alma. Bessie and Lillian can assist until we get enough to start cooking."

Bessie sang gospel songs and prayed aloud, praising Sweet Jesus all day. It was a pleasant distraction as the women worked.

At 4:00, Lenora wiped her brow and remarked, "Let's call it a day, ladies. I want to walk over to the shed and see how many jars of vegetables we sold. Come on, Lillian, accompany me. I want to talk to Pete."

Turning to Bessie and Alma, she said. "We'll see you two in the morning. Go on home to your families."

Pete greeted them with a big smile. "You have a terrific new product, Lenora. We sold about half of what y'all had ready, 'n'this is just the first day. Everybody was excited, especially Mista Ailor and Fred Turner.

"Both a them thank canned stuff'll sell in the summertime 'cause it's easier and faster to cook. But Bill Padgett thinks fresh vegetables will sell better than canned things right now."

"Do ya guess we'd better make about the same this week as we did last week, Len?" Lillian inquired.

Nodding, she replied, "That sounds about right to me, but canned goods won't spoil, so it'll be alright if we don't sell it all at once. We need to accumulate some product for sale this winter."

"Do you think we'll need another building to use for a warehouse, Len?" Pete asked.

"Maybe, but let's not get ahead of ourselves. I'll talk to Will and Papa about it tonight. I want to ask Will about a job for Johnny, too."

When Will arrived home from work, Lenora met him at the door. "Good evening, Mister Presley," she smiled with a flirting wink. "How was your day?"

"Aw, 'bout like usual, nothin' out of the ordinary," smiling as he kissed her lightly. "How 'bout your day?"

"Well, we got good news about our canned goods. Pete said we sold half of what we had prepared, and this was just the first day. He thinks we'll sell the rest of it tomorrow when we get different customers.

"We put up green beans today, and we'll do tomatoes tomorrow. If Pete sells out Tuesday, beans and tomatoes are all we'll have to sell Wednesday."

"Are we still selling the same amount of fresh vegetables?" Will questioned.

"Yes, I believe so. The men have found it necessary to pick more each day because we are canning so many."

"I'll talk with Pete and see if we need another planting. Several of our items will grow another crop before the first frost," Will was smiling. "Looks like the cannery is gonna be successful. I'm happy we can provide some jobs for a few people."

"Speaking of jobs, Johnny Jefferson came home this past weekend. He couldn't find a job in Philly. Lillian wondered if you could help him get a job at the Capitol.

"Bessie thinks that if Johnny finds a job, then Jackie can concentrate on going to school and graduate next year. It's imperative to her to have a high school graduate in the family."

"I don't know if they have vacancies right now. A lot of Senators and Congressmen have gotten jobs for family members and constituents. This recession is hurting everybody.

"I know they don't hire colored folks for security jobs, but the janitorial staff or groundskeepers might have a job opening. I'll ask around tomorrow.

"Roy Ailor knows Johnny doesn't he?" Will asked.

"Yes, they both worked for B&O Railroad. Roy was a conductor, and Johnny was a porter. Roy can probably give you a recommendation."

"I'll stop by there in the morning. I'm eager to hear what Roy's reaction is to the canned goods. And I'll ask about Johnny."

As Will approached Ailor's store on Tuesday morning, he saw Roy sweeping the building's front porch. Stopping the wagon in front of the store, he spoke to his friend. "Mornin', Roy, got a minute to chat."

"Sure, Senator, what ya got on yer mind?"

"My first question is about the new canned products we're selling. Whatta ya think about them?"

"Well, I think all of them will sell very well. I sold about five jars yesterday. My customers were glad to get some things that won't take long to prepare.

"I had a few people asking about green peas, spinach, pinto beans, and carrots. Can you add them to your line of items? Also, my customers asked if you would have pint jars as well as the quarts."

"Yes, I think we can still plant those things this year. It'll be a few weeks, but we'll add them. And I believe we can buy pint jars from the farm supply.

"My second question is about Johnny Jefferson. Len told me you know him from working at the railroad. What can you tell me about him?"

Speaking thoughtfully, Roy answered. "Johnny was well-respected by all B&O personnel. He is honest, dependable, and highly respectful of the customers.

"I believe he will be called back to work when business returns to normal at B&O. Why did you ask about him?"

"Len asked me to recommend him for a job at the Capitol. I wanted to talk to someone who knows him before I recommend him. I am happy to hear that Johnny is a good man. We hired his son and his wife to work for us on the farm."

Chuckling, Roy replied, "I was glad to hear about you hiring Bessie. I rented her a house and wasn't sure she could pay me. But when Johnny got home, I felt pretty sure things would be alright."

"Alright, Roy, you told me precisely what I wanted to hear about both questions. Thank you for your business and your advice."

"Anytime, Senator, I might need a favor some time, myself," Ailor grinned and winked.

The third week of September brought new excitement to the Presley family. Lillian began labor while preparing corn for the canning process. When Lenora realized what was happening, she insisted that Pete help her sister-in-law into the house. "You take care of Lil, Pete. I will send one of the men to get Doc. Phillips.

Following a short period of labor, Lillian presented Pete with a son. The new father was beside himself with joy. James Daniel Presley was the latest member of the family. "I'm gonna call him Danny," Lillian smiled.

Chapter Twenty-nine

THE BARONS VISIT

Entering the Capitol building on a cool October morning, Will stopped to speak to Johnny Jefferson. Since early September, Johnny had been working at the Capitol as a janitor. "Good mawmin', Senator Presley. It's nice ta see ye so brite 'n' early."

"Good to see you, too, Johnny. How's the new job going for you?"

"It's good, Senator. I feel mo' blest 'n' I deserves by de Al'mighty. Now Jackie's back in school 'n/ we a hopin' he graduate. He be de first one in de fam'ly to do dat. The other fo' young'uns is goin' ta school too. We's proud a all a 'em."

"Good, I hope he does graduate. Jackie is a good kid and a good worker. We're happy to have him working afternoons when he's not in school, and Saturdays."

Will went strolling down the hallway and encountered his fellow Virginia senator, J. Harold Walker, from Jonesboro. Walker was a tall, balding man with steel-gray eyes and a small mustache. His demeanor was gruff, and an almost constant scowl adorned his face. He was quite an intimidating figure.

"Good morning, Senator Presley," the senior senator was polite. "Have you met the *Captains of Industry* yet?"

"Captains of Industry? No, I haven't. Who are they?"

"Why, we have the richest men in America visiting the Capitol this week. Four of them will meet with state delegations to get acquainted and tell us about their plans to combat the recession.

"Andrew Carnegie and J.P. Morgan are speaking Thursday morning in the Virginia caucus room. John D. Rockefeller and William Vanderbilt will speak in the afternoon. They want us to have the whole Congressional delegation, not just the Senators.

"It will still be small groups so we can ask questions. I think it's great to hear ideas from these knowledgeable men."

"Yeah, I've got some questions for all of them. Why don't they pay a living wage to their employees? They are thriving and prospering while their workers struggle to keep food on the table. They keep cutting wages because so many folks need jobs.

"It's my understanding that the average industrial worker makes $380.00 per year. These Captains of Industry are making millions. That seems a bit unbalanced to me.

"Charles Graham back in my hometown saw the wisdom of assuring that the people who worked his land profited sufficiently to provide adequately for their families."

Walker frowned and spoke quickly and forcefully. "Now, don't go off making these gentlemen angry, Presley. They are the men who control most of the jobs in this country."

"Uh-huh, and they want to control everything in this country. John Hall, Jim Hall's father from Falls Church, calls them plutocrats. He says the USA is becoming a plutocracy, not a democracy."

Walker began to get more agitated. "Presley, you gotta understand one thing-money talks, and these men have plenty of it."

"It's important to speak truth to power, Senator Walker, and I intend to do just that. People are hurting right here in Virginia. We, you and I, must do everything within our power to assist our constituents. In many cases, their very lives depend on our standing up for them.

"I look forward to hearing these Captains of Industry and speaking my piece to them."

Thursday Morning

When Will entered the Virginia caucus room, he saw Jeremiah Jones and Jim Hall waving to him. Jones called out, "Come on over and sit with us, Senator. We saved you a seat."

"Have you met Bob Weaver? He's our representative from Richmond, and this gentleman is the representative from Charlottesville, Carroll Hoagland," Jeremiah said to Will.

Weaver was a quiet man with a head of dazzling white hair, which belied his age. In his early fifties, he looked much older. The curved stem pipe he smoked added to the aged appearance.

Hoagland was about the same age as Weaver but looked much younger. Slender and cleanshaven, he was a wisecracker who entertained everybody around him with a smiling and friendly countenance.

"Good morning, gentlemen. It's nice to meet you both. I have known Jeremiah Jones and Jim Hall since the days we served in the Constitutional Convention back in '68. We worked in the State Legislature, then here at the Capitol," Will acknowledged his colleagues.

"Presley, I have some serious questions I plan to ask these big money men today-all four of them," Jones looked at Will.

"Yes, me too," Hall informed them.

Weaver, who was a veteran Congressman, nodded his assent and said, "These guys put their pants on one leg at a time just as we do. They will want us to pass legislation on tariffs that will favor their operations. The effect it has on overall business is secondary to these guys."

Hoagland grinned as he said, "I don't put my pants on one leg at a time. I put them over my boots and jump in with both feet."

"Hoagland, you are full of something, aren't you?" Will smiled.

J. Harold Walker addressed the gathering and announced, "Gentlemen, it is my honor to introduce to you the great steel magnate from Pittsburg, Mister Andrew Carnegie."

Polite applause greeted Carnegie.

"Thank you, Senator Walker, for that introduction. I am happy to be with this delegation from the great Commonwealth of Virginia. You are known all over this country as the State of Presidents. Your proximity to our nation's Capital places you in an enviable position of influence, and I hope to influence you today.

"Our nation has been ravaged by a Great Recession that threatens our very existence. Businesses have suffered, and workers have suffered, but the solution to our breakdown is to assist the significant companies.

"Businesses create jobs for workers and are the source of their wages. Help us, and then we will be in a position to grow jobs and wages. It's simple economics."

Walker stood and applauded, but only a few Congressmen followed his lead.

"I have always believed that books and reading are the best things we can do for our communities and the people who inhabit them. Over these last few years, I have provided funds to build and maintain libraries.

"I plan to continue and have identified several sites here in this great state."

Once again, Walker stood and signaled for everybody to stand and applaud. Reluctantly Will, Jeremiah, and Hall stood. "What does he want in return," Hall whispered to the men close by.

Carnegie continued, "Steel tariffs have not risen in several years. Of course, the tariffs protect our industry from imports. And the bounties from the taxes assist us in cash flow. (Bounties are known as subsidies today.)

"I urge you to consider this legislation seriously. It will be useful to the country as we attempt to offset the effects of the recession."

Jeremiah Jones rose to speak and said, "Mister Carnegie, don't you think you could raise the pay of your employees to assist in combatting the recession? Raising tariffs will negatively affect my constituents, who survive by exporting tobacco to Europe. We raise a lot of tobacco in Virginia."

Bob Weaver quickly rose and proclaimed, "Yes, we do raise tobacco in Virginia, and in my Richmond-area district, it's a significant source of our economy. If we raise tariffs on steel, the Europeans will retaliate by raising taxes on tobacco. And let's be honest about it. Surcharges are, in effect, taxes on the consumer.

"I'm sorry, Mister Carnegie, I cannot, in good conscience, vote for any increase in tariffs," Weaver asserted.

Angrily, Carnegie responded, "Raising wages will negatively affect our bottom line at Carnegie Steel. I made that very clear to the union organizers who have threatened us. We will defend our right to set wages at a level that allows us to make a reasonable profit. That's the way the Free Enterprise system works. And the stockholders of Carnegie Steel expect no less from me."

Jim Hall answered him, "Mister Carnegie, may I respectfully remind you that your employees should have some consideration too. As a beneficiary of their labor, your wealth has exceeded even the wildest dreams of the average American.

"Do you not owe these people the opportunity to earn a living wage, so they can adequately support their family?" Hall demanded.

Quickly recovering, Senator Walker proclaimed, "I, for one, appreciate the generosity of Mister Carnegie and the fact that he has graciously shared with folks all over this country. He is a man who was not born into great wealth but has attained it by his ingenuity and hard work.

"I will support his request to receive assistance from this Congress and urge my colleagues to join me in so doing.

"Ler's take a short break, then we'll hear from Mister Morgan before our lunch break."

As Presley, Jones, Hall, Weaver, and Hoagland were chatting, several delegation members offered their agreement to the comments they made. "Thank you, Senator Presley. I agree with you."

"I'm proud of what you said, Hall. I'll vote with you."

"Congratulations, Weaver, that speech will play well to the whole Congress. I hope you'll repeat it at the right moment."

Banging a gavel, J. Harold Walker called the group back to order. "Gentlemen, please be seated. Mister J.P. Morgan, the Wall Street banker, will address us shortly.

"Let's make welcome to the Virginia delegation meeting, J.P. Morgan from New York City." Congenial applause greeted his introduction to the group.

J P Morgan

"Thank you, Senator Walker. I am honored to have the opportunity to speak to this delegation from the great state of Virginia. You were one of the first Colonies to be established in this country and have played an integral role in the history of the United States of America.

"As we continue to face economic difficulties, you once again can play an integral role.

"It is my sincere belief that tariffs are a workable economic tool which can be helpful as we attempt to recover from this recession. Making our industries more profitable will allow them to expand and grow their companies and hire more workers. When people are working, they have money to spend. Thus the economy starts to hum, and the business cycle returns to normal.

"As an investment banker and economist, these are my convictions."

Hoagland rose to ask a question. "Mister Morgan, it has been my observation that you tend to favor only a few corporations when you make loans. Is there a good reason for that practice?"

"Thank you for asking that question, Mister Hoagland. Bankers attempt to make loans in which there is a reasonable assumption of repayment. This current recession started when one bank recklessly made loans on which default occurred. My bank has avoided that costly mistake by selectively choosing our clients."

"I understand your philosophy, Mister Morgan, but by so doing, you have aided in the development of monopolies in a few businesses. Steel, railroads, and oil are dominated by only three companies that exclusively limit themselves to each other.

"This exclusivity allows them to exercise control over most of the jobs and cash flow in the United States. Free Enterprise demands that competition be encouraged. Isn't that right?"

"Theoretically, that is correct, but in a poor economy, I must exercise more selectivity."

Will Presley spoke, "Thank you, Mister Morgan, for talking to us today. I have a constituent who is fearful that we are establishing a dangerous plutocracy-eclipsing our democracy. Is that a concern for you?"

"I've heard those thoughts expressed, too, Senator, but they are overblown and exaggerated. I have no concerns at all about that," Morgan assured him.

"A positive answer from Congress to our request for steel tariffs will bring a boost to our economy and alleviate the adverse effects of the recession. It has continued for too long already. Let's get it done for the good of the United States of America."

"Thank you very much, Mister Morgan," Senator Walker smiled and shook his hand.

"Let's take a forty-five-minute break for lunch, then we'll hear from William Vanderbilt and John D. Rockefeller," Walker dismissed them.

When the five men from Virginia were seated in the Senate dining room, Will spoke. "I assume that Senator Walker wants us to agree wholeheartedly with these Industrial Barons, but I believe it's important that we speak for the working people of Virginia. These Barons are speaking for their self-interests."

Bob Weaver smiled wryly and retorted, " Did he call them Industrial Barons? I've heard them called Robber Barons, but never Industrial."

Hoagland added, "The people in my district are dependent on tobacco exports for jobs and income. These larger new tariffs and bounties will aid the Barons. Still, they will adversely affect the exporters and the growers of Charlottesville. I will listen politely to their speeches, but I will not vote to increase tariffs."

"Carnegie has been one of the worst offenders in fighting unions and has used the President to call in troops to stop union dissenters. Vanderbilt has profited tremendously during this recession by buying the smaller railroads which could not survive and were driven into bankruptcy," Jeremiah Jones stated.

"And J.P. Morgan encouraged Vanderbilt to buy them at bankrupt prices and provided funding for him to do so," Jim Hall added. "Vanderbilt now owns fourteen different railroad lines, the Hudson River steamship lines, and now, some ocean-going vessels traveling to Europe. He controls almost all of the freight business east of the Mississippi."

"I understand Commodore Vanderbilt passed away in January of this year. Is this his son who will speak after lunch?" Will asked.

Hall answered, "Yes, his name is William, and I heard that he inherited most of the Commodore's estate -somewhere close to $100,000,000.00. He's the richest man in the country at this time. He has even more than Carnegie."

AFTER LUNCH

William Vanderbilt

"Alright, Gentlemen, please come to order," Walker instructed as he banged his gavel. "Mister William Vanderbilt is ready to speak. Let's make him welcome."

Warm applause acknowledged Vanderbilt, although no one stood to greet him.

"Gentlemen, I appreciate the opportunity to speak to you today. Thank you, Senator Walker, for inviting me.

"We are talking about the proposed increase in the steel tariffs, now imposed. From the standpoint of industrialists, this increase is something we direly need.

"Imported steel is cheap, poorly made, and offers no jobs for American workers. Our folks, when they earn wages, have money to spend. As they spend, the proceeds circulate to stimulate our economy.

"Besides, revenues generated will accrue to the Treasury Department here in Washington, as well as adding to funds that bounties bring to American business. My company hauls steel to manufacture rails, engines, and freight cars. My railroad engines use diesel fuel refined by Mister Rockefeller, who will follow me at this dais shortly.

"Consequently, many commercial enterprises and their employees will benefit, and we can overcome the recession. I sincerely hope you will consider this formula for combatting our lagging gross national product."

As the applause died out, Will spoke softly to the group. "To hear these fellas tell it, they all are struggling to survive. Aren't these the richest men in the world?" he grinned.

Jeremiah winked, "Yeah, I pity these poor souls who are crying out for help. If they came to my church with these tales of woe, we would take up a collection for them.

"Just give the folks who work for you a raise," Jones opined to his group. "Every one of you can afford it, and that will place more money in circulation without making our trading partners angry," he concluded.

Raising his hand, Will asked to speak. "We have heard these same ideas, and we have asked this question of the others. Every one of you has a successful, prosperous business. Why can't you give raises in wages to your employees? That action would avoid the prospect of retaliatory tariff increases from our trading partners."

"It has been the practice of industry to retain for ourselves the right to set wages for our companies. We must, first of all, maximize profit for our stockholders and our executives."

Jeremiah stood and interrupted, "Your companies and executives have prospered enormously, while your employees have struggled.

"As long as you make no effort to assist in this war on the recession, I will not vote to subsidize you with a tariff increase."

Rising quickly to stifle any further negative comments from his Virginia delegation, Walker introduced John D. Rockefeller.

"Gentlemen, welcome, please, the chairman of Standard Oil Company, Mister Rockefeller. Thanks for coming today, John."

"I'm happy to meet with you today. We have been meeting with Congressional delegations all week, and I must say we have been very well received. Our message seems to be resonating with Congress."

Rolling his eyes and looking at his fellow Congressmen, Jim Hall spoke in an aside. "He hasn't heard from our delegation yet," he snickered.

John D Rockefeller

"The essential industries in our country require continued support from the federal government. Steel, railroads, and refined oil products are prime movers of the economic engine.

"The price supports on oil have enabled us to continue drilling for new sources of crude. Residue from our refined kerosene is processed to make gasoline which powers Carnegie's steel mills. Besides, we make lubricating grease, tar, asphalt, naphtha, and petroleum jelly. We are efficiently using everything that emanates from the refining process.

"Our products provide jobs to manufacture many valuable items from powering steam engines to paving city streets.

"Vanderbilt's trains haul our products in tanker cars to the western states. It should be evident to all of you how interdependent we are on each other.

"As we struggle with the negative aspects of the recession, it is essential that business and government work together. The future of our great republic and its people is dependent on that cooperation.

"In conclusion, steel tariffs and price supports should be approved by this Congress. Are there any questions?"

Weaver stood to ask, "Mr. Rockefeller, we understand that all businesses and corporations must make a reasonable profit to sustain their existence; however, I have one question. How much profit do you consider reasonable?"

Rockefeller smiled and replied, "Just a little more."

Immediately standing to speak, Walker said, "Thank you, Mr. Rockefeler. I trust these representatives of the people of Virginia to take your words of wisdom to heart. I am confident we will take the necessary actions our speakers have shared with us. That will be all, Gentlemen."

Walking out of the meeting, Jeremiah Jones looked around at all of his colleagues. He retorted, "I still say these millionaires should pay their employees a living wage. Money in people's hands to spend is the best way to stimulate our economy. These guys have gotten rich while the workers still struggle. As my momma used to say, "It jist ain't fittin'.""

Hoagland, the Charlottesville representative, asked, "If we pay price supports and tariff bounties to the millionaires, why can't the federal government give some financial aid to working people? Why does it always go to the millionaires?"

"And why do we allow the rich people to monopolize essential businesses? I thought free enterprise encourages competition," Will spoke rhetorically.

"Competition should be encouraged," Hall added. "My economics professor at Yale spent a whole semester teaching the free enterprise system. That's not what we are experiencing in our present situation."

"It seems to me we have a tale of two cultures," Will suggested. "There are a few obscenely wealthy folks, and everybody else is struggling to survive."

Bob Weaver offered, "Maybe we can introduce legislation to change things a bit. At least we can debate these ideas when Congress takes up the bills to accomplish recession relief."

J. Harold Walker ambled by and joined the conversation. "Gentlemen, I want to remind you that Carnegie is selecting sites for libraries. If he chooses one in Fairfax County, Senator Presley and Congressman Hall can appear with him at the announcement. A photo in the local paper would look good.

"Likewise for each of you other Congressmen, whether in Richmond, Charlottesville, or Hampton.

"Then, too, Morgan, Vanderbilt, and Rockefeller always contribute to Congressional campaign funds. Since you are required to run for reelection every two years, I'm confident you'll want to keep that in mind when you vote on the bills in which they are interested. Good day Gentlemen."

Chapter Thirty

SILVER RETURNS

When Will returned to the Capitol to join the reconvened January 1878 session of the 45th Congress, he headed for the Senate dining room.

Smiling as he saw his friends, Jim Hall and Jeremiah Jones, at the entrance awaiting his arrival, he spoke, "I was hoping to see you two this week; I've got questions for you."

"I'm willing to answer your questions if you're buying lunch," Jones grinned.

"Alright, my friend. I'll buy lunch anytime you'll join me. It's always a pleasure hearing your ideas."

Walking into the dining area, Hall whispered, "Oh Lord, there's Senator Walker, and he's waving for us to join him."

"Come on, guys, Walker can't kill us and eat us, too," Will grinned. "His bark is worse than his bite."

As they were all seated, Senator Walker said, "I want to discourage you, gentlemen, from supporting this proposed Grand Bland Plan. It is highly inflationary, and President Hayes has promised to veto it."

"How do you know the President will veto it?" Will queried.

As the Senior Senator from Virginia, I make it my business to know, Presley," Walker smiled smugly.

"Senator Walker, if the return of silver coins increases the money supply, the common working folks will benefit," Jeremiah asserted. "Anything that helps my constituents, I will support."

"Yeah, Walker, this depression has continued for five years, and our entire nation has suffered. The only exception to that is the Robber Baron of Wall Street," Hall offered. "And Grant's Coinage Act of 1873 removed all silver coins from the money supply. It was a contributing factor to the recession."

"Senator Walker, I understand that the proposed law is titled the Bland-Allison Act – named for Representative Richard Bland of Missouri and Senator William Allison of Iowa. Are we talking about the same bill? You called it the Grand Bland Plan derisively, I presume," Presley questioned him.

"Yeah, call it what you want, Presley. By whatever monicker you want to use, this bill isn't good for business. President Grant set the pro-business tone for the Republican Party, and we must fall in line behind our leaders, including President Hayes," Walker insisted.

"Isn't it true that the President has financial interests in industrials and banking, Senator Walker?" Hall questioned. "The short supply of money keeps interest rates high, aiding the bankers. But we farmers need short-term seasonal bank loans, and high interest is detrimental for us."

"Keeping a tight rein on monetary supply keeps inflation in check. Our overall economy should be a concern," Walker stated emphatically.

"That's what we're talking about, Senator," Jones insisted. "The people of my district include everybody, the factory workers and farmers, and not just the wealthy industrialists and bankers. Call me a Lincoln Republican, not a Grant/Hayes Republican. Lincoln called it a government of the people, by the people, and for the people."

"The Bland-Allison Act is a bipartisan proposal, Gentlemen," Hall informed them. "Bland is a Democrat, but Allison is a Republican. Are we going to be on the winning side or the losing side?"

"I can assure all of you that the President will veto this bill. He will not allow it to stand," Walker insisted again.

"I will remind you, Senator Walker, that vetoes can be overridden by Congress," Hall averred. "My law professor at Yale emphasized that fact in several of his lectures."

"You have a snobbish attitude about your Yale law degree, Hall. Don't try to impress me," J. Harold Walker was condescending.

"I am proud of being a graduate of Yale Law School Senator. By the way, Yale will soon announce the new student newspaper, and The Yale Daily News will be the first one in the USA."

"I am a proud graduate of Harvard Law School, myself, Representative Hall," Walker stuck his chest out. "Since my father before me was a Harvard Business School graduate, I got a legacy appointment to Harvard."

Will whispered to Jones, "Guess we're just peons, Jeremiah," as he grinned.

"Yep, but our votes count the same as theirs, peon or blue-blood. We are duly elected, same as them," Jones replied.

When the Bland-Allison Act was introduced in the Senate by William Allison, Senator Will Presley made his first speech on the Senate floor.

"Senators, I rise in support of this bill. It authorizes the United States Treasury to buy two million to four million dollars of silver each month at market prices. Then, silver coins will come from the mint as silver dollars.

I predict they will be in strong demand and become widely used as money once again. The Seated Lincoln silver dollar was very popular before the Coinage Act of 1873 banned its' production. Let's stand up for the working people of America and support this return to silver coins."

Jim Hall made a similar speech in the House of Representatives. By the end of January, the bill, by a wide margin, was passed by both Houses.

As J.Harold Walker had predicted, President Rutherford B. Hayes vetoed the bill. As Jim Hall had indicated, Congress overturned Hayes' veto on February 28, 1878.

Silver mines in Nevada almost immediately returned to mining the ore. Miners returned to work. Railroads hauled the silver cross country to the Philadelphia Mint.

Railroad workers returned to work, and the whistle-stop towns along the way returned to prosperity as the trains ran regular routes through their domicile.

The Philadelphia Mint suspended all operations except the minting of the Morgan Silver Dollar. To meet demand, the minters worked twenty-four hours, seven days per week.

At home in Falls Church, the Presleys and Parkers discussed the Bland-Allison Act and its' impact on the American economy. "I know individuals can have a positive effect on the whole country. Sometimes it's in small steps as we have taken here at Parker's Farm," Harry observed. "Other times, it takes a more robust effort like the Bland-Allison Act."

"Well, I'm proud of our son-in-law," Alice smiled at Will. "He played an important part in the passing of that bill."

"I've always remembered what my Paw used to say. Just do the best you can with what you got. That's all I did. Our friends Hall and Jones were there to assist us too."

"Now that we know what you can do, Will, please remember the rights of women. I want to vote one of these days," Lenora sighed.

Chapter Thirty-one

INNOVATIONS

Will headed down to the barn to hitch the horse to the buggy. Bundled in a heavy wool long coat with a scarf tucked around his neck (Len had insisted on the scarf), he tucked the ends into the opening above the top button. The crisp, cold, late-February morning air smacked him in the face.

Hurrying his walk to the barn, he saw Pete and Harry standing in front of the shed. "What are you two doing out here in the cold? Don't you have a fire in the barn stove?" Will asked.

"Yeah, I built a fire first thing this morning; I seen Harry headin' this way and had a question fer 'im," Pete answered.

"Well, let's head to the barn where it's warm," Harry suggested, "A man my age can catch his death standing out in cold weather like this."

"Exactly what I was thinking," Will said. "I'm freezin' out here."

"I've got some bricks heatin' on the stove, Will. You can put 'em in the buggy when ya start to the Capitol. They'll keep yer' feet warm."

"What's happening in D.C. these days?" Harry asked Will when they entered the warm barn.

"We're debating a bill to raise greenbacks to the same value as silver and gold coins. As you know, greenbacks fluctuated for less than face value after the war. Gradually, we've raised their value. He informed them that this bill would make a greenback the same value as the Morgan silver dollar. In effect, it will increase the money supply nationwide – very much like the minting of silver coins did."

"Why'd they call 'em greenbacks?" Pete was curious.

Chuckling, Harry answered, "As the war continued, the value of paper money fluctuated depending on whether the Union Army won or lost a battle.

"Since the value fluctuated according to the perception of whether the government could redeem them if presented for redemption, people said they were backed by only the green ink on the back – hence the nickname greenbacks.

"Throughout the war, I was paid in greenbacks."

Will interjected, "We attempted to raise the number of greenbacks in circulation by 400 million dollars in '68, but Grant was adamantly opposed. He claimed it would be inflationary.

"Many farmers in the Midwest and Western states clamored for more greenbacks and even formed a Greenback Party. Their influence has been the impetus for the bill we're considering now."

"Hey Will, are there any efforts to install a telephone in the Capitol? I remember that we saw one at the '76 Exposition in Philadelphia. A man named Alexander Grahan Bell demonstrated it."

"I do remember that Harry, and early in "77, President Hayes had one installed in the White House. The problem was that the only phone available for him to call was at the Treasury Department," Will laughed.

"Is it true that a whole network of phones has already been installed in Massachusetts?" Harry asked.

"Yes, and it seems to be growing more widespread. I'm hopeful that soon a phone will be installed at the Capitol, enabling us to call the White House. Now the only thing we have is a telegraph, and we have to stand in line to ask the operator to send a wire for us."

"Have you heard of Thomas Edison?" Harry asked Will.

"Yeah, he's the guy who invented the machine that records voices on a piece of tinfoil. I believe he calls it a phonograph. That's the strangest thing I've ever heard. I can't see anything it'll ever be good for. What use is it?" he asked rhetorically.

"I was reading in the Washington newspaper about him. They say he's working on an electric light bulb. Now that's something we could use.

"These kerosene lanterns can be dangerous. Many fires have started from lanterns that were overturned. The big fire in Chicago began when a cow turned over a lantern in a barn. It burned down half the city of Chicago," Harry informed them.

"Yeah, ya gotta be keerful with fire in a barn," Pete noted. "We had a fire in 'er barn at Roaring Fork. Some hay we had fer tha mules was burned by a spark from tha stove we had in ther," Pete remembered. "Nearly burned tha 'hole barn down afore we cud git it put out.

"As I was saying, Harry, 'bout tha first of March, we gonna hafta start plowin' 'n' gittin' tha ground ready fer plantin'. When we gonna git 'er crew back in ta start workin'?"

"Let's watch the ground and make sure it's thawed out before we start plowing. Winter here in Northern Virginia isn't over until closer to the middle of March. We'll check it out and let our people know when it's time to come back."

"Say, Will, Alice was reading about a new store up in Utica, New York. A fellow named F.W. Woolworth opened up a whole store where everything sells for a nickel. Calls it the F W Woolworth Great Five Cent Store. Do you think we could get one of those here in the city? It'd be great to have a store like that for people to shop – especially working people and poor folks," Harry said.

"Don't know, but it would be nice to have one here," Will smiled.

"Alright, men, I'm headin' out to the Capitol. Where are those warm bricks, Pete? I'm gonna need them today."

Chapter Thirty-two

WHITE HOUSE EASTER EGG ROLL

Lenora greeted her husband with unexpected glee as he returned from the capital one early evening in March of 1878. "Did you know about the Easter Egg Roll, Will?"

"Only that it had been discussed with many jokes attached. Some say the President is trying to get children's votes since he may not be as successful with their parents in the future. Others think he has laid enough eggs to have an executive team of egg rollers."

She laughed, although she didn't see the humor, and said, "It is going to happen. I read about it in the Sunday paper. On Monday after Easter, April 22nd, the White House will open the grounds for all children who wish to bring their Easter Eggs. The paper said there would be games or contests, and the President would greet the boys and girls himself."

"I don't see any harm in it. If it is a nice day, we should take the children," Will suggested.

Lenora grabbed him and kissed his cheek. "I was hoping you would say that, Will. They will be so excited."

"If they are any more excited than you, sweetheart, I might not be able to handle it."

"You are no fun at all, Mister big shot Senator," she quipped while poking him in the ribs.

The children anticipated Easter this year almost as much as Christmas. Mimi would ask Lenora several times each week, "How many more days until the Easter Egg Roll?"

When Friday, April 19th, arrived, Mimi convinced her brothers it was time to collect eggs. Ronnie thought that was girls' work and suggested something more manly like bird hunting but conceded after his mother's rebuke.

"You won't get away with that nonsense in this house, boys. First of all, nobody is too good to do any job that needs doing. Men and women may have some traditionally different roles. Still they pitch in and do whatever it takes as a family when they care about each other."

"But you can't even vote, Momma," Randy said before he thought about the consequences.

Ronnie pretended not to hear and took Mimi's hand. "Let's go get some eggs."

Randy did not utter another word for many hours.

Lenora told Lillian about this conversation, and they both had a good laugh while the children were busy outside.

"I guess those lads are feeling the wrath of Momma right about now," Lillian snickered.

"Sometimes you have to get burned to learn not to touch the stove," Lenora smiled.

On Saturday, the Presleys and Parkers joined together for an egg dying event. Lillian oversaw the hard boiling of the eggs. Harry instructed the boys in the collection of natural items to be used for the extraction of dyes. Alice and Lenora supervised the coloring process with Mimi's assistance. Surprisingly, Ronnie and Randy asked to participate in all aspects of the project with no comment about gender roles. Will had assumed the role of family researcher and pontificated from what he had read.

During supper, Will shared the following information about the origin of colored eggs at Easter. "The early Christians of Mesopotamia began the custom of dyeing Easter eggs. Red was used to represent the blood of Jesus Christ that was shed on the cross. An English King, Edward I, had 450 eggs colored or covered in gold leaf to be distributed on Easter in 1290. Egg rolling was also a traditional Easter egg game played in many European countries where children rolled eggs down hillsides at Easter. The tradition was taken to the New World by European settlers."

The Easter Sunday service at church was beautiful and inspiring. The Nave was resplendent with Lillies. Fresh candles had been placed in shiny brass candelabra, each adorned with greenery and carefully arranged on the altar and in the windows. The Rector wore a white Chausable over the usual Alb. The parishioners had risen to the challenge by donning their best clothing and hats for the occasion.

During his homily, the Rector mentioned that the egg is a symbol of Easter, representing the resurrection of Jesus. The rolling of Easter Eggs also stands for the rolling away of the stone at his tomb. Additionally, early Christians abstained from eating eggs and meat during Lent; therefore, Easter was the first time they were allowed to eat eggs in forty days.

Driving home from church, Ronnie asked his father, "Why are some things used to stand for something else? Why don't we just say what we mean?"

"Good question, Son. I would dare to guess that people have always found a shorthand way of communicating larger ideas. Simple words that we can visualize can help us to understand other ideas or concepts that are not as easy to picture in our minds. We call these symbols."

Randy was listening and wanted examples. "What symbols do we use all the time, Daddy?"

Will thought a moment and said, "I can think of two you will recognize immediately, the cross and our flag.

"When we see the cross, what comes to mind? Probably our church or, more importantly, the faith that we have in the life and message of Jesus Christ.

"When we pass our country's flag waving in the breeze, it should remind us of the self-evident truth's established by our Founding Fathers in the Declaration and Constitution. It should cause us to stop and think about the ideal that we have yet to achieve and encourage us to keep working for a more perfect union."

"I see what you mean. Those symbols would certainly stop a long-winded discussion or sermon," Ronnie said It as both parents laughed.

Monday Morning, Capitol Hill

The buggy was filled with smiling children anticipating a new and hopefully fun-filled experience. They were each proudly carrying a basket full of colored eggs. "I think our eggs will be the prettiest ones," Mimi grinned.

As they parked their buggy, they noticed several young men wearing badges who seemed to be directing traffic.

Groups of children were beginning to arrive from several points, all being led to the highest rise of the property on the front of the White House lawn.

Will spotted his friend, Congressman Jeremiah Jones, with his wife, Janie, and their two children, Samuel and Cora. Introductions were made, and the children began comparing the colors of their eggs.

Everyone was in good spirits as they climbed the hill together. Samuel, age ten, had teamed up with Ronnie and Randy. Cora, age five, quickly attached herself to Mimi, who was happy to be the big girl for once.

One of the young guides approached Jeremiah at the top of the hill where the games were scheduled. "I'm sorry, Sir, but you and your family will need to go around to the back lawn."

Rendered speechless for a moment, Jeremiah asked, "Why?"

"We were told this area is for white children only, and we are supposed to make sure there is no trouble."

Indignantly, Jeremiah replied, "Well, you have a hell of a way to keep trouble from happening. I am an elected representative, a member of the Congress of the United States, and you're telling me to go the back lawn?"

Will heard the voices as they became louder and walked over to his friend. "What's the problem?"

The startled young guide recognized Senator Presley and turned bright red. "I was ordered to make sure only white children were allowed on the front lawn, Sir. I don't mean no disrespect."

"No disrespect, Hell!" Jeremiah said with gritted teeth.

Will stepped between the two and said, "These people are with me, and they are not going anywhere. If your boss has a problem with that, tell him to come to see me. Now, why don't you continue with the better part of your job and ensure that all of our children have a good day? Thank you."

Jeremiah took a few deep breaths and gained control of himself. "Thank you, Will, but you should not have to do that, and I should not be put in such a humiliating position in front of my wife and family. Just what does a man have to do in this country to be treated as an equal human being?"

Despite this ugly moment, all the children enjoyed the games, met the President, and made new friends.

On the drive home, Ronnie asked Will, "Why was that guide so mean to Mr. Jeremiah? Isn't he an elected official just like you?"

"He most certainly is, and he is an outstanding representative. The answer to your question will require a lot of words. Remember what I told you about symbols?

"Representative Jones salutes the same flag that I salute. He took an oath to uphold the Constitution just like I did. There is no logical reason that he should be treated differently. That is why we must continue the hard work of moving us ever closer to the ideals we all profess to believe. Someday, that flag will wave over a nation that believes the ideas it symbolizes, but unfortunately, not yet."

Chapter Thirty-three

SWING LOW SWEET CHARIOT

Walking down the road from the school and singing a song that she heard her mother, Bessie, singing, Lucy Jefferson was heading home on a beautiful mid-May day. It had been three years since the Presley and Parker families had befriended her and her parents and siblings.

Lucy was a tall, slender girl, much like her mother. Her long narrow face and pointed nose, along with braided pigtails in her hair, made her pretty. Her boyfriend, Jasper, sometimes walked her home, but today had to do errands for his mother.

This year, 1880, Lucy had finished the tenth grade and earned excellent marks in all areas of study. Her teacher, Miss Duncan, encouraged her to apply for a job teaching Primary school students. If hired, she could start training younger children in the Fall. It was exciting to think she could add to her family's income.

Although Virginia's Jim Crow laws mandated segregated schools for blacks and whites (separate but equal), it did provide more opportunities for black teachers.

Jackie, her older brother, graduated from the twelfth grade and would attend Howard University in the Fall. Senator Presley had helped arrange for him to be admitted and agreed to pay tuition for him. He would pursue a degree in Agriculture.

Life was good.

Four young men graduated from the white high school and were celebrating. Billy Randolph sneaked a bottle of his father's bourbon to add to their party. Jimmy Boatman, Walter May, and David Miller passed the bottle around while Billy drove the buggy looking for a shady spot to pull off the road and park.

"Hey boys, do you want some smoked ham?" he laughed. "I've heard these black girls love to do the deed. Here's one walkin' down the street. Ask her if she wants to party with us, David. I'll stop when we get beside her."

Hearing the buggy approaching, Lucy moved to the side of the road to give ample room to pass. As she turned to face the street, it stopped.

"Hey girl, do you wanna party with us today? We're celebrating school being over," David smiled.

"Huh-uh, I got to get on home and take care of my little brothers and sister. Ain't got no time for no party."

"Aw, come on, girlie," Billy pleaded. "We'll have a lot of fun. Do you want a swig of bourbon?"

"I don't drink no liquor. I go to church. I'm a Christian 'n' all my family is too."

"You know it ain't very often a darkie gets a chance to party with white boys. Are you turnin' us down, girl?" David was insistent.

"Now y'all know whites 'n' blacks ain't supposed to be mixin' 'n' minglin'. You could get in trouble. Besides, I got a boyfriend who wouldn't like it neither," she was almost sobbing.

"Come on, girl, we won't tell nobody if you won't. You're gonna like it, I promise you," Billy grinned slyly.

"No, I ain't goin' nowhere with you boys, and if you don't leave me alone, I'm gonna scream." Unexpectedly, she started to run.

"Hurry up, Billy, don't let her get away," Walter shouted.

Jimmy hurriedly jumped from the wagon and chased her. Catching up, he swooped her into his arms and carried her to the buggy.

"Please, let me go. I gotta get home 'n' take care of my little brothers 'n sister. They're by themselves 'til I get home," she pleaded.

"You ain't goin' nowhere 'til we have some fun, girl. Now shut your mouth. This won't take but a few minutes, then we'll be finished with you."

Struggling to free herself, she screamed. "All of you are in trouble. You can't treat a girl like this. It's against the law."

"Don't you talk to me like that, you Jim Crow girl," Jimmy yelled. "Won't nobody believe you over us?"

David spoke up, "I'm first. I'm the one who asked her."

"Huh-uh, I caught her before she got away. I'm first," Jimmy demanded.

"Ain't nobody gonna be first. 'Cause, you ain't doin' nothin' to me," Lucy sobbed. "I ain't done nothin' to any of y'all."

Spotting a clump of trees hidden from the street, Billy drove the buggy there, then ordered, "Tear her dress off and pull her underpants down. We'll make this quick."

When all four boys had their fill of Lucy, they left her lying in the grass, bleeding and sobbing. "Why'd they do that to me? I didn't do nothin' to them."

Slowly, she got up and walked home. When she got there, she cried uncontrollably. "I didn't do nothin' to them boys," she said to Eddie, who met her at the door.

"What'd they do to you, sister?" Eddie asked with tears in his eyes.

"It was awful stuff, Eddie. They hurt me. Where's Jimmy 'n' Susie?" she worried about the other children.

"They out playin' wit Zeke's kids. We wondered where you wuz," he replied.

"Momma's gonna be mad 'cause you tore yo dress she made for ya to wear to school."

"That ain't all she's gonna be mad about, Eddie. Them boys hurt me bad."

"D'ya know any of 'em?" Eddie asked.

"I just heard some names. I've seen them around the neighborhood but don't know any of 'em."

"Are ya gonna tell the lawmen about it?"

"It won't do no good. They ain't gonna do nothin' to no white boys for messing over a black girl. Just have to run a little faster next time."

When Bessie arrived for work the following day, she was crying. Lenora looked at her and walked over to comfort her. "What's the matter, Bessie?" she asked softly.

"Four white boys took advantage of my Lucy yesterday. They hurt her, Miss Lenora," Bessie was angry.

"How did they hurt her? Tell me about it."

"They forced her to do what she didn't want to do. All of them had their way with her. It was in a clump of trees down by the creek.

"She was walkin' home from school mindin' her own business. One of them grabbed her and put her in their buggy. They tore her clothes off her and took turns with her. She was bruised 'n' bloody when I got home.

"Johnny, he wants to kill 'em, but that won't do no good. He'd just get hisself arrested.

"Jackie, say he gonna get a ax handle and beat 'em up. He might do it too."

"Do you know who they wuz, Bessie?" Lillian asked.

"Not fo sho Missy, but Lucy heard some names. They say they wuz graduatin' from high school."

"Lillian, see if you can catch Will before he leaves for work. He needs to talk to the sheriff."

"Alright, Len, he's prob'bly at the barn a gettin' a buggy ready."

Will burst into the Cannery and shouted, "What's goin' on with Lucy?" He listened as Bessie repeated the story, then said, "I'll stop at the sheriff's office and demand that he arrest these boys. Do you have any names?"

"She only heard first names, but no last names. They did graduate yesterday from high school. They can probably figger it out," Bessie reasoned.

"Is R.F. Broadwater still the sheriff of Fairfax County, Will?" Lenora asked. When he nodded assent, she continued, "You and Daddy voted for him in the last two elections. He should be receptive even if you drop in without an appointment."

"Yes, I feel certain he will see me, but not so sure he will take any action against these four boys. We'll see what happens."

As he entered the Sheriff's Office, Will was greeted with a big smile from the deputy at the front desk. "Good mornin', Senator Presley. What brings you here today?"

"I need to talk with the sheriff, Deputy Brock. Is he in his office this early?"

"Yes, he's usually the first one to arrive. I'll tell him you're here, Senator."

Entering Broadwater's office, Will received a warm greeting from the sheriff. "Good morning, Senator. What can I do for you this fine day?"

"I have an employee whose daughter was assaulted by some high school boys yesterday. They sexually assaulted her, and she suffered some injuries. Her parents are treating her at home, but these boys must be held accountable."

"Of course, Senator, who are they?" he quizzed

"She only has first names, but all four graduated from the high school. It should be easy enough to identify all of them. Billy, Jimmy, Walter, and David."

"OK, Senator, I will personally handle this investigation as a favor to you. I am up for reelection in November, and I'm aware of your past support. I'll do my best to get to the bottom of this."

One Week Later

A page in the Senate Office Building knocked on Will's door. "Senator, a note was delivered with instructions to give it to you."

"Thank you, Richard, 'preciate it." Will acknowledged him.

> Senator, I have made an investigation of your complaint from last week. Please stop by my office at your earliest convenience, and I'll share my findings.
> R.F. Broadwater Sheriff of Fairfax County

"Hello, Deputy Brock, I need to see the Sheriff."

"Of course, Senator, I think he's expecting you to stop by today," the deputy was deferential to the Senator.

"Come in, Senator. I have some information about the alleged assault you reported last week," the sheriff smiled slightly. "It seems there's a difference of opinion about the incident with the black girl. You didn't tell me she was black."

"It doesn't matter that she's black," Will shouted. "All of our citizens have a right to expect law enforcement to protect them and to punish those who abuse them. The 14th Amendment guarantees the right of every citizen to due process of law, and I demand this young lady's rights be protected."

"Now, Senator, the boys tell a different story. That makes four against one. This Lucy Jefferson person asked to join their party. She was happy that white boys were interested in her.

"These boys all come from preeminent families in our county. The Randolph kid is the son of a county commissioner. Jimmy Boatman's father is one of my deputies. Walter May's daddy works at the War Department in D.C, and David Miller's mother works at the White House.

"Do you believe that a judge and jury would accept the word of a black girl against the word of fine upstanding white families?

"I cannot find enough evidence to bring charges against these boys." He whispered in an aside to Will, "especially with an election coming up this Fall."

When Will arrived at home, he stopped in at the Cannery and shared the news from the sheriff. Lenora wrinkled her face in anger, but Bessie was nonchalant.

"Johnny, he always say, don't get mad, get even. I reckon that's what him and Jackie gotta do."

Two Days Later

Lenora read the local newspaper to Will: "Local man severely beaten by an unknown attacker. Beaten with an ax handle, Billy Randolph, son of a Fairfax County commissioner, is hospitalized and in serious condition. The Sheriff's Office is searching for the assailant.

"Will, you don't think....." Lenora hesitated. "Surely Johnny nor Jackie did this."

"I don't know, Len. Not sure I want to know. But at any rate, the Randolph boy deserved it."

Encountering Sheriff Broadwater in the Fairfax County courthouse two weeks later, the sheriff spoke to Will. "Senator, if you know anything about these assaults on the four boys you accused of attacking your black friend, you had better tell me what you know. All four of them are injured, and two are in the hospital. It looks like someone is seeking revenge."

"I know nothing of which you speak, Sheriff. But I must say, they had it coming.

"As you said earlier, an election is upcoming, and black men vote too. It would be wise *if this case remains unsolved, just as the case against the boys who committed the heinous* assault on Lucy remains unsolved."

"I'll keep that in mind, Senator."

In the sheriff's election of 1880, William Ayre, Jr. succeeded R.F. Broadwater.

Rufus Brown led the campaign in the State Legislature to appoint Will Presley to a second term as United States Senator from Virginia.

Chapter Thirty-four

ANOTHER ASSASSINATION

Tuesday, July 5, 1881

A loud knock on his Senate office door caused Will to look up from the document he was reading and answer, "Come in, please." When the door opened, Jim Hall and Jeremiah Jones entered with shocked and sorrowful looks on their faces.

"What's going on, men?" Will asked apprehensively.

"We just got word that President Garfield has been shot," Jones exclaimed. "He was at the Baltimore and Potomac train station on Saturday preparing to take a short New England vacation for Independence Day and to escape the intolerable heat here in the Capital. Mrs. Garfield has been sick but has improved in the last few days.

"Secretary of State Blaine drove the President and Lucretia to the station in his carriage."

"Who did the shooting, and why would anybody want to shoot the President?" Will shouted.

"A man named Charles Guiteau was arrested at the scene as he tried to escape. He said God told him to shoot Garfield and that Chester Arthur was destined to be President.

"A reporter for the Washington newspaper told me Guiteau's family thinks he's insane," Hall offered.

"I heard one of Garfield's staffers say that Guiteau had written a speech after the President was nominated in Chicago. The address was supportive of Garfield but never delivered. Nor did it ever show up in print.

"Guiteau showed it to our leader, then asked for an appointment to a consulship in Vienna or Paris. That request was rejected; therefore,

Guiteau became enraged, claiming that his speech was the major factor that accounted for the President's election," Hall told them.

"He's been stalking Garfield since the Inauguration in March. He chose Saturday to carry out his plan."

"Was anyone else shot or injured?" Will questioned. "Did they take the President to the hospital?"

Jones answered, "The last report I heard was that he was taken to the White House to be treated. His doctor's name is Bliss, and he probed the wound with his hand, trying to find the lodged bullet in the abdomen but could not find it. They said he would try again upon arrival at the White House.

"It seems that the President has survived for now but lost a lot of blood. He'll get good care and rest at the Executive Mansion."

"What is known about this Charles Guiteau?" Will searched for answers.

"Not very much for now, but I'm certain the D.C. newspaper reporters will find some answers about him," Hall asserted.

On his way home from the office, Will stopped at a newsstand and bought the Washington newspaper. The front-page story was about the shooting and an extended biography of Charles Guiteau.

When he arrived home, he asked Lenora to read the article aloud so both of them could hear the story simultaneously.

Lenora read: "Guiteau was born in Freeport, Illinois. He was the fourth of six children born to Luther Wilson Guiteau and Jane August Howe. The Guiteau family was of French Huguenot ancestry.

"In 1850, they moved to Ulao, Wisconsin, where they lived for five years. While there, his mother died of postpartum psychosis after her sixth child was born. Soon after, the family moved back to Freeport.

"Guiteau attempted to enroll in the University of Michigan but failed to pass the entrance exam. He had not prepared himself for college and could not master the algebra and French that were required.

Lenora continued to read, "In June 1860, Charles joined the Oneida Community – a utopian religious sect located in Oneida, New York, which practiced group marriage.

"After five years, he was rejected by the group, and he subsequently renounced them and their leader, John Humphrey Noyes."

"This guy is kind of nutty," Will exclaimed.

"Here's another article on the back page about him. It says he worked at a Chicago law firm as a clerk, then passed a cursory bar exam. Although admitted to the bar, he only argued one case in court, which he lost. Most of his work was collecting bills.

"Will, where do you think they found all this information?" Lenora wondered.

"I assume a background check was done when he asked for the appointment to Vienna or Paris. Presidential staffers talk daily with reporters, and lots of information is passed on to the public."

Monday, September 19, 1881

Entering his office in the Senate Building, Will was immediately informed that President Garfield had died.

"The President and Lucretia had traveled to Elberton, New Jersey, for a vacation trip. Two months after the July 2nd shooting, he succumbed. His body was wracked by infection, and he had a high fever," Will's office assistant, Dennis, told him.

Chester Arthur

"That same day, at his home in New York City, Chester A. Arthur was sworn in as the 21st President of the United States."

On the next day, September 20, Guiteau was officially charged with murder. He had previously been charged with attempted murder.

When he arrived home from his Senate office and shared the news of Garfield's death, Lenora was inquisitive. "What do you think caused the infection, Will? Could they have prevented that?"

"Well, I was told that Doctor Bliss stuck his hand and a pair of forceps into the President's body in an attempt to remove the bullet. It's possible those actions somehow caused the infection," he surmised.

"It would be tragic to think that the doctor's actions caused the death of the President. But it has been two months since the shooting," Lenora shook her head.

"The bullet remaining in his body could have caused the infection, too. I'm certain that's the reason the doctor made such a concerted effort to remove it," Will reassured her.

Guiteau was indicted on October 14, 1881. His trial began on November 17, 1881, and on January 25, 1882, he was found guilty of murder. The President's assassin was hanged on June 30, 1882.

Chapter Thirty-five

THE EVOLUTION OF GEORGE WILHELM PRESLEY

Actively involved in all discussions during the Party's June Convention, Will listened, suggested, debated, and was newly energized at the possibilities for the future.

Between sessions, he found himself absorbed in introspection. "In two months, I will attain the age of forty-four, the exact age at which we lost our Paw in a logging accident. J.W. Presley did not live to see all the changes in his family, country, and world.

"It is probably a blessing that he missed the war and the tragic losses it brought, but I hope and want to believe that he would have been proud of his third-born son.

"Here I stand with opportunities Paw never had. What will I do to justify my good fortune?

"I cannot squander the chance to do something meaningful, to leave something, anything that might benefit not only my immediate family but potentially leave a positive effect on future generations.

"To be in a position to lead, I need to have more knowledge. I need to know more than what I read in the newspaper or hear from other politicians. I need to understand the thinkers of the past who have influenced the present through the arts and politics.

"Our Maw taught all of us to read, and she gave us the tools necessary to get as much information and knowledge as we chose to obtain. She was determined to equip her children with the ability to pursue whatever opportunities presented themselves. In her honor and for my own family, I pledge to put all my spare time to good use by immersing myself in the thoughts of the great people who came before me."

Will did not share his epiphany with anyone, but it did not go unnoticed by his wife and family that he began bringing books home every week. Whenever there was a quiet moment, he could be found with his nose in one of those books and his mind entirely focused on whatever he was reading.

When their father was reappointed to his second term as a United States Senator from Virginia, Mimi entered third grade. The twins, Ronnie and Randy, were in high school. The Presley children found many things to occupy their attention among their friends, school, and the bigger outside world.

Occasionally, Mimi would crawl into Will's lap and say, "What's ye reading, Daddy?" Will could never resist this little angel and would stop long enough to share a brief idea of the subject matter in age-appropriate language and imagery.

"I'm reading the thoughts of some very wise people, Mimi. People who can make me think differently about very ordinary things. Here is an example, 'When it is dark enough, you can see the stars.' That is only one of many memorable things said by Ralph Waldo Emerson, a famous writer from the northeastern part of our country."

"What does that mean, Daddy? Why do you want to read what somebody you don't even know has to say?"

"You ask excellent questions, sweetheart. Let me try to answer as best I can. First, I think he is reminding us that we overlook many beautiful things around us because we are constantly being distracted. When we shut out all those distractions, we can begin to see and appreciate the important things. Does that make sense?"

"I guess it does, Daddy. Is that kinda like I forgot about the old doll Grandma Sally gave me because it was buried under a pile of newer things in my toy chest?"

"I believe you have the idea, Mimi. How did you feel when you pulled out all the newer toys and found that doll.?

"I loved it, Daddy. It is still special to me."

"So, does that answer your second question about why I would want to read something a stranger wrote?"

"Not exactly. Can you help me understand, Daddy?"

"Again, I will try. Part of education is keeping our minds open to new information or new ways of looking at the world. Our education should not stop when we finish school. I don't ever want to stop learning, and I wish the same for you."

Will did not have a tutor's advice nor an official reading list to guide his continuing education. Consequently, his reading selections were arbitarily dependent on what was available in the Senate library or what he happened upon when browsing a bookstore in the capital city.

During his time in the Senate, he acquainted himself with politicians, philosophers, scientists, poets, and novelists from the old and new worlds. He made intentional and obvious selections of the writings of our country's founding fathers, i.e., Washington, Jefferson, Madison, etc.

From George Washington

It being among my first wishes to see some plan adopted by which slavery in this country may be abolished by law.

When the freedom of speech is taken away, then dumb and silent, we may be led, like sheep, to the slaughter.

When one side only of a story is heard and often repeated, the human mind becomes impressed with it insensibly.

From Thomas Jefferson:

The price of freedom is eternal vigilance.

If a law is unjust, a man has not only a right to disobey it; he is obliged to do so.

From Thomas Paine

We have it in our power to begin the world over again.

From Benjamin Franklin

We are all born ignorant, but one must work hard to remain stupid.

An investment in knowledge pays the best interest.

If everyone is thinking alike, then no one is thinking.

From John Adams

Liberty cannot be preserved without general knowledge among the people.

From James Madison

The day will come when our Republic will be an impossibility because wealth will be concentrated in the hands of a few. When the day comes when the nation's wealth will be in the hands of a few, then we must rely upon the wisdom of the best elements in the country to readjust the laws of the nation to the changed conditions.

From Abraham Lincoln

You must remember that some things legally right are not morally right.
   It is a sin to be silent when it is your duty to protest.
   If anything links the human to the divine, it is the courage to stand by a principle when everybody else rejects it.
   However, it was pure serendipity through which he discovered thoughts and phrases that etched their way into his heart and memory. "There is so much to read, to learn, to think about," Will considered and felt overwhelmed. "What a gift Maw gave us by first teaching us to read. That gift is the key to opening all the doors we choose to unlock."

From Voltaire

It is difficult to free fools from the chains they revere.
   Common sense is not so common.

From Emerson

To be yourself in a world that is constantly trying to make you something else is the greatest accomplishment.

From Thoreau

To have made one person's life a little better, that is to succeed.
   The only people who ever get anyplace interesting are the people who get lost.

From Walt Whitman

The truth is simple. If it were complicated, everyone would understand it.
   Re-examine all that you have been told; dismiss that which insults your soul.

From Dickens

It was the best of times. It was the worst of times. It was the age of wisdom. It was the age of foolishness. It was the epoch of belief. It was the epoch of incredulity. It was the season of light. It was the season of darkness. It was the spring of hope. It was the winter of despair.

Will reread Mr. Dickens' words several times and thought, *"The writer lived in a different city on a different continent, but he describes what we are experiencing right here and now. Maybe that is the way things always are, but those of us with a voice need to work to make it no longer true."*

Chapter Thirty-six

ELECTIONS 1880

After Sunday morning service, Will and Lenora stepped out of the church and saw John Hall and his wife waving. Smiling and waving back, they approached their friends.

"Good morning, Senator and Mrs. Presley. Have you got a minute to chat?" Hall inquired.

"Of course we do, John. We always have time for you and Marian," Will smiled broadly.

"Jim is coming to our house this afternoon after dinner to talk politics. I'd like to have you join us, and Mrs. Presley is welcome to participate too. What I want to discuss will affect your entire family. Harry and Alice might be interested, also. Bring them if they are available," John smiled conspiringly.

"Now you've piqued my interest, John," Will agreed,

"Mine too," Lenora answered, "I'll talk to Mama and Daddy just as soon as we arrive home. I feel certain Daddy will want to hear what you have in mind."

Pete and Lillian agreed to sit with the children. The Presleys and the Parkers drove to Hall Manor for a meeting to discuss some political maneuvers.

John opened the door before they could knock and ushered them into the parlor.

When everyone, including Jim Hall and his wife Susan, was seated, John spoke. "Have any of you ever attended a national convention to select Presidential candidates?"

Looking around at the group, every one of them shook their head, and John continued. "The Republican National Convention is convening in Chicago on June 2. Because I am a member of the Virginia Republican Board of Governors, I can choose a few delegates to the Convention.

"We can ride a Pullman car for the overnight trip and stay in a four-star hotel. The Tremont, the Palmer House, the Sherman, or the Grand Pacific were all rebuilt after '71 when they had the Great Fire.

"All have elevators, fine dining, and great views of the city. The Tremont is where Lincoln received the Republican nomination in 1860. He made a speech from its balcony to crowds of people on the street below.

"The Interstate Exposition Center will be the meeting site, but the Tremont will be the headquarters hotel, and it's my preference. But, if you have other ideas, I'm open to suggestions.

"In addition to selecting our nominee for the race in November, we can have input into the party platform. Tariffs will be a big issue. Chinese immigration, monopolies, and Women's Suffrage are other major topics."

"Now you have my attention, John," Will smiled. "Jim, Jeremiah Jones, Bob Weaver, Carroll Hoagland, and I were discussing monopolies and tariffs recently. Is it possible to get these other people I mentioned to be appointed as delegates?"

"Mr. Hall," Lenora spoke. "I have advocated for Women's Suffrage for many years. Could I be allowed to speak to the committee?"

"The answers are yes and yes. If we want to make changes for the better, folks who are ardent in supporting causes must be heard.

"These men you mentioned, are they members of Congress?"

"Yes, they are, Dad," Jim Hall answered. "And every one of them is a friend of mine. It will be a joy to have them joining us at the Convention."

Chicago, June 2, 1880

When Will and Lenora checked into the *Tremont*, they saw their group standing off to the side. "Where's Jeremiah?" he asked of no one in particular.

Jim Hall dropped his head and cursed under his breath. "They did not receive a reservation for him – so they said. But I made all the reservations at the same time. Jeremiah was referred to a small hotel across the street. They did not state it straight out, but it is obvious they don't want blacks to stay here."

"Isn't there anything we can do about this discrimination? Jim, you're the lawyer," Will asked angrily.

"I'm afraid not, Presley. A private business can choose its customers."

When Jeremiah and Janie rejoined the group, Janie was furious. "That place they sent us to is just a flop-house. They had half-dressed women sitting all around the lobby."

"They think we negroes don't belong in a four-star hotel with decent folks, I assume," Jeremiah frowned.

John Hall spoke to his group when they had gathered in the Convention Hall. "I apologize for your ill-treatment Jones. I had no idea we had these prejudiced people running this hotel. We'll make the best of a bad situation."

He continued, "Of the 14 men in contention for the Republican nomination, the three strongest leading candidates are Ulysses S. Grant, James G. Blaine, and John Sherman. Grant has already served two terms as President from '69 to '77 and is seeking an unprecedented third term in office.

"His backers are the *Stalwart* faction of the Republican Party, which supports political machines and patronage.

"Blaine is a senator and former representative from Maine. His backers call themselves the Half-Breed faction of the party because they are more moderate.

"Sherman, the brother of Civil War General William Tecumseh Sherman, is presently serving as Secretary of the Treasury under President Rutherford B. Hayes. He is a former senator from Ohio and is backed by delegates who do not support the Stalwarts or Half-Breeds."

"We will hear nominations almost every night until June 7th, when we choose the nominee. With 14 men in contention, it will be a long tiresome process. But, in the meantime, we can be in committee meetings on the Party's platform and make our views known.

"Also, for Will and Jim, we'll set up adjoining hospitality suites and invite our state legislators to join us for cocktails and *hors d'oeuvres*."

"What is that?" Jeremiah asked.

"Yeah, I was wondering, too, John," Will grinned.

"It's just a fancy name for snacks to nibble on while they are sipping our great Virginia bourbon and wine.

"We will ask them to vote for another six-year term for Will in the Senate and vote for Jim when J.Harold Walker retires in '82."

On June 8th, on the first ballot, Sherman received 93 votes. Grant had 304, and Blaine had 285. With 379 votes required to win the nomination, none of the candidates was close to victory, and the balloting continued.

James Garfield

After the thirty-fifth ballot, Blaine and Sherman switched their support to a new dark horse candidate, James Garfield – a retired Union Army General and a sitting member of the United States House of Representatives from Ohio. Garfield won the nomination on the following vote by receiving 399 votes, 93 higher than Grant's total. Garfield's Ohio delegation chose Chester A. Arthur, a Stalwart, as his vice-presidential running mate. Arthur won the nomination by capturing 468 votes, and the longest-ever Republican National Convention was subsequently adjourned. The Garfield–Arthur Republican ticket defeated Democrats Scott Hancock and William Hayden English in the close 1880 presidential election.

November 1880

Awaiting the arrival of his friend, Jim Hall, Will meditated on the events of his first six-year term as a Senator from Virginia. This first term had been a time of learning for him. He found many things about politics rewarding and satisfying, but others not so much.

Jim Hall would accompany him to Richmond to attend a session of the State Legislature which would choose a Senator for the next six-year term. With the help of their friend Rufus Brown, Will would seek another term as Senator.

Although he had met many of them at the convention, he found it was not easy and a bit frightening to solicit votes from the State Legislators. The United States Constitution designated that Senators were not chosen by direct election of the voters of Virginia. The elected State officials chose United States Senators. It was far easier for him to make speeches to large groups of people than ask an individual to vote for him.

Hall, on the other hand, relished the one-on-one interaction with legislators. His background in a Yale fraternity served him well as a politician.

Rufus Brown, a former slave, had a loyal following among the State legislators. Unfortunately, his lack of name recognition and campaign donors hampered his bid for the House of Representatives from his district. Not deterred by his lack of success, he vowed to run again in '82.

"Senator Presley has been a good Senator for the people of Virginia – all the people, black and white. He gets my vote for the appointment, and I hope yours too," Brown shared with his friends. "Maybe in '82, I'll join him in D.C."

J. Harold Walker, the senior Senator, still had two years left on his fourth six-year term. Although not widely known, Walker had heart problems and told some close associates that this would be his last term.

Speaking on behalf of Will to several legislators, Hall said, "I would be thrilled to serve the people of Virginia as their junior Senator when Walker retires. Presley and I have worked very closely since our days at the Constitutional Convention in '68. We will be a good team in the United States Senate. Let's reappoint Presley, and then I'll join him next term."

Republicans picked up several seats in the House, taking a majority of the chamber for the first time since the 1874 elections.

In the Senate, Republicans made small gains at the expense of the Democrats. Still, neither party had a majority due to an independent Senator and a Readjuster Senator. The two parties ultimately agreed to share power.

Chapter Thirty-seven

ARTHUR IS PRESIDENT

Monday, January 2, 1882

Will smiled and spoke to his office assistant, "Happy new year, Dennis. Did you have a big celebration at your house?"

"Yes, Sir, we did. My mom cooked a big meal of beans and cabbage and cornbread. Dad has made that menu a traditional one every year. He says it brings good luck and prosperity."

"I heard that back home in North Carolina when I was a boy. Traditions are comforting and soothing. At the beginning of a new year, there are always issues that make us stressed."

"Senator, I have a message for you from Congressman Hall. It was delivered about ten minutes ago." He handed the note to Will.

"Thank you, Dennis." Will was polite and respectful.

The message read: Can you meet my father and me in the Senate dining room for lunch? He's at the Capitol today meeting with some Virginia politicians.

"Dennis, send a note to Representative Hall telling him I will be in the dining room at noon."

Turning the corner leading to the dining room, Will saw John and Jim waiting at the entrance. "It's a pleasure to see you today, John. What is so important to lure you to the Capitol?"

"I'm here today on behalf of the Republican National Committee. We are putting together a slate of candidates for the election this Fall. My effort is a fundraising mission for some Senatorial and Congressional candidates. Also, I want to lobby for some issues important to our party and the country."

"Let's go in and find a seat so we can talk privately," Jim suggested.

As soon as they were seated, John asked, "Senator, how serious are you about electing Congressmen from Virginia who will be helpful to our agenda?"

"Well, yes, John, I want to have colleagues who will vote with us. Why do you ask?"

"It's going to be necessary to aid these men in their campaigns. Congress members must run every two years, and that means fundraising. Are you in a position to donate to some candidates from Virginia?"

"Yes, of course, I am. My campaign fund has increased since I became a Senator. Somebody told me people like to support a winner.

"I have contributed to State Legislators because they have a more difficult time raising funds. And they are the ones who choose Senators," he grinned. "But it is definitely to our advantage to have a majority in Congress.

"Jim and I have a friend named Rufus Brown serving in the State Legislature, and he served in the Constitutional Convention back in '68. I would like to see him elected to the House. He has been a friend and ally to us from the beginning when we first met him," Will told John.

Jim added, "And he has supported Presley in his appointment to the Senate, Dad. We need him in the House. When J. Harold Walker retires this year, Rufus will support me for that position."

"Alright then, let's get him elected," John smiled.

"The other thing I want to mention to you is that President Arthur has a schedule for his term, which he considers essential.

"Workers in the western states are loudly complaining about Chinese laborers who work for low wages. They proclaim that the Chinese should be prohibited from emigrating to the United States. The President calls it the Chinese Exclusion Act.

"I saw a draft of this legislation last week," Jim Hall offered. "It proposes to forbid the entry of all Chinese workers, both skilled and non-skilled—especially miners or those in mining support jobs.

"Many of these Chinese immigrants are male, but few are female. That's not a formula for peace and contentment."

"Do you mean that just because of their national origin, they want to discriminate against them?" Will exclaimed.

"I cannot endorse that kind of bias against any ethnic group. I don't know much about the Chinese, but I know they are human and should be rightly treated.

"My father and my mother were both immigrants to this country. If they had been banned, I would not be here today.

"This proposal is astonishing to me because most of these complainers are recent immigrants themselves. It seems to me to be selfish, greedy, and hypocritical.

"I must oppose the President on this one," Will said adamantly.

(Congress passed the Chinese Exclusion Act on May 6, 1882.)

John added, "Also, Arthur is interested in the Pendleton Civil Service Reform Act."

"Dad, could you explain that more fully so that the Senator and I can understand what is involved in this proposal?" Jim asked.

"Surely I can. As you both know, the patronage system has been used by every administration since Andrew Jackson. Both Democrats and Republicans have taken advantage of patronage.

"President Andrew Jackson used the phrase coined by Senator William Marcy of New York to the victor belongs the spoils. Friends and allies of the party in power are given well-paying federal jobs but are expected to return the favor by donating campaign funds to the party. Also, they are encouraged to influence their friends and neighbors to do likewise.

"For many years, the primary source of funding for campaigns has come from federal employees. That is why we are seeking alternate sources. Many businesses and business owners are financially able to assist in financing candidates for public office, and the party wants to be part of that effort.

"President Hayes disliked the patronage system and attempted unsuccessfully to pass bills to outlaw it. Senator George Pendleton from Ohio has again proposed a Civil Service Act requiring about ten percent of federal employees to be hired based on testing and merit rather than patronage. Pendleton's proposal would also prohibit an employee from being fired for political reasons."

Hall continued, "Presley, you and Harry Parker, by all accounts, have been highly successful with the expansion of Parker Farm Produce and Cannery. Are you interested in participating in this effort?"

"Yes, John, we have done very well, and you readily consented to help us with the launch of that expansion. I will not give you a definite yes without talking to Harry, but I am receptive to the idea.

"We have been able to add twenty men in the garden and orchards, effectively doubling our workforce. In the Cannery, we started with four people and now employ ten women. Several of these women are widows and single mothers who need an income source.

"We consider ourselves blessed by the Almighty and are happy to contribute to assist in overcoming the recession of '73.

"Lenora and I have devoted our careers to helping the downtrodden and oppressed in our effort to follow the teachings of Jesus.

"I do like the idea that government employees can have some security in their jobs and not be susceptible to the vagaries of an election. Do you think this Pendleton Act has a chance to be passed? Will President Arthur sign it if it passes?"

"It is my opinion that the bill will pass, but we need your support in the Senate and yours, Jim, in the House. This current bill will cover one-half of postal employees and three-fourths of Customs Service employees," John stated.

"I know that President Arthur is a Stalwart Republican and a strong believer in patronage. I would be a bit surprised if he signs it," Will said.

"There is a lot of support for Civil Service Reform in this country – especially among Democrats, who now control the Congress. The President wants to sign this bill."

The 47th Congress, on January 16, 1883, passed the bill with a majority of 38-5 in the Senate and 155-47 in the House. As the year progressed, Arthur added more federal workers to the Civil Service roster.

Jim Hall received the Senate appointment vacated by Walker. Even though Democrats gained a majority in the House, Rufus Brown was elected as the Congressman from his district.

Chapter Thirty-eight

MOURNING FOR A MENTOR

On March 29, 1882, Monday morning began as most workweeks in the Senate offices but was soon interrupted with an urgent message for Senator Presley.

Dennis displayed an unusually serious grimace as he rushed into Will's office. "Sorry to barge in, Senator, but I knew you would want to get this wire as soon as possible. It's from your sister, Maggie."

"Don't worry, Dennis, just let me have it," Will said, grabbing the wire from his assistant's trembling hands.

> Maggie wrote.
> We need you here, Will. Preacher Henderson had a stroke Saturday night, and he is in a bad way. Doug has been with him almost constantly and is not very optimistic about a recovery. Maw is beside herself. Please make arrangements to come to Graham as soon as possible.

"I'm going home, Dennis," Will said, shaking a little as he put on his overcoat. "I will be taking a trip and will update you on my return date as soon as I have more information. In the meantime, tell anyone who asks that I was called away on a family emergency."

"Yes, Senator, I will take care of everything. Please let me know if I can be of any assistance."

The drive from the Capitol to the Parker Farm seemed much longer than usual as Will's mind raced to the worst possible scenario. "I have to see John again. Since Paw died, Pastor John Henderson has been my mentor, my confidant, and my stepfather. He has guided me through unpopular decisions, listened to my agonized confessions of guilt, and has always encouraged me to believe I have something of value to contribute to the world."

Rushing through the front door, Will called out to Lenora but found the house empty, and he realized she was probably still overseeing the cannery employees. Running down to the work areas near the produce shed, he yelled out, "Lenora, I need to talk with you."

Lenora dropped what she was doing and walked rapidly toward her husband. "What's wrong, Will. Why are you back home so soon?"

"Come with me to the Parker house. I don't have a lot of time to make plans, so everyone should hear this at the same time."

"Now I am apprehensive," she said, taking Will's hand and trying to keep up with him as he almost ran toward her parent's house.

"Alice, get Harry. We need to talk," Will almost shouted, pushing open the front door of the Parker house.

"Sit down, children. I'll get him," Alice said. "It must be important for my always polite son-in-law to barge in unannounced," she thought.

Gathered around the fireplace, they waited as Will shared the bad news and laid out his intentions.

"I need to make a trip to Graham and would like Lenora to accompany me. I need to talk with John and provide some support for Maw. We will stay until we know what is happening. During our absence, I need to feel comfortable that all the Farm and the Cannery operations continue on schedule. I need your help," Will said, bowing his head into his hands.

"Don't worry, Son. I can supervise the activities. Pete and Bessie both know what needs to be done, and I will check in with them several times each day," Harry promised.

Alice added, "Between Lillian and me, we can take care of the children and the house. Meals will be here, and we will make sure they have clean clothes and do their homework. Just get yourselves together, leave as soon as you can, and don"t worry about the home front."

"Give Sally and John our love and keep us updated as much as you can," Harry asked.

"Thank you so much," Will said, hugging his in-laws.

Will and Lenora packed their bags, conferred with Pete and Lillian, and spent some after-school time with the boys and Mimi before preparing the carriage for the ride to the train depot in Washington.

They tried to explain John's condition to their children without being too pessimistic. "Why can't we go see Grandma Sally?" Mimi asked, pulling at her Daddy's pant leg.

"Grandma Sally is very busy taking care of Preacher John right now, but I'm sure she would love to see you another time," Lenora answered.

"We are counting on all three of you to be helpful to Pete, Lillian, Grandpa Harry, and Grandma Alice while we are gone. Show them how grown-up you are," Will added as he brushed his hands across the three young heads.

Will had reserved two train tickets and had wired ahead to rent a carriage in Asheville. Lenora hurriedly packed for both of them while fending off complaints and pleas from the boys and Mimi.

Leaving on the last train out of Washington, D.C. that afternoon, the Presleys would be sleeping overnight in coach with an expected midday arrival in Asheville, NC. Another five hours by carriage would get them to Graham on Tuesday afternoon. "This will be a long and tiring trip, Lenora," Will said. "But still much shorter than the one we made on our trip to Memphis back in '65."

Lenora laughed at his attempt to be positive. "Yes, with all the improvements in the speed of trains, I'm expecting to run down to Asheville for a short shopping trip one of these days." Will flashed his crooked Presley grin and was glad for the temporary break to lighten the stress.

Will's napping was periodically interrupted by nightmare reminders that persisted after twenty years. "I need to talk with John. Please don't let us be too late," he silently prayed.

Exhausted yet glad to set foot on his native ground, Will met his sister, Maggie, at the front door of the parsonage.

"Maw won't leave John's side," Maggie wept as she embraced her big brother.

"Is the good Dr. Mahan available?" Will asked.

"Yes, I'll ask him to talk with you in the parlor. Come on inside. Lenora, I'm so glad you came with Will."

"What can I do to be of help, Maggie? When was the last time any of you ate?" Lenora asked, hugging her sister-in-law.

Maggie walked to John's bedroom and asked her husband to go into the parlor and bring Will up to date on John's condition. Then she took Lenora into the kitchen, where the two women began searching the larder for something they could prepare for supper.

Dr. Doug Mahan sat with Will and explained that Pastor Henderson's condition did not show much promise. The stroke had left him paralyzed on his right side, and he could not feed himself or even move about without help.

"Your Maw cannot handle him by herself. Maggie has been staying with them, and I come in and out daily; however, we may need to move both of them to our house, where we have plenty of room and regular support on staff. Miss Sally doesn't want to move. She is holding out hope of a complete recovery, although I have tried to explain the unlikelihood of that happening."

"Thank you for being honest with me, Doug, and thank you for all that you do for John and Maw. It is times like these that I feel so helpless being so far away."

"Try not to worry, Will. You can feel confident that Maggie and I will be here for your mother despite what the future holds. If John does not survive, Sally will have a place with us."

"Doug, do you think you can talk Maw into letting me have a few moments alone with John?" Will asked pleadingly.

"I will certainly give it a try, but she will want to have some time with you first. I'll tell her I need to examine John and ask her to come in here with you for a while."

Sally's eyes were swollen from sleep deprivation and weeping. "Oh, Will!" she cried as she threw her arms around her third-born and sobbed into his chest.

When she regained the ability to speak, Sally sat next to Will and thanked him for coming to be with her. She told him, "I know that it was hard for you to leave your job, the farm, and the children to make this long trip, Will, but it means the world to me. John will be so pleased that you are here."

"Maw, could you allow me to have a little time with John? He has been a significant influence in my life, especially after we lost Paw."

"Of course, Son, but he may not be able to talk very much."

The sight of the strong figure of authority who had shared so much advice and wisdom through the years now lying shrunken and helpless sent a shock through Will's senses and a dagger through his heart.

Pulling a chair close to John's left side, Will leaned in and said, "Afternoon, Pastor."

John Henderson opened his eyes and mumbled something that sounded like, "Will?"

"Yes, Sir, it's me, the Prodigal Son."

Henderson attempted a smile, but the paralysis warped it into a one-sided sneer. He moved his left hand a few inches toward Will, who grasped it warmly.

"Don't struggle to talk, John. Save your energy for the recovery process. I am asking a favor, one I probably don't have the right to ask, but you are the only person I trust to hear what I am about to say."

John patted Will's hand in agreement and managed to mouth, "Go on."

"John, you have been my Pastor, my guide, my friend most of my life. You have allowed me to share some of the nightmares and guilt that I bear from my time in the war; however, there are still some things I have never confessed to you or anyone else."

John was listening and intermittingly squeezed Will's hand with all of the remaining strength he could muster.

"Since those horrible days, it has been my central ambition to somehow atone for my actions through work in the public arena. It may be impossible to balance the scales, but I need someone I trust to know the heinous crime that lays heavy on my heart. I don't expect you to offer me absolution. I only want you to listen and let me know you understand."

Will was sweating, and he could not raise his head to look into the eyes of John Henderson. He stumbled for the words to complete his confession. "John, it's about that day at Gettysburg. I told you that my unit was directly opposite the field from a unit containing boys from Graham. I told you how sick I felt when I saw boys wearing grey caps lying in the mud. I told you I did not want the medals they forced on me. I just wanted to run away from it all. What I did not tell you has to do with some of those fallen soldiers from Graham."

As Will bowed his head even lower, he felt Henderson's hand pulling him closer. As he leaned in to understand the weak garbled voice, he heard John say, "I know, Son. I know."

Wiping his wet eyes, Will stared at John. "You know?"

"Yes, Son. It was not your fault," although voiced haltingly. It was clear to Will. "You are a fine man, Will."

The two men sat silently for several minutes, after which Will said, "Thank you, John." Nothing else needed to be said. They understood one another.

After supper, Will and Lenora sat in the parlor with Maggie and Sally catching up with events in both families. Doug examined John again before he and Maggie returned home for the night.

Sally felt comfortable enough to get some sleep while Lenora and Will took turns checking on John.

Wednesday was primarily uneventful as Maggie, Lenora, and Will took turns sitting with John. Dr. Doug examined John mid-morning and noticed no change in his condition. John did make a few attempts to sit up and eat but was easily fatigued.

At 2:00 in the afternoon, Sally's scream was heard throughout the house. Everyone ran to John's room to find Sally leaning over the bed, trying to wake him.

"What happened?" asked Maggie.

"He seemed to be fine when all of a sudden, he grabbed his chest with his left hand and started gasping for breath," Sally whimpered.

Lenora ran across the town square to Doug's office and told him to come quickly.

Doug raced to the parsonage and checked all vital signs confirming that Pastor John Henderson had passed away. It was most likely from a heart attack and complications of the stroke.

The funeral was set for Friday morning at the Graham First Methodist Church. Attendance was at an overflow level.

Matthew Hale, an interim pastor, officiated. Eulogists included Doug Mahan's father, Johathan, the current Mayor of Graham, Frank Graham, and several long-time friends.

Dressed in black, Sally sat quietly in the first pew on the right between Maggie and Will. Her hands remained folded in her lap. Will remembered her sitting in that exact position next to his father's coffin. "She loved and lost two of the finest men I have ever known," Will thought. "Blessings and curses seem to be an everlasting part of life."

All the other members of the Presley family from Roaring Fork and Graham sat in the next pew.

Pastor John Wesley Henderson was laid to rest on April 2, 1882, behind the church he had served for over fifty years.

The ladies of Graham outdid themselves, providing a sumptuous meal following the services. Condolences were abundant and well appreciated but tiring.

Will and Lenora spent Friday evening with Sally, Maggie, and Doug. Sally brought Will up to date on his other siblings and nieces and nephews. He was surprised to learn that Buck's boy, Jedediah, who had turned twenty-five in March, was no longer living at the farm.

"Jed just up and left home just like you, Will. Nobody knows where he went. His Mama worries about him every day but doesn't know where to look.

Saturday morning, Will and Lenora loaded their rented buggy and started the trip back to Asheville. There would be another overnight train ride before they were home again.

Chapter Thirty-nine

TARIFF ACT OF 1883

Exiting the building at Falls Church, Episcopal, Will spoke to John Hall. "I want to talk with you about the tariff situation. Can you come by my office at the Capitol in the morning?"

"Sure, Senator, what time should I arrive?"

"Come before lunch. Then I'll treat you to lunch," Will smiled.

Arriving at 10:00 am. John Hall knocked on the inner-office door, and Will quickly opened it. "Come in, John. I'm glad you could make it today. Please have a seat and get comfortable. This could take a while."

"I appreciate the invitation. Senator. I always enjoy the time I spend talking with you. What's on your mind?"

"This ongoing debate about tariffs. The questions of what and how much to add has me in an uproar. We talked about this at the Republican convention in Chicago in '80. Our stance then was to phase out or reduce all tariffs, but we have regional differences. It seems the Northern states are for and Southern states are against them.

"Here in Virginia, we export many agricultural products and don't import much at all.

"The President is going to appoint a commission to study the issue. I want to be a part of that body. As a member of the Republican National Committee, can you get me an appointment to the commission?"

"Well, I can certainly recommend to the President that you be appointed, but I can't guarantee it. Is there anyone else you want to serve with?"

"Yeah, Senator Jim Hall, but I assume two Senators from the same state would not be chosen. Representative Bob Weaver from Richmond is very interested in this issue and has some strong opinions on it. Can you get him on?"

"That is another possibility. I'll add Bob to the list. Didn't he accompany us to the Convention in '80?"

"Yes, he did. He was the tall fellow with the dazzling white hair."

"I remember him," John smiled. "I'll see that these recommendations get to the President today."

Ten Days Later

"Good morning, Sir," Dennis, Will's office assistant, greeted him as he entered the outer door. "There's a memo here with the Presidential Seal on the outside. It's addressed to you."

"Thank you, Dennis," Will hurried into his office to read the memo.

> Dear Senator Presley, it has come to my attention that you are interested in serving on the commission to study the tariff situation. Consequently, I am appointing several government officials and a few business people.
> Since you are the highest-ranking person in government to be appointed, I want to ask you to serve as a ranking member. If you find this to be satisfactory, please send me a memo affirming your acceptance.
> Chester A, Arthur
> President of the United States of America

> Mr. President, I am pleased and honored to be asked to serve as a ranking member of the Tariff Study Commission. I gladly accept your appointment and will faithfully and diligently serve you and my country in this position.
> G. Wilhelm Presley
> Virginia Senator

> Dear Senator Presley,
> Thank you for accepting the appointment to the Tariff Review Commission. I have appointed twenty-one members to the group. Some are Republican, some Democrats, some from the North, some from the South - business and political men. The Commerce Secretary will chair the body and lead the discussion. He will report to me, and then we will proceed to implement the recommendations. The body will be assembled on May 1, 1882.

Chester A Arthur
President of the United States

The first meeting convened in a Congressional Room at the Capitol and proved to be contentious and extended.

Will spoke to Bob Weaver, "I'm not sure we'll ever reach any agreement on changes to the tariffs."

"Yeah, I know what you mean, Senator. These industrial northern states' representatives are holding the line on what the Robber Barons told us they wanted."

"Of course they are. The rich guys are in control, but we need to protect our tobacco and cotton exporters here in Virginia and throughout the South. These issues have not changed one iota.

"President Arthur is not enthusiastic about cutting tariffs, but he realizes that changes need to be made. Most of the present taxes on imports are in the range of thirty-five to forty percent. That raises the price of imported steel and fuel oil products, but it puts money into the treasury and provides bounties to the manufacturers, which adds to their bottom-line profits."

"What do you think about the proposal to put tariffs on fruits but not on vegetables?" Weaver inquired.

"Well, we grow apples, pears, strawberries, and grapes, but we also grow tomatoes. Some tomato importers say tomatoes are vegetables and not fruit, as some contend. I'll vote for the tariffs on fruit and hope that tomatoes will be classified as a fruit."

The Tariff Act of 1883 was passed on March 3, 1883, with only minimal changes. Some items were increased, and some were reduced, but the total taxes were reduced by only 1.4%. Critics called it the Mongrel Tariff Act of 1883.

(Later, the Supreme Court would rule that tomatoes should be classified as vegetables and not subject to the tariff on fruits.)

Chapter Forty

AMERICAN FEDERATION OF LABOR

As they sat down at the dinner table, Pete asked Will, "Can we talk business at the table, or should I wait until after dinner?"

"You have piqued my interest, Pete," Lenora smiled. "What do you have on your mind? Maybe Lil and I should hear it since we both work at the Cannery."

Will grinned, "There's no way to avoid it now, Pete. Spit it out."

"One of the new guys, Freddie Casteel, was talking about a labor union that asked Congress for a law calling for an eight-hour workday. I never heard anything about that when I was in Roaring Fork. We worked until it got dark and we couldn't see any more. Then we quit for the day."

"Yes, that was the National Labor Union. It was in 1866, just before Will and I left Memphis," Lenora related. "But Congress was struggling with the Reconstruction Act of 1867 and not interested in labor laws.

" They did pass a law to that effect in California in 1868, but not a national law."

"Why did this come up now, Pete? Are our employees complaining?" Will worried.

"No, not really. I asked some of the older guys to stay and finish work on a corn patch before going home. Casteel said he had worked in California, and they got paid extra for work over eight hours."

"Don't we pay our people extra for extra work, Pete?" Lenora asked.

"Yeah, we do, and nobody has ever complained about working overtime, but I don't want no trouble."

"There is a strong labor movement now in the big-city factories. A group calling itself The Noble Order of Knights of Labor has organized several different crafts and trades and is asking for eight-hour workdays and more pay for workers. Maybe they need unions there, but we are fair with our people and want them to be happy and prosperous as we are," Will declared.

"We always turn in extra hours our ladies in the Cannery work, don't we, Len?" Lillian asked.

"Yes, we do, and Papa always pays them more," Lenora stated emphatically.

"I don't believe labor unions are an issue with us here on Parker's Farm, but it is becoming an issue with the big industrialists," Will related. "When Irish workers demand more pay, the big bosses replace them with Chinese or Blacks and pay them lower wages. The Captains of Industry control the labor market.

"Then, too, many unions are primarily for white, protestant, males, and the minority groups are excluded from the unions. It seems that there is bias and bigotry even there among the working-class people.

"The one exception to this is the Knights of Labor group. They include minorities and women, and children. These folks are the ones who are abused most by the big bosses."

"Will, who is this group which calls itself the American Federation of Labor?" Lenora questioned. "I read about them in an article in the Washington newspaper last week."

Will replied, " That's the group formed by Samuel Gompers. His organization combines several associations of workers into one group. They believe that a larger body of folks can have more clout with the big bosses.

"Steelworkers, railroad people, miners, oil drilling and refineries, textile workers, and even farm laborers are uniting for collective bargaining with the corporations."

"What does collective bargaining mean?" Lillian wrinkled her brow.

"It means that they negotiate as a group with the companies who pay them. They ask for higher wages, eight-hour workdays, break time to rest and eat lunch or dinner. And the companies are beginning to respond to these desires of the working folks.

"This American Federation of Labor or the AFL as they call themselves has combined the different bodies of laborers into one group, and they're gaining concessions for all of them at once. It's an excellent idea for those people who by themselves don't have much leverage to entice their employers to compensate them better, but there is strength in more significant numbers.

"Me and Pete ain't never worked for a big company, so I cain't understand why they have to have unions speaking to the company for them.

Down at Roaring Fork, Billy Bob could always talk to Mr. Graham and say what we needed. Paw J.W., did that too. Here at Parker's Farm, we can talk to you or Mr. Parker," Lillian added.

Lenora joined in the conversation, " When there are two or three thousand workers, it's not that easy, Lil. Also, these Robber Barons who own big companies insist that they have the right to set working hours and wages to maximize profits. Working folks cannot question their decisions. Employees are a commodity to be used at the discretion of the company.

"Many laborers are required to work twelve-hour days and work six or seven days per week. Children and women are paid lower wages and told by the boss that they are not the primary wage earner in the family.

"According to the Washington newspaper, some Europeans advocate Socialism. This system, where the government owns the businesses, allows the government to regulate wages, workday hours, and medical expense payments.

"Our system, Free Enterprise, retains those rights for business owners. But some components of the Socialist system could help us bridge the wealth gap that is so prevalent today. Specific rules and regulations applied to businesses by federal law would not allow multi-millionaires to exploit folks the way they are doing now."

Will added, "The Great Railroad Strike happened because there were no unions to negotiate with the Barons. Many people were murdered, and much property was destroyed. Federal and State troops quelled the strikers and sided with the corporations.

"Unions attempt to bridge the gap between management and labor, thereby eliminating the need to strike. Strikes and violence have been averted simply by talking things out by the two parties.

"We in Congress are passing laws to encourage cooperation among the opposing factions. Management is slowly discovering the advantages of keeping a satisfied workforce. Some are offering retirement plans and medical expense plans for their people.

"Charles Graham of Roaring Fork was way ahead of his time in recognizing the enlightened self-interest of a satisfied group of employees.

"Some smaller groups of skilled workers are maintaining their independence from the AFL. Silversmiths, goldsmiths, blacksmiths, bakers, tailors, and Pullman Car employees have their groups of members, but their goals are the same as the big organizations.

"Unions have had an impact on our economy and working conditions, but much remains to be done," Will concluded.

Chapter Forty-one

SUFFER THE LITTLE CHILDREN

"Will, I cannot believe what I have been reading and hearing about young children working in factories in our cities," Lenora said with an urgency in her voice. "Something has to be done about this outrage."

"Slow down, Lenora. At least let me take off my coat before you give me another assignment," Will replied with a smile, hoping to get one in return.

Child Labor in Factories

"This is serious, Will. I was unaware that children as young as five years old were forced to work long hours in often dangerous conditions. Their education stops so that they can add a small amount of income to their struggling families."

"Children have always helped their families by doing whatever work they were capable of doing, Lenora. I started working in the garden and tobacco patch when I was even younger than five.

"We Presley children were fortunate to have a mother who began teaching us at home as soon as we could sit in a chair. She managed to fit in our learning around all the chores we had to do each day. Once we had mastered the basics of reading and writing, she continued to encourage our curiosity.

"Farming would not be possible without all family members sharing in the work. Hard work is not a bad thing."

"Working on a farm under the supervision of your parents is very different from crawling through underground tunnels while breathing in coal dust or climbing on moving machinery with no safety precautions. I don't think you understand, Will."

"Oh, but I do understand, Lenora. Life was dramatically changed when people who had known nothing but farming moved to the cities.

"The destruction left behind after the war eliminated many opportunities for low-income families to survive. Even those owning small parcels of land struggled to feed their families. Those without any land of their own soon found it impossible.

"The growing industry in more northern cities became a magnet for the desperate. There were plenty of jobs, even though most paid very little. Affordable housing was usually cramped and in disrepair. People were forced to double up in small quarters. There was no space or opportunities for children to roam, play, or even help with the chores. It became necessary to send all family members out into the workforce at whatever small wage they could earn.

"Owners and managers of mines and factories were happy to use the additional help of these young people and pay them the bare minimum. Their small size was a significant advantage in the mining operations. Their tiny, nimble fingers were welcomed in both textile and tool-making industries."

Lenora was now crying. "So once again, the people with money and power take advantage of those without either. Why do we allow this to continue, Will?"

"My sweet Lady," Will said, taking Lenora into his arms. "Your big heart and sense of fairness are just two of the many things I love about you.

"Will, are other people not interested in doing something about these horrible conditions? Surely I am not alone in feeling outraged about the treatment of our children," she posed as she wrung her hands and looked at her husband for support.

"No, Lenora, you are not alone. There have always been and will most likely always be people of goodwill who see injustice and try to do something about it. Such people often meet with harsh opposition and sometimes ridicule."

"Why would anyone be opposed to protecting children, Will?"

Will shook his head, trying to gather his thoughts before attempting a response to such an innocent question.

"It doesn't make sense to me either, sweetheart. I can only guess. It is probably a combination of ignorance and self-interest."

Lenora looked puzzled and was waiting for elaboration.

"Ignorance can be attributed to lack of exposure or personal choice. People who have only been exposed to sheltered and protected atmospheres have little knowledge of how others live and are ignorant of their environment. People who are exposed to more diverse conditions sometimes choose to remain ignorant because they perceive a personal social or economic benefit from what we see as injustice."

"I feel like screaming," Lenora said.

"It might give you some hope to know that child welfare organizations are working toward legislation that would protect children from harsh and dangerous conditions.

"England had a head start in the area of labor legislation, especially in factories where they made some improvements in the treatment of apprentices.

"Here in America, the New England states began addressing some labor regulations at a later date. I read that Massachusetts was the first to recognize the necessity of regulating factory labor. They passed a law in 1866 stipulating that no child under ten should be employed in a manufacturing establishment. No child between ten and fourteen should be engaged unless he had attended some public or private school at least six months during any year of employment. No child under the age of fourteen should be allowed to work more than eight hours in one day. These restrictions carried fines to any employer, parent, or guardian found in violation of the law."

"Well, that sounds like a good start but only in one state. What about all the rest of us?" Lenora asked.

"One step forward and two steps back," Will responded.

"The Massachusetts law was repealed the same year it was passed.

Will reminded Lenora that it should not be news that the noblest efforts can be easily reversed.

"Remember what happened after the war, Lenora. We were so eager to put things right during Reconstruction. When Lincoln was assassinated, the plan was quickly dropped, and political compromises were made, which affect us to this day."

"What this country needs is some women in charge for a change. We are used to getting things done with few resources and very little help from anyone."

Will chuckled and hugged his beloved wife.

Chapter Forty-two

THE SALVATION ARMY

"Good morning, Alice, and you too, Lenora." Marian Hall greeted them as they entered the Falls Church Parish Hall on Saturday morning.

"Good morning to you, Marian," Lenora smiled, and Alice nodded.

"It looks like we have a larger than usual crowd today," Alice noted.

Poverty

"Yes, we do," Marian responded. "There's been another round of wage cuts down at the Potomac river docks. The roustabouts who load and unload the supply ships and the teamsters who drive the wagons to deliver the products to warehouses had their pay cut again this week. Big city factories have reduced pay for employees, and many of them have been replaced by folks willing to work for less. Any job is better than no job," I've heard them say.

"But that creates a need for more food supplements for working people trying to feed their families. What did you bring us today?"

Lenora frowned and answered, "The usual baskets of fruit and vegetables and canned goods we bring every week, but maybe we need more."

Marian nodded and said, "Yes, we do need more. Can you help us?"

Alice replied, "Of course we can. Lenora, why don't you drive back to the farm and get another load. Pete and some of his men are there filling baskets for Monday morning sales. Ask them to fill the wagon with an identical load to the one these men are unloading right now. I'll stay here and help Marian dispense the food we have here already."

"Alright, since it's only a mile back to the farm, I should be back in less than an hour." Lenora was concerned.

She hurried back to the farm.

"It seems that even though the Great Recession is officially over, working folks continue to struggle to survive," Alice lamented. "Why is that the case, Marian?"

"It's simply a fact of life that the few people who have plenty of everything don't worry about those who have practically nothing," Marian retorted.

"Of course, there are exceptions to that. We are doing as much as one church parish can, but churches can't care for all the needs.

Wealth

"These Robber Barons are accumulating unbelievable amounts of wealth, while the people who work for them are barely able to survive. I heard John say the other day that William Vanderbilt inherited Commodore Vanderbilt's estate. The Commodore was his father, and the estate amounted to one hundred million dollars while the railroad and steamship laborers who work for him earn about three hundred dollars per year. Yet he cut wages to that level because some immigrants were wanting jobs and offered to work for less."

"When we started this effort here at the church, we were serving mostly mothers with small children whose husbands had died or just went off and left them alone. Now we are serving intact families who can't earn enough," Marian stomped her foot.

"Will was saying last week that the Salvation Army opened a ministry in the city downtown. Of course, they primarily focus their programs on street people, those who are homeless and unchurched," Lenora said.

Marian replied, "I've heard about them. Didn't they start in London ministering to drunkards, pickpockets, gamblers, and prostitutes?"

William and Catherine Booth

"Yes, William Booth, a Methodist minister, and his wife Catherine started preaching on the streets of London. The church leadership frowned upon their unorthodox approach to ministry, but they won many converts to Christianity," Alice revealed.

"Eliza Shirley, who had worked with the Booths in London, moved here in '79. Along with her parents, who had arrived ahead of her, she started a mission in Philadelphia. Now they have branches in New York and here in our city.

Alice continued, "I have read newspaper and magazine accounts of their work. Today, we have so many people in need but not enough programs to meet all the requirements."

Marian frowned and said, "It seems so strange that with all the wealth in this country, that we have so many people in need. Is there a solution?"

"One would think that the Barons with their great wealth would donate money and resources to help these needy people," Alice was indignant.

"And Will doesn't believe there is any sentiment in Congress to involve the government in assistance to poor people," she shook her head.

Lenora arrived back at the church, and the men unloaded her wagon once again. "I told Will and Pete how the need for food had increased so much lately, and they were sympathetic. We'll help all we can," she assured Alice and Marian.

On Monday morning, Will walked out to the Shed to check on Pete and his crew of men. "How's it going this morning, Pete?" Will greeted him.

"We're right on schedule, Senator. We'll have everything ready when our first customers arrive today. Why are you out this way so early?"

"I want to make an excursion into downtown today to check out the Salvation Army operation. I understand they are open and serving the needs of homeless folks and the city's neediest. Are you available to accompany me? Can your men do without you for a while this morning?"

"They can. Henry is here to take charge, and all our experienced workers are on the job."

"Good. I want to meet the managers of the D.C. mission and find out if they can use anything we can provide them. They offer meals to their patrons every day, so I'm confident they need vegetables and fruits.

"We might be able to make small financial contributions to help cover other necessary purchases," Will concluded.

They finally found the location of the Salvation Army mission and were somewhat taken aback. The building was decrepit and appeared to be barely usable. In slums, dirty, ragged, unshaven men were milling around the front door waiting for the call to enter and eat.

"Where can I find the minister in charge here, fellows?" Will inquired.

"That would be Cap'n Johnson, Sir," a man wearing an old Union army cap replied. "He's probably in the kitchen checking on dinner. They serve it every day at high noon.

"Say, ain't you Senator Presley, Sir?"

"I sure am, mister. Do I know you?"

"Probably not, but I was at Gettysburg when you was there. I was a Private 'n' you was a Sargent but got promoted. I knowed you was a hero there. Killed two Rebs just before they was about to overrun our lines. You ain't changed much 'cept fer a little gray around the temples. Maybe you put on a few pounds."

"I wasn't a hero. I just did my job but hated killin' people." Will dropped his head and winced at the memory. He still had nightmares where he dreamed of shooting his brothers. It happened on Cemetery Ridge on the outskirts of Gettysburg, Pennsylvania. Haunted by his memories, his only choices were to kill or be killed.

Unexpectedly, he was roused from his thoughts by a shout from the back of the room. "Hey, Uncle Will and Uncle Pete. I didn't 'spect ta see you'ns here. What y'all doin'?"

"Good gosh! Is that you, Jedediah?" Pete was astonished.

"Yeah, Uncle Pete, it's me."

"You're a long way from home, boy," Will marveled. "How long have you been in these parts?"

"I reckon it's been nigh onto a year now. I left home right after we put the 'backer in the barn. I told my Maw I'm tarred of workin' for Uncle Billy Bob, 'cause he don't do me right.

"Adam 'n' Thomas help him in the loggin' 'n' me 'n' Johnny, Junior worked the 'backer patch. I'm older than him 'n' worked 'backer a lot longer, but Uncle Bill Bob put him in charge 'cause he's Willadeen's boy.

"Uncle Will, I left home kinda like you done. Wuddn't shore what I wuz gonna do. I hopped on a freight train in Asheville and headed north. Hid out in a boxcar, 'n' talked to some other guys huntin' a job, too.

"When we got to the D.C. freight yard, three of us went in the foreman's office 'n' asked fer a job. He hired us all on the spot.

"They made me a switchman in the yard, 'n' things wuz goin' real good. Then one night, one of the boys got caught stealin' stuff outta a boxcar. They fired all three of us right then 'n' there.

"I tried ta tell 'em I didn't steal nothin', but they wouldn't listen ta me. Then I couldn't find no other job. Nobody would hire me 'cause they said I wuz a thief.

"I didn't have no money to pay the boardin' house where I wuz stayin', so the only thing I could do wuz live on the streets.

"I wuz real glad when the Salvation Army opened up. I already knowed most of the songs they sung. I reckoned they wuz Methodists like me. I told Cap'n Johnson - he runs this place - that I wuz a Methodist back home 'n' he lets me do some jobs 'round here. I clean tables 'n' warsh dishes. I got a bed ever night."

"We came here to talk to the Captain. I believe Johnson is his name," Will informed Jed.

"Yep, Ross Johnson is his name. Come on 'n' I'll introduce y'all to him," Jed offered.

"Cap'n Johnson, I want you to meet my two uncles from Roarin' Fork farm. They both live up here now.

"This here's Uncle Will Presley 'n' this other one is Uncle Pete Presley.

"Captain Johnson, Pete, and I run Parker's Farms over in Falls Church. We raise vegetables and fruits to sell to grocery stores and the War Department here in the Capital.

"In addition, we donate some fresh produce to needy families in our community through our church. Also, our cannery preserves both vegetables and fruit for winter consumption. We are including some of those in our donations.

"We read about the work you are doing to fill the needs of the oppressed in our city, and we'd like to assist in that effort."

"I am incredibly grateful for your offer, and we will gladly accept it. This will be a big boost to our operation in the Capital, and I will promptly inform Sister Eliza of this development.

"May I ask, Sir, are you Senator Presley from Virginia?" Captain Johnson inquired.

Modestly, Will acknowledged the question and nodded his head. "We are looking for ways to contribute to those less fortunate than we are, Captain, and we admire the work you are doing. Thank you for coming to Washington to aid our needy folks.

"Maybe someday we can figure out a way to get the federal government involved, but for now, we just have to do the best we can with what we got, as my Paw used to say."

Looking at Jed, Will said, "Come on, Son, you're goin' home with us. Pete, can you find a job for him on the farm?"

"Sure can, Boss man. Jed, can you drive a wagon?" Pete cast him a sidewise glance.

"Now you know I can drive a wagon-you seen me drive our 'backer crop to Asheville to market year after year, Uncle Pete."

"We have two deliveries per week to the War Department 'n' one on Saturday to the church. If we're addin' another one to the Salvation Army, that's a full-time job right there. We'll keep him busy the rest of the time, fillin' basket for the shed," Pete grinned.

"Where am I gonna sleep, Uncle Will?"

"Pete, can you make him a bed in the hayloft? The place smells bad, what with the mules and all, but the hay makes a soft bed," Will winked at Pete.

"Yep, that hayloft makes a good place to lay down. Me 'n' Lil was in the hayloft a lot before she married me," Pete chuckled.

"We'll find a room for you in Parker's house, temporarily. Later on, you can find a boarding house room," Will instructed.

Will was happy to have the opportunity to help Buck's youngest son. Somehow he had to make amends to Buck's family for that awful day at Gettysburg.

Chapter Forty-three

THIRD GENRATION

On January 21, 1884, Mary Amelia Presley (Mimi) celebrated her thirteenth birthday with her parents, grandparents, brothers, Uncle Pete, Aunt Lillian, Jedediah, cousin Danny Boy, and a beautiful cake decorated by Grandma Alice. She was treated like a princess even by Ronnie and Randy, who usually enjoyed teasing her.

Will noticed Lenora's expression and took her aside while the others were busy with presents. "Why do you look so sad, Sweet Lady?"

"I'm not sad, Will, just feeling a bit old. Our baby girl is becoming a young woman, and our precious twin boys will be graduating from high school in a few months. They will be leaving us for college in the fall. It's all gone by so fast," she said, trying to control a catch in her throat and the sudden wetness in her eyes.

"My Maw already had three grandchildren by the time she was your age, Lenora. You have all of that to look forward to in the future.

"In my eyes, you are just as beautiful as the day I first saw you twenty years ago at the Boarding house. Some people think I married a child bride," he said, gently kissing her on the cheek.

"Oh, Will Presley, how you do go on! You always know how to make me smile."

Hand in hand, like young lovers, they rejoined the group as presents were being unwrapped.

A prominent theme appeared to be developing. First, a square package wrapped in muslin tied with a pink ribbon revealed a lovely booklet of landscape paintings by famous American painters.

Next, her brothers handed her a long tube of brown paper that held various paintbrushes, some delicately small and some quite broad. Mimi smiled and politely thanked everyone but seemed somewhat puzzled.

Will excused himself and returned with a sizeable wooden apparatus with three supporting legs and a flat panel at the top sitting on a small shelf. He spread the legs in a triangular format for stability.

Finally, Lenora placed two packages on the shelf of the wooden triangle. One was a large rectangle and one a smaller square. A cloth drape covered both.

"What is it?" Mimi almost squealed.

"It is your easel, darling," Will responded.

The boys had remained quiet beyond their capacity to restrain themselves. "Look," Ronnie said. "It is your special painting equipment."

"See, you have watercolor paints, brushes, and the kind of paper real artists use," Randy shouted.

"Your teachers have told us you display an interest in and a talent for art," Will said proudly.

"We went together to give you something special for your birthday, and that's not all," Lenora added.

"Tomorrow, we are taking you to visit the Corcoran Gallery of Art in the city. They have a great collection of paintings by American artists."

Mimi could not control her excitement. "Can we go first thing in the morning, Daddy?" she asked, twirling around and waving her new paintbrushes.

Corcoran Art Gallery

The Corcoran Gallery of Art was opened to the public in 1874 with much excitement. William Wilson Corcoran commissioned architect James Renwick to design a public museum to display his private collection of American Art. The building sat imposingly at the corner of 17th and Pennsylvania Avenue. With a permanent endowment from the Corcoran estate. The Gallery's stated mission was f*or the perpetual establishment and encouragement of the Fine Arts.*

The Presley/Parker crowd arrived in two carriages early enough to be among the first visitors Sunday morning.

"Think they will miss us sat church?" Lenora giggled.

"No, they will just wonder why that second pew on the left is empty," Will laughed.

The elaborately framed portraits and landscapes enthralled Mimi. She would get lost gazing at scenes of farms, rivers, woods.

Ronnie and Randy ran from room to room and were easily bored, although they did spend more time than was necessary examining a few nude statues.

"Is this going to take all day?" Ronnie asked after only an hour.

"I'm tired of looking at pictures of old people who are probably already dead," Randy added.

Ronnie prodded his father for more information. "Why would a rich man spend all his money building a big building just to fill it with flat pieces of canvas covered with paint? Who is Mr. Corcoran, Pa?"

Will took the boys to a seating area to talk with them while the others continued their tour.

"From what I have read about Mr. Corcoran, he had an extensive collection of art in his home and decided to create a space where everyone could enjoy what he had been looking at privately for years.

"That was the charitable part of his gift to the public. His other reason may have been that he wished to be remembered for some grand gesture. Undoubtedly, Mr. Corcoran was aware of the significant charitable gifts made by the wealthy industrialists and businessmen, such as libraries and schools. He chose to promote art."

"But Pa, what good is art?" Ronnie asked as he shrugged his shoulders. "It's just a lot of pictures on the wall or some carved figures standing around in a garden."

"Sons, I am not an artist, and I have had no formal education in art, so I can only tell you what I feel.

"When I see a painting of a lovely scene such as a mountain covered with snow or a lake with a family of ducks, I have at least two feelings. First, I become calmer. I smile and remember where I grew up or where I have visited. Second, I greatly admire the artist who created that feeling with only a brush and different paint colors. Art makes you look at the world differently."

"Can we have another look?" Randy asked sheepishly.

"Sure, let's go, boys."

Father and son walked behind the rest of the family and stopped here and there to discuss what they saw and how they felt.

After another hour, Ronnie dared to speak again. "I see what you mean, Pa, but I had more fun in the other museums that show trains, big machinery, or new inventions with moving parts."

"I enjoy those, too, Son. Your mother and I will be happy to see you explore your interests as you continue your education, but we don't want you to limit that to what you already like. Part of education is broadening your range of experience and knowledge."

"Each of us has some seed of creativity that we find a way to express. You both have created new games. You have made things out of sticks and stones. Your mother and grandmothers often use their ideas to make clothing or quilts.

"There are many ways to use that urge to make something or express something. Some people make music, write books, invent tools, paint pictures, or carve marble."

"What you see today is one of the ways people have chosen to express themselves using the visual arts. Please take it in and add it to your understanding of creative diversity. Ten years from now, you will remember this day fondly because you shared it with your sister, who is so excited."

Will thought about what Lenora had said on Mimi's birthday about their children growing up and leaving them for the bigger world soon.

"We have a few more years with Mimi, but the boys will leave the nest by fall. I hope we have been good influences on their thinking by the way we have lived; however, I suddenly feel the need to make clear how we see the world and what we think is important."

He was determined to make good use of the next seven months to enrich his sons' real-world education and to challenge their thinking skills.

The Next Weekend

"Lenora, I will be taking the boys on a field trip this weekend."

"Do you want all of us to go?"

"No, this is a Father-Son educational expedition."

She looked puzzled but did not argue. She had plenty of work to do between her church food pantry obligations and her oversight of the canning preparation work on the Parker farm.

"Where are we going, Daddy?" Ronnie asked as they loaded the buggy with blankets, some biscuits, and a jug of cider. "It's not another art museum, is it?"

"You will see in an hour or so."

They drove from the farm into the city, where they recognized several marble buildings after crossing the bridge. When they did not stop near the Capitol or the museums, Ronnie and Randy looked at each other and shrugged. "Where are we going?" Randy asked.

The scenery began to change as they drove through a residential area that did not look like their home, the Parker home, the Hall home, or any other white family home they had seen. Instead, they saw crowded streets lined with shabby unkempt wooden structures. There were mothers hanging clothes out of upstairs windows and small children wandering alone through narrow and dusty roads. The children were wearing dirty clothes and did not appear to be playing or having any fun.

Slum Life

On one corner, they spied a vendor selling apples and a few vegetables. Will parked the buggy and said, "Let's have a walk, boys."

Ronnie and Randy were wearing their usual school clothing, nothing fancy but compared to the children on this street; they appeared to be wealthy young gentlemen. One young lad approached Ronnie tugging on his sleeve. I'm hungry, Mista. Ye got a nickel fer me?"

Will bought a bag of apples from the vendor, who was not well dressed for the cold weather. What teeth he had left seemed to be chattering as he handed the apples to Will and seemed highly grateful for a sale on this dreary winter day. Will told Randy to fetch one of the blankets from the buggy, which he gave to the older man.

The next thing they knew, they were surrounded by more than a dozen young boys. Will instructed the boys to divide the apples among them and then to return to the buggy.

Will continued driving the buggy through the areas housing the poor of the city. The depressing scenery was repeated in each locale. Before leaving the town, Will drove past two factories where tired workers of all ages could be seen coming and going. All of them appeared to be in ill health and to be poorly equipped for the weather. Several of the factories were belching heavy smoke making it difficult to breathe even while outside.

The boys were silent for a long time on the ride home, and Will allowed them space with their thoughts.

After crossing the river, Randy finally spoke.

"Daddy, how can they live like that?"

"What we saw was worse than the places our farmhands live, and these folks weren't even black," Ronnie seemed confused.

Trying to conceal his disappointment, Will responded, "Well, boys, you have raised two important questions today.

"The answers will require more than a few words. but believe me, you will be hearing them."

"How was your trip?" Lenora asked as the boys ran into the house and passed her without speaking.

"Did something bad happen?" she asked Will.

"Actually, something good happened, Lenora. Our two sons were forced to confront how the other half, or maybe two-thirds, live more than a hundred years after our Founding Fathers proclaimed that all men are created equal, that their Creator endows them with certain unalienable rights."

"Did you have to frighten them to let them know that some people don't live as well as we do? Couldn't they just have read about the poor?"

"Perhaps, but my Paw always said, 'Some things ye jist have ta learn by livin'. It was the quickest and most vivid way I could think of to make my point that they have lived a privileged life."

"But Will, we wanted them to have a good life. Is that a bad thing?"

"No, not in itself. I certainly want my children to have more advantages than I had, but I also want them to understand that with privilege comes some responsibilities.

Will developed a reading list for his sons to complete over the summer. He included *A Tale of Two Cities* and *Oliver Twist*.

"I will suggest that they read as a team so that we can discuss the content as they progress through the books. It is essential that they not only understand the stories but the social and economic significance of each. It will give us vital time together as a family before they embark on their post-secondary education."

Lenora listened with admiration. "I'm so proud of you, Will. You have come so far from the young fellow I met and fell in love with who was still suffering the scars of warfare.

"I think you should also share with our boys the kind of life you and your family had in Roaring Fork. They are old enough now to understand the grueling decision you were forced to make when the war started and the paths you have taken in the aftermath of that horrible experience."

"Thank you, my sweet lady. I knew I was marrying above my station and have worked hard to be worthy of you. Our children are blessed to have you as their mother."

With Lenora's advice in mind, Will used the remaining winter months to hold evening fireside chats with his sons, during which he told them stories of his youth and early adult life. Mimi sat on the fringe of the circle and listened.

The boys talked privately about the eye-opening information they had recently learned from their father and their increased respect for him.

Eventually, the conversation turned to college. Ronnie has expressed an interest in the law and was encouraged by John Hall to apply to Yale.

Randy had visited the University of Virginia and had a feeling that was the place for him.

Will and Lenora advised their sons to explore all options during their freshman and sophomore years before committing to a major.

Secretly, Will was very proud when Ronnie expressed interest in law as an opportunity to help put things right.

Lenora was delighted that Randy would be studying a little closer to home and might pursue something in agricultural management.

"I believe my Paw, J.W. Presley, would be mighty proud of his third-generation," Will said, holding Lenora close.

Chapter Forty-four

ELECTION 1884

"Good morning Senator Presley," Jim Hall spoke as he prepared to sit at the Senate dining table Will occupied.
"Do you mind if I sit with you while we have lunch?"
"Glad to have your company, Senator Hall," Will smiled at the feigned formality between these two long-time friends.

"I got a wire from my father this morning. He's trying to compile a roster of Virginia delegates to the Republican National Convention this year.

" The *Grand Pacific Hotel* will be the headquarters this time, and there appears to be an interesting race for a Presidential nomination. President Arthur is not as popular as an incumbent should be."

"Yeah, I've read some editorials in the Washington newspaper and the Richmond newspaper. The Civil Service Act was not popular among his Stalwart supporters. They enjoyed the patronage system that goes back to Andrew Jackson.

"Then, too, the ongoing scandal in the Post Office Department has hurt his image. Bribes have been paid for the acquisition of Independent Star Routes.

"Yes, that is true," Hall replied. "But that political impropriety is not new nor unique to the Arthur administration. That transgression started way back in the first Grant tenure. It was ongoing with the Garfield/Arthur officials for sure but should not be a deal-breaker."

"Well, we'll see what happens when we get to Chicago. What are the dates for the convention this year?"

"The dates are June 3-6, and the meeting will be convened in the *Chicago Exposition Hall,* the same location as the '80 convention."

"Are Jeremiah Jones and Rufus Brown attending as delegates this time," Will asked.

"Yes, I talked with both of them this morning. Rufus is excited because this will be his first convention," Hall smiled.

"Who is making the hotel reservations?" Will furrowed his brow.

"Dad will make them, and he assured me that unless our black colleagues are allowed to stay in the same hotel with us, we'll refuse to book our rooms with them. He is going to start with the Grand Pacific, where headquarters will be."

"Good. I'm happy to know that John agrees that all men are created equal, even the black ones," Will stated emphatically.

June 3rd

"It sure looks like a lot of people are here at the convention," Lenora said to Will.

"Yes, I heard John Hall say there are 1600 delegates and alternates, and 6000 spectators. But this Exposition Center has plenty of room to handle a crowd of this size."

Jim Hall spoke to his group from Virginia. "There's some political maneuvering taking place here on the first day. With 820 official delegates, it will take 411 votes to secure the nomination.

"Speaker Blaine from Maine appears to be the front runner even though Arthur is the incumbent President.

"Some of Blaine's supporters want to test the waters to see how much support he has. They will nominate a man named Powell Clayton as temporary chairman of the convention, but supporters of Senator George Edmunds from Vermont will propose John R. Lynch, an African American from Mississippi, to chair the meeting."

"This evening, Lynch was named to oppose Powell as chairman of the convention. Theodore Roosevelt, from New York, gave a rousing speech in support of Lynch. In a surprising vote, Lynch was chosen by a vote of 424 to 384," Hall excitedly exclaimed. "Hey Presley, are you surprised?"

"Yeah, a little bit, but it doesn't bode well for Arthur. I've heard that Arthur's and Edmunds' supporters are trying to form a coalition to oppose Blaine, but Arthur's people can't guarantee his voters will go for Edmunds if Arthur doesn't win the nomination. It seems the second choice for many of them is Blaine."

Nominations June 4th

"Well, it's midnight, and they've finally adjourned," Rufus Brown shook his head in disbelief. "That was quite an experience."

"Yes, these conventions can be real knockdown, drag-out battles," John Hall shared with the group. "The longer it takes at the roll call vote on the 6th, the lesser Arthur's chances for renomination becomes.

"I think we should stay with him through the second ballot, then jump on the one who appears to be the eventual winner.

"It always pays to back a winner," he smiled wryly.

Jeremiah joined the conversation. "When the roll call got to Maine, and that ten-minute demonstration started, you could feel the momentum strongly for Blaine.

"But when New York was called, the crowd was not enthusiastic for Arthur, and Martin Townsend's speech was weak and uninspired. What happened?"

"Townsend was selected to make the speech at the last minute, so he was not well-prepared," John told them.

"Seconding speeches by Harry Bingham, John Lynch, and Patrick Winston were weak - especially Winston's. So, Arthur got no help there."

Will asked, "I heard that neither Arthur nor Blaine are in Chicago. Wouldn't it be better if they were here advising their supporters?"

"Maybe, but it is customary for the candidate to wait until election night to make his appearance before the convention," John answered.

"Do you think it will hurt us to stay with Arthur through the second ballot, John?"

"No, we are expected to be loyal to him, but on the third ballot, we should be better able to pick the eventual winner," he assured them.

Balloting June 6th

"OK folks, listen up here," John Hall quieted his delegation from Virginia. "When the roll call starts, Senator Presley will announce our votes for President Arthur. Presley is the highest-ranking elected official from Virginia.

"On the second round, Senator Jim Hall, the second-ranking elected official, will announce our continued support for the President.

"If it goes to the third or fourth round, our governor will announce our vote. Before he makes his announcement, we will poll the delegation to decide who gets our endorsement.

"Any questions?"

"Yeah, Mista Hall," Rufus Brown asked. "How many rounds do it take?"

John chuckled and answered, "That depends on how quickly the momentum shifts, Rufus. And whether some of the lesser candidates withdraw their names. We have eleven nominations, including General William T. Sherman and his brother, John Sherman, Lt. General Phillip Sheridan, and General John Logan.

"None of them are serious candidates, but vanity could compel them to leave their name in the competition for a few rounds."

As the roll call vote wound its' way down to Virginia, Will stepped to the podium and loudly proclaimed:

"Mister Chairman, Virginia, the state of presidents, proudly casts all 26 of our votes for the continuing President of the United States." His voice crescendoed, "CHESTER A. ARTHUR."

Loud applause erupted throughout the hall, and John Hall winked at him and mouthed, "Great job, Presley."

The first round ended with Blaine in the lead at 384 votes. Arthur followed with 278, and Edmunds was third with 93.

"It looks like a three-man race, John," Will shook his head.

"Yeah, Presley, and it doesn't bode very well for the President. Blaine will probably be our nominee, but we'll stick with Arthur for one more round," Hall replied.

Jim Hall cast the second-round vote for Arthur, and the total was Blaine 349, Arthur 276, and Edmunds 61.

"I think you're right, Mista Hall," Rufus and Jeremiah both agreed with John. "It sure looks like Blaine is gonna take it this time."

In the third round, the Virginia delegation switched to Blaine. Blaine received 375, Arthur 274, and Edmunds 53.

"The momentum is clearly with Blaine," John Hall informed the group. "This next round, we will coalesce around Blaine, and he will be our nominee."

"Well, the fourth round is now over, and you were right, John," Will smiled. "Of course, I never doubted your political acumen and shrewdness. But I am a bit surprised at the margin Blaine gained so quickly. The vote was 541 for Blaine and just 207 for Arthur."

"John Logan did not do well in the Presidential nomination, but he swept the field for the Vice-Presidential nomination," Jim Hall noted. "He received 780 out of the 810 delegate votes. That's impressive."

"I am convinced that we have a strong slate of candidates to oppose the Democrats. A Democrat has not been chosen as President since James Buchanan in 1856," John said smugly.

The Election

"Wow, that was a wild up and down ride. I would never have believed that both candidates had so many scandals in their closets," Lenora said to Will. "Grover Cleveland appeared to be such a moral and upright man.

Grover Cleveland

"He was elected mayor of Buffalo, New York, then, governor of New York state, and now President of the United States, yet he fathered an illegitimate child."

"Many people have things in their past that they hope are never made public. (Will remembered the events at Gettysburg.) President Cleveland cleaned up much of the corruption in New York left by the Tammany Hall scandal. People called him Good Grover until Blaine's supporters discovered he was paying child support to a woman who claimed he fathered her son.

"When the claims were made, he told his followers to tell the truth. He paid support money for the child, but there was no actual proof he was the father. He claimed that his law partner Oscar Folsom could be the baby's father. The boy was named Oscar Folsom Cleveland."

"A Washington newspaper reporter wrote that Blaine had taken bribes from an Arkansas railroad company. He expedited a federal land grant to build a line from Little Rock to Fort Smith. They paid him more than $110,000.00 (1.5 million in today's dollars). That's a small fortune, Will," Lenora exclaimed.

"Rumors about Blaine's shenanigans have abounded for several years, but then that Mulligan fellow found a letter to Blaine from the railroad company. The letter concluded with *burn this letter*. Democrats chanted, *burn, burn, burn this letter*.

"He got all the Democrat votes and a bunch of reform-minded Republicans who were called *Mugwumps*.

"Cleveland won with 48.9 % of the popular vote and Blaine captured 48.3%, but Cleveland got 219 electoral votes."

Will chuckled, "I heard some folks in the Capitol Building chanting *Ma, Ma, where's my Pa*. Some Democrats chanted back, *Gone to the White House, Ha, Ha, Ha.*"

"The Washington newspaper reported that a Republican minister in New York who backed Blaine had preached a sermon condemning Cleveland. He proclaimed that *rum, Romanism, and rebellion* supported Cleveland. This slam on Catholics and southerners infuriated the church people – especially in New York. There was speculation that the New York vote, only a 1200 vote margin for their Democrat governor, won the electoral college for him."

The next day in the Senate Dining Room, Will and Jim Hall discussed the election's outcome and concluded that the country was headed in a different direction.

"With the first Democrat in the White House in twenty-eight years, we'll have a hard time getting our agenda approved. Maybe we can make him a one-termer," Hall suggested.

Chapter Forty-five

CLEVELAND IS PRESIDENT

Will, I've been reading this new book by Mark Twain. You might remember that he wrote The Gilded Age, which Mama gave us for Christmas one year.

Will nodded, and she continued. "His newest book is being serialized in *Century magazine* – titled *The Adventures of Huckleberry Finn.*

"I believe our children should read it–the boys especially. They have his other one, called *The Adventures of Tom Sawyer.* They don't like to read, but these books are exciting and informative about life in the South.

"Since they're in college now, they need to have some knowledge of other parts of the country. I have copies of Century magazine to give them.

March 4, 1885

Seated at the East entrance to the Capitol Building, Will and Jim Hall watched Grover Cleveland take the oath of office.

"He certainly is a big man, isn't he?" Will observed.

Jim replied, "Yeah, I heard somebody say he weighs 275 pounds. He drinks a lot of beer and smokes cigars, too.

"Did you know his first name is not Grover?" Hall grinned.

"It's Stephen, but he's used Grover since he became an adult. He was called Stephen Cleveland in grade school and didn't like it."

"Who told you all these trivial facts about the President?" Will asked as he smiled.

"I was having a drink with a reporter for the Washington newspaper. He researched Cleveland's background for an article he's writing. A lot of people are interested in every tidbit of information they can find on the President," Hall confided.

"Yeah, and every tidbit of dirt they can find, too," Will shook his head. (The events at Gettysburg crossed his mind, again, and he hoped nobody ever publicly revealed his secret.)

Hall continued, "When he moved into the White House, Cleveland, a bachelor, was uncomfortable with the surroundings. He asked his sister to move in and act as hostess at social events.

"Not happy with the food he was served in the White House, he wrote to a friend of his: I must go to dinner, but I wish it was to eat a pickled herring, a swiss cheese, and a chop at Louis' instead of the French stuff I shall find," Hall chuckled.

In June 1886, Cleveland, a 47-year-old bachelor, married Frances Folsom, the 21-year-old daughter of his law partner, Oscar Folsom. The ceremony was conducted in the East Room of the White House, and he became the only sitting President to be married there.

Six Months Later

Will and Lenora discussed Cleveland's first year in office. "How do you feel about the Democrat President so far," she asked Will.

"I wouldn't say this publicly, but he has done some things I like.

"He has stated that he will not replace any Republican appointee who is doing a good job. In the past, under the *Spoils System,* folks were replaced by party affiliation, and many good managers were lost.

"So far, he has chosen people solely on their merits, and I like that.

"And he has reduced the number of employees by not filling vacancies because many departments were bloated by hiring to repay political debts.

"I hope he sticks with that policy throughout his term." **(He did not)**

"What is this *Tenure of Office Act* I read about in the paper?" Lenora asked.

"Well, to my understanding, it was passed in '67 and stated that any appointee subject to the advice and consent of the Senate could not be removed without the Senate's approval. He seems to be ignoring it, and I suspect a repeal is forthcoming," Will explained.

"For most of us Republicans, he is too conservative. Being the leader of the Bourbon Democrats, he opposes high tariffs, which I like, but he is also against Free Silver, subsidies to farmers and veterans. These folks are the backbone of our nation and sometimes need our support.

"He has vetoed some Civil War veteran pensions that Congress authorized. And he said in a speech:

"I can find no warrant for such an appropriation in the Constitution, and I do not believe that the power and duty of the general government ought to be extended to the relief of individual suffering, which is in no manner properly related to the public service or benefit. A prevalent tendency to disregard the limited mission of this power and duty should, I think, be steadfastly resisted, to the end that the lesson should be constantly enforced that, though the people support the government, the government should not support the people. The friendliness and charity of our countrymen can always be relied upon to relieve their fellow citizens in misfortune. This has been repeatedly and quite lately demonstrated. Federal aid in such cases encourages the expectation of paternal care on the part of the government and weakens the sturdiness of our national character, while it prevents the indulgence among our people of that kindly sentiment and conduct which strengthens the bonds of a common brotherhood."

Lenora frowned and said, "But Will, we are well aware that the President is very wrong in this belief. Our church has been aiding poor and hungry folks for some time. Yet, the needs we see are far more extensive than our resources will allow.

"The Salvation Army is feeding and housing a few people in a few cities, but millions more are being allowed to suffer and die from malnutrition and exposure to the elements.

"Our working people are struggling to survive. Mothers and even children are forced to work in factories to supplement the father's wages to meet basic needs.

"If we meet the needs of our citizens, the federal and state governments must take on these issues.

"Our President was reared in the family of a Presbyterian minister. His needs were always taken care of by his church, so he cannot relate to ordinary working people."

Will shook his head and responded, "Len, you and I have had this conversation many times before. If we go back to the term of Grant in the White House, there has been no sentiment for the federal government to be involved in the personal lives of our folks."

"Yes, I know. It seems that the government just wants to use common people, then throws them away when they are no longer useful. Our wealthy industrialists are like-minded and probably influence the thinking of the politicians," Lenora was angry and venting.

"At present, the Treasury Department has an enormous surplus of funds which could be used to assist needy people. We do, as you just said, have an abundance of needy folks, too. Many needs are going unmet, but the President had these words for Congress in his last address:

"When we consider that the theory of our institutions guarantees to every citizen the full enjoyment of all the fruits of his industry and enterprise, with only such deduction as may be his share toward the careful and economical maintenance of the Government which protects him, it is plain that the exaction of more than this is indefensible extortion and a culpable betrayal of American fairness and justice ... The public Treasury, which should only exist as a conduit conveying the people's tribute to its legitimate objects of expenditure, becomes a hoarding place for money needlessly withdrawn from trade and the people's use, thus crippling our national energies, suspending our country's development, preventing investment in productive enterprise, threatening financial disturbance, and inviting schemes of public plunder."

December 6, 1887.

"President Cleveland is pushing Congress to reduce tariffs. This action will reduce the revenues the Treasury is now receiving. There's not much chance of increasing spending to supplement the wages poor people are earning.

"Perhaps, when the next President is elected, he will be more empathetic with the plight of our workers," Will smiled wryly.

"The President is adamant that we need to improve our coastal defenses. He is proposing to spend 127 million dollars (3.7 billion in 2020 dollars) on upgrading them.

"He wants new breech-loading rifled guns, mortars, and naval minefields at the harbors and river estuaries. Many of them will have armed forts as protection.

"His spending priorities are not the same as mine, but he's the President, not me," Will concluded.

Spring 1888

Seated in the Senate Dining Room with John and Jim Hall, Will asked about the upcoming Republican Convention. "Where will it be convened this year, John?" he inquired.

"We're back in Chicago again this year, but in the Auditorium Building on June 16-25," John answered. "I think this will be my last one. At my age, these long days and nights are getting to be too much for me," he chuckled. "Next time, you and Jim are on your own.

"If they will accept Rufus and Jeremiah, I would like to stay in the *Palmer House*. It's a real upscale hotel."

"Yeah, Dad, I like the idea of staying in different hotels. The Convention is the only chance we get to go to Chicago."

"Why is it always in Chicago?" Will asked.

"Chicago is centrally located and equidistant for everybody to travel. There's good rail service there, too," John explained.

"Who is running, and what issues will be in the platform?" Jim asked.

"There's a crowded field again this time. When you don't have an incumbent, the field is wide open."

John continued, "Blaine is the frontrunner going in, but he lost in '84. I believe somebody else has a better opportunity to capture the nomination this year.

"Russell Alger, John Sherman, Walter Gresham, and Chauncey Depew have all been mentioned."

"Dad, I heard that Fredrick Douglas has been invited to address the Convention, Any truth to that?" Jim asked.

"Yes, he has, Jim, and that's a historic decision. No black man has ever been a featured speaker at a major party Convention. When you don't have the White House, innovation is in order, Douglas won't get the nomination, but he will garner a lot of votes for the party."

June 25th

"Well, that was a surprising end to this convention," John spoke to his Virginia delegation. "Benjamin Harrison was a Senator from Indiana. He lost his seat when conservative Democrats took over the Indiana legislature. A dark horse candidate for President, he made a rousing speech declaring himself a Living and Rejuvenated Republican.

"After seven rounds without a majority, the tide turned to Harrison on the eighth ballot. He won with 544 votes, including all of ours.

"*Rejuvenated Republicanism* is the campaign slogan," John summarized for a reporter who interviewed him after the meeting adjourned near midnight.

Benjamin Harrison

Benjamin Harrison, along with his running mate Levi Morton, defeated incumbent President Grover Cleveland.

For the third time since Rutherford B. Hayes in 1880, the President served only one term and failed re-election. Harrison would become the fourth one-termer in 1892 when Cleveland returned to defeat him. Cleveland is the only President of the United States to serve two non-consecutive terms.

Will Presley had won a Senate appointment for his third six-year term in '86. He would serve until 1892.

Jim Hall was returned to the Senate in 1888 to serve until 1894. Virginia Republicans rejoiced.

Chapter Forty-six

HARRISON IS PRESIDENT

"Hey, that Inaugural Address was surprisingly short," Jim Hall exclaimed to Will. "I had a professor at Yale who reminded us of the speech made by President Harrison's grandfather, William Henry Harrison. As the ninth President, his Inaugural Address was the longest in history. This one was half as long."

"The heavy rain contributed to the brevity of the speech. And I was thrilled to see Cleveland holding Harrison's umbrella to protect him." (Will remembered the heavy rainfall on the Gettysburg hills that long-past July day in '63.)

"Yes, but he effectively touched on all the issues we will face in the coming four years. Brevity should be the watchword for politicians and preachers, too. After twenty minutes or so, folk's minds start to wander, and you lose your audience.

"My stepfather, John Wesley Henderson, told me that, and he was right. I've noticed it in my speeches," Will related.

"Harrison credited the influences of education and religion as significant factors in our prosperity as a nation. He urged the cotton and mining areas to expand their industrial base as the Eastern states had done. For continued growth, he promised a protective tariff."

Jim replied, "I found it interesting what he said about commerce. Here are his exact words. I wrote them down."

> "If our great corporations would more scrupulously observe their legal obligations and duties, they would have less call to complain of the limitations of their rights or of interference with their operations."

"Maybe there's an opportunity to eliminate these monopolies the Robber Barons have created for themselves," Hall continued. "Senator John Sherman has been talking about an *Anti Trust Act,* which now seems possible relative to the President's remarks."

"Isn't Senator Sherman a brother of General William T. Sherman?" Will asked.

"He is indeed his brother," Hall answered.

Will continued, "I was delighted to hear him express his support for pensions for disabled veterans. This stance is the exact opposite of President Cleveland's position. Harrison is advocating for veteran's disability pensions regardless of the cause of their affliction.

"Many injuries suffered in war are not just physical. Most participants in battle have mental problems associated with killing and with watching their friends and brothers die. Some soldiers never recover from these problems. I can attest to this from my experience.

"We are obligated to these men to aid in their quest to deal with the aftermath of war. They sacrificed for their country. Now their country must repay them," Will was adamant.

"We've got four territories in the northwest who are seeking statehood, Presley," Hall added. "North and South Dakota, Montana, and the state of Washington. This country is growing fast, and things are gonna change here in Congress. With forty-two states, we'll have eight more senators and several more Congressmen.

"It's gonna get interesting," Will shook his head.

"Are you and Lenora attending the Inaugural Ball this evening? I heard that John Phillip Sousa's Marine Corps band would play," Jim said.

"Yes, Lenora is looking forward to it. Maybe we'll see you and Susan there."

Next Week

During a lull on the floor of the Senate, Will walked over to his colleague and said, "Hey Jim, what do you think of Harrison's reluctance to name Blaine Secretary of State? He's held that job before and knows it well."

"Yeah, but Blaine tends to dominate when he sees the opportunity. To preclude Blaine's involvement, Harrison will name other cabinet members before he appoints Blaine. I think it's an astute move on his part to wait before calling Blaine," Hall replied.

"Yeah, he's gonna do it his way. Blaine dominated the selections during Garfield and Arthur's Administration. These party bosses have done that far too long," Will acknowledged.

"The President seems to favor Civil War vets, his fellow Indiana natives, and Presbyterians. I reckon it's hard to overcome our inherent biases," Will shook his head.

Parker's Farm

Will pulled his buggy into the barn when he arrived home. Harry and Pete were engaged in a lively conversation while Henry, Lenora, and Lil listened intently.

"What's gonin' on?" Will asked.

Lenora acknowledged Will and hugged him tightly.

"Roy Ailor was here today talking about the newest canning processes," she answered her husband. "It seems that the larger companies are automating and speeding- up their operations. They're using tin cans because they can be sealed by solder.

"Roy said the tin cans prevent breakage and stack better on the shelves. He thinks we should consider changing from glass jars to tin cans."

"What do you think, Harry?" Will asked.

"Well, it would involve spending a lot of money which we don't have, but eventually we'll be forced to do it if we remain competitive."

"You fellows are the bosses," Pete acknowledged. " But I think we should look into it and see what all is involved.

"Roy said, H J Heinz and Borden Milk Products are using tin cans now, and other companies follow them," Pete related.

Harry thought for a while before responding firmly, "I appreciate the fact that you, Pete, are interested in keeping us competitive. I'm not sure we need to hop onto each new trend the minute we hear about it. We are doing quite well with our canning business."

"I didn't mean no disrespect, Mr. Parker," Pete said, hanging his head.

Will could see his brother's embarrassment and stepped in to support him. "Harry, it sometimes makes sense to step out ahead when new possibilities present themselves. We are all proud of being part of the Parker Farm and Cannery business and want to ensure that it remains profitable for a long time."

Lenora squirmed with discomfort, feeling caught between her father and her husband. She could see Harry's face becoming flushed. "Maybe we should talk about this after supper in a more comfortable location," she suggested.

"You don't have to protect me, Lenora. I fully possess my faculties, and I have been running this farm before any of you were even born. Tin cans may have advantages; however, they are not nearly as attractive as our glass jars, where you can see what you are planning to eat. A label on the outside will tell you what's supposed to be inside, but how do you really know?"

"I don't think any company would get by with false representation for very long. If you bought a can with a label saying corn, you would not be too happy if it turned out to be greens," Will said, trying to soften the atmosphere with some levity.

Harry was breathing faster than usual as he raised his voice to say, "I've heard enough for now. You Presley boys are both hardworking and intelligent. You have been a great addition to my business and our family.

"You have pushed me into doing things I had never planned to do. While it is true that most of those things have been successful, I remind you that this will remain my farm and my business until I leave this world for a better place."

With that, Harry turned around and began walking toward the house. Everyone watching and hearing this exchange stood awestruck. They had never listened to the mild-mannered Harry Parker raise his voice or demonstrate such obvious displeasure.

A few yards away from the Parker house, Harry stumbled and fell to the ground.

Will, Lenora, and Pete rushed to his side. "Daddy, are you alright?" Lenora cried out as she knelt by his head.

Hearing no response and noticing only a low level of breathing, Will and Pete lifted Harry and carried him the rest of the way into the house.

Alice met them at the door. "What happened?" she anxiously asked.

"He was walking home and fell," Lenora answered.

"Let's put him in his bed and send Henry to get Doc. Phillips."

"He should have Doc Watson, his heart specialist," Alice said, wringing her hands.

"We will get Doc Watson later, Alice. It would take almost two hours to get him here, and we don't have time to wait."

Lenora and Alice were busy trying to make Harry as comfortable as possible. They propped his head up with several pillows and placed cool cloths on his forehead to bring down any temperature. Both women insisted on remaining by Harry's side until the doctor arrived.

Meanwhile, Will and Pete went into the gathering room to talk. "I feel terrible, Will," Pete said with great remorse.

"I know, Pete. So do I. The last thing in the world I would want to do is to upset Harry. He has been more than generous to me from the very first day I met him.

"He allowed me to marry his only child and take her five hundred miles away for a dangerous experiment. He welcomed us back to his home, helped us build our own house. He and Alice have been the most loving grandparents to our children.

"They welcomed my mother and my step-father into their home for a visit when I became a Senator.

"Harry has been an ally and a mentor. He has made it possible for me to have a completely new life. He was the coach leading me into public service, and he has been behind me in every step of my political career."

Pete added, "They invited Lillian and me to become part of their family and gave me a chance to be more than a dirt farmer. He gave me responsibilities and encouraged me to think I was capable of leading. Why did I say anything?" he shook his head.

When Henry returned with Doc Phillips, Harry had opened his eyes and tried to utter a few words. Alice managed to get him to swallow some cider. The doctor performed the usual vital sign checks and talked with Harry for a few minutes.

Leaving Alice with Harry, Doc Phillips met with Will, Lenora, and Pete in the parlor. "You should try to get him back to the hospital where Doc. Watson can do additional tests as soon as possible. I would not try to move him yet. Try to keep him comfortable. Make sure he has fluids, and most importantly, keep him calm, no excitement."

"Alice, would you let me talk with Harry alone for a minute?" Will asked.

"Not now, Will. I have instructions to keep him calm, and it seems that is not what was happening down by the barn, " she replied curtly. "Come back after supper, and we will see if he is up to it."

"I'm staying here, Will. You and Pete can finish up with the workers and go to our house. Lil can fix some supper for you. I need to be here for Momma and Daddy."

Will knew that Lenora was both frightened and angry. "She probably blames me for what happened to Harry," he thought.

Lillian tried to explain the afternoon's events to Mimi, who was working on a senior essay. She would be graduating from high school this spring. In the fall, she would begin her study of art at the Corcoran School.

"Oh, no. Can I go over to see Grandpa Harry?"

"Your Grandmother, Mrs. Parker, asked us all to wait until after supper. She will let us know when he can see people."

"He's not going to die, is he?" Mimi asked with tears on her cheeks.

"We are all praying for him, Mimi. That's all we can do right now," as she hugged her niece.

Will came in and embraced his crying daughter. He tried to act optimistic but could not swallow more than a few bites of food at the supper table.

Harry had managed to pull himself up in bed and drink some chicken broth. "Alice, I want to talk with my son-in-law. Please go get him."

"Lenora, please get your husband over here now. I am not leaving."

Will ran faster than he had in years and nodded at Alice as he was waved into Harry's bedroom.

"This is between Will and me, ladies," Harry said, addressing his wife and daughter. "Please leave us alone until I call for you."

Expecting the worse, Will approached Harry with trepidation. "Harry, I am so sorry, I . . ."

"Stop right there, Son. I guess you think my condition is your fault. Well, I have news for you, Senator. You don't have that much power. You may carry a lot of weight on the hill, but here you are, merely the husband of my only child. By the way, I love you like a son," he smiled.

"I can never repay all that you have done for my family and me, Harry. I couldn't live with myself if I thought I had done anything to hurt you. I apologize for pushing you into changes that you did not want to make."

"Just listen to me, Son. I may not have very long to tell you all that I wish to make clear. First, neither you nor Pete is responsible for my weak heart. I am a seventy-five-year-old man who has smoked most of my life and doesn't take health advice well from my wife or doctor.

"I have had a wonderful life. I married the woman of my dreams who gave me a beautiful, feisty daughter. That daughter gave me you and three precious grandchildren.

"I have been blessed with a successful business, which you have tried to bring into the current times. I have had the pleasure and pride of watching you develop into a respected public official.

"This afternoon, I popped off at you because old folks need some time to think about dramatic changes before committing. You all looked at me as if I were a relic of another time. It was my Alamo stand. I guess you didn't think the old guy had it in him," Harry chuckled.

"When I go to meet my maker, I will feel comfortable that you will carry on the work I began and make it better. Please tell Pete I didn't mean to scare him. He is a good man, just like his brother."

"Thank you, Harry. You must know by now how much I respect you. You should also know that I love you and Alice. Your grandchildren love you and will also make you proud. Don't be talking about meeting your maker yet. You have more work to do. We all need you."

Harry had a few more good days and was happy to spend them talking to Alice, Lenora, Will, and the other family members.

Nine days after his fall, Harry Parker passed away gently in his sleep.

Dr. Watson confirmed that his death was not caused by an argument or by a fall. His weakened heart had kept him going longer than medical evidence would have predicted.

Memorial services were held at Falls Church Episcopal Church. A tremendous outpouring of respect and love was offered to the family from parishioners and the community.

John Hall read the scripture, and Will gave the eulogy.

Burial was in the church cemetery.

The next day in the Senate Dining Hall, Will shared with Jim Hall: "This will be my last term in the Senate. Harry's gone now, and I must assume my role as the patriarch of the family.

"Alice has always looked to Harry as her leader, so as I assume the position as Director of Operations at Parker's Farm, many others will look to me for guidance.

"Randy has finished his college work in Agriculture but has no practical management experience. Ronnie is finishing law school and will probably join a prominent D.C. firm.

"Jeremiah Jones has been an excellent legislator, and I hope to help him succeed me in the Senate. I will do everything in my power to make that happen.

"Lenora and I have many goals that we have yet to achieve for our country, so in the next three years, I will concentrate on those.

"Women still are not allowed to vote.

"Blacks continue to be discriminated against and are not accorded the full privileges of citizenship.

"The wealth of our country is controlled by a handful of people. We have a few millionaires, but most of the rest are struggling to survive.

"With the Industrial Revolution, this should have been the Golden Age, but with so few sharing in the gold, it's only gilded around the edges. It's no wonder that Mark Twain called this the *Gilded Age*.

Chapter Forty-seven

FAREWELL ADDRESS

December of 1892 would mark the end of the legislative career of Senator George Wilheim Presley. Regardless of how political winds might be blowing, he had decided shortly after Harry Parker's death to complete his term and retire to oversee the Parker enterprises.

Within months following Harry's passing, the family had reorganized their living arrangements.

Alice had insisted that Will, Lenora, and Mimi move into the Parker house. "I'm rattling around in this big old place. It was meant to be a family home, not a lonely widow's retreat. Harry would have insisted."

Randy had graduated from the University of Virginia and was coming home for his apprentice period as the future Operations Manager for Parker Enterprises.

He was now engaged to marry Miss Amanda Nell Dawson from Richmond. They had met at a debutante ball last year, and the relationship developed into wedding plans. "Amanda's father owns a large building supply company, and he had tried to entice Randy to come work for him," Lenora told Alice.

"I hope he doesn't change his mind about coming back here," Alice worried. "I guess he will have several opportunities as a new graduate of such a fine school."

"Randy made it clear to his bride-to-be that he already had solid plans for their future, and if she wanted to marry him, she would learn to love Falls Church," Lenora shared with a smile. "That's my boy!"

Senators were still being appointed by State Legislatures or the General Assembly in the case of Virginia. The Democrat, Grover Cleveland, received all twelve of Virginia's electoral votes in the General Election of 1892; consequently, Will might not have been appointed for another term. That probability did not influence his decision. Will now had a new mission, to preserve and enrich his wife's family legacy.

As he began clearing out his office before the holidays, Will revisited all he had seen, heard, done, and learned since 1870. He resolved to leave a written summary of his legislative career in the form of a farewell address which he would deliver aloud during the final session before the Christmas recess.

Will contacted Senator John Sherman, a lawyer from Ohio, who would remain the majority leader until the 1893 term. He requested permission and a time on the agenda for his farewell address.

Having secured his time slot, Will spent every spare minute over the next several weeks thinking and writing draft after draft of what he wanted to say.

After supper one evening, Lenora said, "Will, what are you daydreaming about? I don't think you have heard a word I said tonight."

"I am mentally outlining my final speech before leaving office. There is so much I want to say, and I'm having a bit of trouble putting it all in order and condensing it so as not to put everyone to sleep."

"Will, you are a natural storyteller. If you are just yourself, people will gladly listen. I hope we all get to hear that speech. I want Momma, our children, and Pete to be in attendance?"

The Presley family piled into the Senate visitor gallery anticipating Will's turn to speak.

Senator Presley walked to the front of the chamber, placed a printed copy of his address in the Vice President's hands, and turned to smile at his peers and visitors.

"Mr. Vice President, Senators, family, and friends, I am honored for the opportunity to speak to you as I exit my political career.

"My story is an American story made possible only in our wonderful country. Allow me to share parts of the journey I have traveled and what I have learned along the way. To avoid putting you to sleep, I will concentrate on highlights and eliminate minute details. My wife often accuses me of padding the story for dramatic effect."

There was laughter and some applause in the chamber.

"I was born on a small North Carolina farm where my parents worked as sharecroppers. My father came to this country under a contract of indenture. My mother was also an immigrant from England whose parents were recruited to provide tailoring and seamstress work for the town.

"In 1861, I left my home because I could not take up arms against our country to help preserve the institution of slavery. Unable to find employment, I found myself on the other side in the Union Army fighting against my brothers, figuratively and literally.

"Although I take no pride in the medals I received, doors were opened for me. I found a job in the War Department.

"When the war ended, I wanted to do something to help restore our union. My brand-new wife and I took an assignment in the Reconstruction efforts. We were stationed in Memphis, Tennessee, where our mission was to build schools for the former slaves who were now free to improve their lives.

"After President Lincoln was assassinated, the Reconstruction plans quickly disappeared. Lenora and I completed our term and relocated to her home area in Virginia. Our new goal was to be active in passing the 14th and 15th Amendments to the Constitution.

"I was neither a highly educated man nor a trained orator, but somehow my local impromptu talks made an impression, and I was encouraged to become active in the political realm.

"I cannot take credit for the opportunities that opened up for me. Many fine people, including my late father-in-law, supported me along the path and boosted my confidence.

"My entry into the legislative arena was with an appointment to the Virginia Assembly where I participated in the required rewriting of the State Constitution.

"Thankfully, my new home state was readmitted to the union, but this was not without controversy. As you know, the war between the states left us with a lingering threat to the goals set forth by our Founding Fathers

"I was honored to be elected to serve two terms in the House of Representatives as a Congressman from the eighth district of Virginia in 1870. During that period, I was blessed to become friends with many others who were also elected to represent the views and needs of their constituents.

"My appointment by the Virginia Assembly sending me to this chamber in 1874 was an almost unbelievable event. My mother was able to travel to see me inaugurated. Her pride was humbling as she spoke at length about how proud my father would have been to see the son of a sharecropper in the United States Senate.

"And that is my American story and the American Dream. Our beloved country is founded on a noble idea, one that we are constantly challenged to pursue.

"Maybe I'm a sap, but I took the following words seriously: *We hold these truths to be self-evident, that all men are created equal, that they are endowed by their Creator with certain unalienable Rights, that among these are Life, Liberty, and the Pursuit of Happiness.*

"Those of us having the privilege of serving in this elite body should not forget that we are charged with securing those rights.

"Each of us has a story. Each of us has encountered ups and downs along the way, both successes and failures. Each of us has been influenced by the particulars of our life experience, and our attitudes and opinions have developed.

"One of the lessons I have learned is the word change can ignite either joyful anticipation or angry resistance. Where a person stands depends on where he sits.

"I have found that most people don't really like change unless it is their idea."

An outpouring of laughter ensued, giving everyone a break in Will's dissertation.

"Change is uncomfortable. Change requires us to think. Change may necessitate doing things differently than we have always done them. Change may cause us to disagree with our friends or families. Who wants all that trouble?

Another round of uneasy laughter.

"Change can also open doors for us, lead us to something more beautiful and rewarding. There is always a risk of allowing change to happen.

"There is a natural tendency for most of us to become even more resistant to change as we age. That's the way we have always done it. If it was good enough for my parents and good enough for me, why change?

"That resistance would have prevented railroads, electric lights, and many discoveries that have made us healthier and made our lives easier.

"Change needs champions, respected people of influence who can educate their circle of friends and constituents about the need for and the value of specific changes.

"The slow pace of change has been a hard pill for me to swallow. It is not unusual for the young to be impatient for changes to occur. I must confess to falling prey to that disease, of wanting change tomorrow.

"Someone warned me early in my career that politics is the art of the possible. We have to work together for the common good. Working together means that we have to debate all proposals and eventually agree to do what is possible at any given time.

"The process is often tedious and laborious, but it usually moves us forward, even if only a tiny amount at a time.

"Another hard lesson that I continue to learn is that ideas that seem clear and reasonable to me do not necessarily seem that way to other people. Am I crazy? Wait, don't answer that."

Laughter and a few hands were raised.

"That's alright; I'm used to getting puzzled looks, often in my own house."

Applause.

"That brings me back to us, Senators. We have the privilege of and the responsibility to promote necessary changes that move us closer to the American dream.

"What I am trying to do is to challenge you in this august body to take advantage of your platform and influence while you have it.

"In the pages of history, we will each be, at best, a sentence or two. However, we can leave a legacy of courage and hope.

"For good or bad, we leave a legacy with our children.

"Our children learn from us how to think. They will learn from us to cherish our country's ideals or to ignore the Founders' words if they are inconvenient.

"They will learn from us to respect all people or to place people in categories of worthiness.

"They will learn from us the responsibility that comes with their privilege to do something to contribute to the common good of society.

"I know what I want my children to learn. I want them to hold up in honor the grand experiment that is the American idea. I want them to be advocates for the rights of all people. I want them to choose love over hate. I want them to inspire others as they move through life with hope, joy, and humility.

"I am betting that you want the same for your children and all the children in our country. They will be the next generation and will either secure and advance our special American mission in this world or neglect it and watch it die.

"There is much work ahead to fully achieve the ideals left to us in those sacred documents. Each generation has the responsibility to do its part in moving forward.

"The final question I wish to leave with you is, are you willing to dedicate your time in office to the main task of preserving our form of government?

"Dr. Franklin once cautioned that our Republic is a beautiful thing if we can keep it. Democracy is a messy form of government. Some would say it is the worst form except for everything else. It demands that we debate, even argue, to make decisions that move us closer to a more perfect union.

"It would be easy to throw up our hands in frustration and look for one strong leader to follow. That might be simpler, but it is not what this country is about.

"When things get complicated and divisive, there will often be a tendency to believe that we might be better off with an authoritarian form of government.

"Resist that urge. Don't give up your voice. Our children's future depends on those of us who are elected to public service.

"Always remember the oath you took to defend the Constitution against all enemies foreign and domestic. Do not take the easy way out.

"As I thank you for your friendship and your work, I bid you and those who come after us goodbye with a challenge.

"Use these limited but special times that you now enjoy moving the line closer to the goal. You will always meet with argument and resistance, but you can persist in doing the right thing.

"I still trust in the Idea of America and in the form of government established to support that Idea. I also trust in the essential goodness of all people and hope that you, especially because you are elected leaders, will choose light over darkness.

"Thank you for indulging me in this moment of self-reflection. God bless each of you, and God bless America."

The address was followed by a standing ovation from the Senate and tears of pride in the eyes of the Presley family.

Chapter Forty-eight

EPILOGUE

Following his retirement from the Senate, Will remained busy with oversight of the Parker Farm and Cannery business. In the quiet times of reflection, he would daydream about his father.

He would imagine what the family patriarch, James William Presley, would have experienced and seen if he lived to 1893.

What did he miss? What became of the family he and Sally created. What happened to the United States of America?

Between 1830 and 1901, his adopted country's myriad changes set the backdrop for the Presley family's destiny.

In quiet moments, Will Presley remembered his past life in Roaring Fork. Then he considered all that brought him to the present and imagined how his father might have viewed all that transpired.

When J.W. died in a logging accident, he was only forty-four. He missed both the tragedies and the ecstasies that were to occur in the life of his progeny. "When we lost Paw, I thought of him and Ma as older folks. Now, I'm older than Paw was then," Will thought with a smile. "Funny how you see things differently depending on where you are in life."

Blessedly J.W. missed the Civil War. He did not suffer the agony his wife had to bear alone. The pain of losing four children, two on the battlefield (Buck and Johnny), two in town after the war had already ended (Matt and Lizzie), adding to her grief. His third-born son, Will, opted to leave home rather than participate in the senseless violence of civil war and was presumed deceased for five long years.

Sadly, he missed the joy of watching his beloved wife, Sally, achieve her dream of expanding her school to include more children.

He missed seeing their daughter, Maggie, marry the town's physician.

After his death, his wife, Sally Presley, remained a widow for almost two decades and then married John Henderson, a close family friend and the local traveling minister in the Graham, N.C. area.

Sally set up a larger school and trained her remaining daughter, Maggie, to become her assistant and ultimate replacement upon moving into town.

He missed welcoming more than a dozen grandchildren into the family.

He missed the pride of watching his third-born son become a United States Senator, inherit through marriage a substantial farm, and become a successful entrepreneur.

J.W. was not there to see his grandson, Ronnie, become a degreed lawyer with a career in the center of the U.S. government.

He did not attend his grandson Randy's graduation from the University of Virginia and become head of a growing canning enterprise.

He missed the joy of watching his beautiful granddaughter, Mimi, complete her college degree in art history, which led to positions in Washington, D.C. galleries.

"When I count all the blessings we have had, I regret that Paw was not here to share the joys. He would be bursting with pride that the family he started has persevered and in many cases flourished."

J.W. missed the scientific discoveries, technological inventions, and the movement from an agrarian to an industrial society.

The many innovations in the way we travel, communicate, live our daily lives, and entertain ourselves would have brought a smile to his lips or shake of his head. "I coulda used tha rite thar," Will could hear him saying.

"Just imagine Paw riding in a railroad car over much of the road that carried him from Charleston to Asheville.

He also missed the social, economic, and political changes as the nation grew and struggled with making its stated principles a reality.

Of the seven male children born to J.W. and Sally Presley, Will was most similar to his father in physical appearance and personality. His usually tousled sandy hair, sky blue eyes, and quick crooked smile immediately attracted other people to him. The initial positive impression was solidified by his open honesty, concern for others, and his gift of storytelling.

Will's lingering sense of responsibility for so many unfortunate events prodded him to seek service opportunities throughout the remainder of his life.

In many ways, Will saw himself as an extension and continuation of his father. Much as his father before him, Will dared to take a risk for an unknown future. When others attempted to persuade him to conform to peer pressure, he refused to alter his sense of right and wrong.

With his wife, Lenora, Will sought avenues of influence which led to his political career. He followed this unlikely path, not for personal acclaim but because it gave him a platform from which he could be a champion for the two fundamental principles he held dear to his heart: ALL MEN ARE CREATED EQUAL and LOVE YOUR NEIGHBOR AS YOURSELF.

Never forgetting the family he left behind, Will took opportunities to assist those who needed a chance at a different life.

His younger brother, Pete, found the courage to take his new wife away from the only home they had ever known and learn that he could lead others.

When he discovered his nephew, Jedediah, homeless, jobless, and friendless, he made a place for him.

Trying not to squander his brief moments in the limelight and his circle of influence, Will managed to suggest alternative courses when he saw legislative trends going backward. He knew he was only one vote, but he felt compelled to attempt changing attitudes.

In the back of his mind, Will was always thinking, "What would Paw think of me? How would he feel about my choices? Would he forgive me for the things I cannot forgive myself for doing?"

He did gain some solace from John Henderson's final words to him. "I know, Son. I know. It was not your fault. You are a fine man, Will."

As he lifted his consciousness out of his memories, his past mixture of losses and gains, he asked himself, "What if anything have I learned? What can I do with what I have learned? Maybe I should write a book or tell my story to someone who can write a book."

When Will shared this germ of an idea with Lenora, she had a suggestion.

"Tell your story to Mimi. She has a new typewriter and would be glad to spend time with you to record your thoughts. If you get it all on paper, it can be there forever.

"Not only our children and grandchildren will know, anyone who reads can benefit from your experience. Just as we have learned from those who lived before us, others can learn from our generation.

"Every life has a story, Will, but every story does not get told. It takes a storyteller to send it out into the future."

"What would I have been without you, Lenora? Will asked, embracing his wife.

"Thankfully, we will never know," she laughed.

Mimi was honored to serve as her father's recording secretary. Over the next year, the two of them spent spare moments together with Will remembering and Mimi typing.

Will told his daughter, I have learned some things the hard way. As my Paw always said, "Somethings you just gotta learn by living."

"Everyone I have met, fought with, worked with, lived with has left a sentence or a paragraph in my collected book of life. Some people have disappointed me, some have surprised me, others have inspired me."

"Mimi, it is one of the many blessings I have received to have the time to sit with my beautiful daughter and recall my life's journey. I will tell you everything I remember about my parents and siblings. I will share the winding road I have traveled to be here with you today. If any of what I tell you sounds boastful, please change it. If some of it is too sad, feel free to soften it."

"No, Daddy, I won't change a word. It means the world to me to sit with you and record your story."

"Alright, sweetheart, buckle up. Here we go.

"I have learned that life is a journey of continuous learning opportunities. People will detect themes and patterns that remain constant even when the background changes if people pay attention.

"For example, we are all connected fundamentally. When Thomas Jefferson wrote ALL MEN ARE CREATED EQUAL, he did not mean we are all the same. Each of us enters the world in a specific time and place and with individual talents and traits.

"He indicated that we all have value in the sight of our maker and that because of that, we should be afforded respect and the opportunity to use those talents to the best of our abilities.

"Although he did not use these exact words, I believe he would have included men and women of all creeds and colors in that sentence.

"I learned from Pastor Henderson and the Good Book that we are all God's children and that WE SHOULD DO UNTO OTHERS AS WE WOULD HAVE THEM DO UNTO US.

"I hold those words from the Founding Fathers and from the Scriptures to be absolute requirements as a member of the human race and a civilized society.

"Another thing I learned the hard way is that it is easy to spout a belief in something, but it becomes difficult to stand firm on that belief when tested. Liberty carries with it certain obligations.

"Sometimes it becomes necessary to upset your friends or even family to remain true to yourself. When that happens, you can try to use your influence to change minds or attitudes. If that does not work, you may have to do something unpopular.

"If we want to keep the unique experiment that is this country, we each are obliged to speak up for what is right. We have a long way to go to achieve the ideals laid out for us, and it may take many generations to get there. What we can do now within our circles of influence, big or small, is to stand up for what is right.

"Each of us has a part to play in the drama that is America. If we take that duty seriously, we will work together to move closer to fulfilling the dream a little bit at a time.

"It is also a human truth that we all get distracted from the big things while we are taking care of the small things. That's why leaders are essential. We need leaders to remind us of where we should be going. Like the good shepherd, a leader can help us focus on the right road and avoid the dangerous side paths."

EPILOGUE

Will and Mimi worked together in spurts over the next decade, compiling his experiences, memories, and thoughts into his story. His work, her work, and unplanned events would interrupt their efforts for short periods.

In 1889 the family made their final trip to Graham to attend the funeral of Sally O'Connor Presley Henderson. She had continued teaching until the age of seventy and passed away peacefully at the home of her daughter at seventy-five.

Will Presley lived to see the Parker Cannery become a significant player in the processed food industry on the east coast. It was so rewarding to watch Randy take full charge, allowing Will to retire to his reading. His nephew Jedediah proved he was a quick learner with ambition. He apprenticed with Uncle Pete and prepared to replace him as Production Manager eventually.

In 1901, Will experienced the third Presidential assignation during his lifetime, William McKinley.

In 1911, the family lost Will Presley to a heart attack. Lenora was devastated but continued as the titular head of the family. She knew her husband would have expected it from her.

Lenora was thrilled to accompany Mimi and Lillian to be the first Presley women to cast a vote in the presidential election of 1920. She thought how Will always reminded her of the importance of holding on to the dream, never giving up, always marching forward.

After her father's death, Mimi continued editing his story and finally published it in a three-volume series.

Acknowledgments

Writing as a chosen activity is a commitment to continuous learning. Whether you are a professional career writer, an aspiring newcomer to the world of creative writing, or a pair of retired nerds looking for intellectual stimulation, writing challenges you in so many ways.

We, if you haven't guessed, fall into the third category. The original impetus was a desire to leave family history for our children; thus, we each began with our memoirs. That cathartic process opened a new world to us.

We offer our gratitude to the following individuals:
- Martha Woodward for introducing us to the world of self-publishing,
- Chris Cawood for his creative writing class, feedback, and mentoring,
- David Hunter for his friendship, example, and inspiration,
- Sylvia Sheh for her professional assistance in cover design and internal formatting.

We also acknowledge the following as resources:
- Wikipedia and the worldwide web
- Knoxville Writers Guild
- Writers Digest

About The Authors

A native of Knoxville, Tennessee. Ronald E. Pressley enjoyed two successful careers spanning fifty years. Traveling the southeast, he represented various products both at Trade Shows and directly with customers. Simultaneously, he served as a Minister of Music for multiple East Tennessee Baptist congregations.

As a life-long learner, he retains intense curiosity and interest in history, philosophy, and politics. Ron is now deeply involved in making his goal of sharing his experiences, thoughts, and inspirations through the written word a reality.

Straight Outta Lonsdale, 2017, Memories of a Working-Class Family (A Memoir)

Straight Outta Lonsdale II, 2018, Voices from Lonsdale (An anthology)

Blood Brothers, A Family Divided, 2019, co-written with his companion, Nancy P. Holder, was his first novel.

Blood Brothers II, Reconstruction, Racism, Riots, Ratification, 2020, also with Nancy P. Holder

Blood Brothers III, Jim Crow, and the Gilded Age, 2021, with his wife, Nancy Holder Pressley

Coming Soon:

Cotton Mill Man, now in the process

All are or will be available on Amazon.
You may also contact Ronald by email. ronaldpressley12@gmail.com

Nancy Holder Pressley was born in Washington, D.C. After graduation from Carson-Newman College, she enrolled in additional studies at the University of Tennessee and East Tennessee State. For most of her life, East Tennessee has been home.

First, as a Social Worker and later as a Human Resource Manager/Consultant, her professional career afforded many opportunities to put words on paper. She explained the missions, programs, and policies of numerous companies, institutions, and organizations.

Now retired, she is enjoying sharing observations, perceptions, and,, inspirations in her voice.

The Fourth Quarter, 2018, Reflections of a Septuagenarian. (A Memoir)

Blood Brothers, A Family Divided, 2019, written with her companion, Ronald E. Pressley, is her first novel.

Blood Brothers II, Reconstruction, Racism, Riots, Ratification, 2020, also with Ronald Pressley

Blood Brothers III, Jim Crow, and the Gilded Age, 2021, with her husband, Ronald Pressley

Coming Soon:

Beltway Baby, a collection of essays and poems

December Love, Story of unexpected blessing in the Fourth Quarter

All are or will be available on Amazon.

You may also contact Nancy by email. nancypholder@gmail.com

Made in the USA
Columbia, SC
20 April 2023

4946638d-3c2e-4639-9d7c-a24a9a3717b9R01